MELVIN BURGESS

DOING IT

ANDERSEN PRESS • LONDON

This edition first published in 2014 by
Andersen Press Limited
20 Vauxhall Bridge Road
London SW1V 2SA
www.andersenpress.co.uk

2 4 6 8 10 9 7 5 3 1

First published by Andersen Press Ltd in 2003

British Library Cataloguing in Publication Data available.

ISBN 978 1 78344 063 4

Typeset in Adobe Garamond by Palimpsest Book Production Limited,
Falkirk, Stirlingshire

Printed and bound in Great Britain by CPI Group (UK) Ltd,
Croydon CR0 4YY

With thanks to Mr Knobby Knobster

1
either or

'OK,' said Jonathon. 'The choice is this. You either have to shag Jenny Gibson – or else that homeless woman who begs spare change outside Cramner's bakers.'

Dino and Ben recoiled in disgust. Jenny was known as the ugliest girl in the school but the beggar woman was filthy. Her teeth!

'You are so gross,' said Ben disgustedly.

Jonathon acknowledged the compliment smugly and nodded. He was the King of this.

'At least they're both female,' said Dino.

'I'd take the homeless,' said Ben, after a moment's thought. 'She wouldn't be so bad once you'd cleaned her up.'

Jonathon shook his head. 'You have to take her as is.'

'Agh! You're the one who thinks of this stuff,' Dino pointed out. But that was the delicious horror of it. You had to make a decision. You had to consider it yourself.

Ben squirmed as he tried to focus his mind on the actuality. It was beyond a matter of taste. Disease came into it.

'Can I shag her from behind?'

'No, from the front. With the lights on. Snogging and everything. And you have to do oral sex on her too.'

'*Jonathon!*' hissed Dino.

'You never said anything about oral sex,' said Ben.

'Oral sex until she comes.'

Ben winced as his mind shrank back like a slug on salt. 'You are *disgusting*. Well, if I could have her cleaned up, I'd do the tramp, but if she has to be filthy, I'd do Jenny. *But* . . . if you had to leave Jenny out on the street for a few months until she was as dirty as the tramp, I'd do the tramp. What about you?'

'I'd take Jenny,' said Jonathon promptly.

'That's just because it's the only way you could get a shag.'

'She's ugly, but I bet her body isn't too bad. It'd be all right once you got going. And the tramp would have rotten teeth and smelly breath, bits of old kebab rotting in her teeth. Cold sores, probably. Ulcers, that sort of thing.'

'Yuk.'

'OK, Ben,' said Dino. 'What about . . . Jenny or Mrs Woods.'

They hissed with laughter. It was a clever one. Mrs Woods was at least sixty, obviously hated anyone under the age of twenty and her breath smelled of tinned cabbage – but at some time in the distant past, she might well have been a bit of a looker.

Ben paused. 'Are they both clean?'

'More or less.'

'Mrs Woods,' said Ben boldly.

2

'Mrs Woods?' said Dino, acting appalled. 'I mean, Jenny is ugly, but Mrs Woods is *old*.'

'Old is better than ugly,' said Ben definitively. The other two looked at him curiously. That was Ben; he always knew exactly what he wanted.

'You're really quite weird, aren't you?' said Jonathon. 'Nothing is worse than old. What about personality? Jenny's quite a nice sort of a person, but Mrs Woods is a monster.'

'Yeah, but she wouldn't be a monster if I was shagging her, would she? She'd be . . .'

'Friendly?' suggested Jon.

'Yeah.'

'So old is better than ugly and personality doesn't come into it?' asked Jonathon.

'We're talking shags here, not marriage. No one mentioned having to talk to them,' pointed out Ben.

The boys laughed.

'I'd do Jenny,' said Dino.

'And me,' said Jon.

Ben shrugged and smiled. 'Ah, but at least I got to shag a teacher,' he teased. 'And she'd be experienced.'

'A woman as horrible as her would probably be prepared to do anything,' Jonathon agreed.

'Let's not go there. OK,' said Ben. 'My turn. Mrs Woods or . . . Mrs Thatcher.'

Dino sighed. He hated this. It was, in his opinion, one of the few things he wasn't any good at. 'OK,' he said. 'Mrs Thatcher. She's uglier and older . . .'

'And she's had a bit of a stroke,' pointed out Jon.

3

'. . . but you'd have to see Mrs Woods at school every day, whereas with Thatcher, you'd never have to see her ever again. Definitely Thatcher.'

'Coffin snatcher.'

Dino grinned sheepishly.

'I'd do Mrs Woods. Thatcher's practically dead,' pointed out Jon.

'I know one,' said Dino happily. 'The Queen . . . or Deborah Sanderson?'

'Not Deborah again!' protested Jonathon. The Queen was hideous, no one in their right mind would sleep with her even if they were eighty years old and called the Duke of Edinburgh, whereas Deborah's only crime was that she was a bit on the plump side. She and Jon were good friends. The theory was that Jonathon fancied her to bits and was too embarrassed to admit it.

'You have to answer,' insisted Ben.

'Deborah, then.'

'Ah ha!'

'But only because *anything's* better than the Queen.'

'Bollocks,' said Ben. 'It's because you fancy her. The Queen is obviously far more attractive. I'd rather sleep with the Queen, any day. What about you, Dino?'

'The Queen, definitely.'

'You lying bastards! You're only saying that to wind me up!'

'No way. I mean, Deborah! Fat!'

'Plump!' hissed Jonathon.

'Still, you know what they say. Fat Girls Are Grateful For It,' said Ben.

'Yeah,' said Dino. 'She's probably the only woman living who'd be prepared to sink to your level. I knew you fancied her all the time.'

'Right.' Jonathon pointed a finger at Dino. He had one that would see them off all right. He'd been saving it up. 'Either you can sleep with any woman – OK? Any woman, at any time. They can't say no. No matter how beautiful and gorgeous, all you have to do is ask. At your disposal. And they have to do whatever you want them to. *Anything*. But. You ALSO have to be buggered. Once a year for twenty minutes. On the radio.'

'On the radio? Why not on telly?' demanded Ben.

'Because on the radio you'd try and keep really quiet so that no one would know it was you, but you wouldn't be able to. Little noises would escape. Oh. Oh. Oo. Ow. You know. Mmm. Ah. Mmm. Woo. Ah. Na-ha. And if you don't, then you get no sex ever. Never. No one. For life.'

Dino tried to think about it, but he couldn't. No sex was impossible. So was being buggered.

'I'm not answering that.'

'You have to.'

'No way. I'm out. Anyway, you asked it, you have to answer it.'

'Easy. I'd take the endless women and the buggery. It'd be worth it.'

'Me too,' said Ben. 'Think of the rewards! Anyone. S Club 7. Kylie. Jackie Atkins . . . ?'

'Poofs,' said Dino weakly, but he'd already lost.

'OK, you,' Jonathon pointing his finger at Ben.

But Ben spread his hands and smiled. 'No thanks. You win. Again.'

'You can't just back out!'

'Yes I can. I know what you're going to say. The same as last time. My dad or my mum. I'm not doing either of them.'

'Ugh! No! That's not fair. No family,' insisted Dino.

'That's the rules. You're allowed to say *anything*,' said Jon. 'So I win again. Wimps.'

'I won really,' said Dino, 'because both of you took it up the arse.'

'You might like it,' said Ben. 'You never know till you try.'

'Twice the chance of scoring on a Saturday night,' said Jon. 'I'd rather not.'

'It probably means you're a suppressed homosexual, they're always the ones that hate it the most.'

Dino pulled a face. 'I might as well be.'

'Still no punanni,' said Ben sympathetically.

'You should get a girlfriend. Punanni is usually found in the same vicinity. Unless you get one of those plastic ones,' Jonathon pointed out.

'Shut up,' said Dino; and Jonathon did.

'Give it up, Dino,' advised Ben. 'She isn't interested.'

'I'm not thinking of her,' insisted Dino. 'There just isn't anyone else I fancy at the moment.'

'What a stupid waste,' said Jonathon. 'Half the girls in the school are wetting themselves for him, and there he is, mission impossible, Jackie Atkins or nothing. Only the most gorgeous will do for our Deen.'

Dino shuffled his feet and smiled.

'You'll probably get it before I do,' he said. He left Jonathon smiling fondly at this thought and headed off home.

As he left the cloakroom, Dino paused to look at himself in the mirror. He liked what he saw. Jackie was the most gorgeous creature in the school – with one possible exception: himself. Dino was It. He had dark hair speckled with honey blond, even features with just a hint of rough, a wide mouth, full lips and deep golden-brown eyes. Girls fell into them and disappeared without ever being seen again.

But Jackie was more than gorgeous; she was sensible. She already had a boyfriend years older than her and she thought that Dino was a prat. Dino knew better. As the two officially most gorgeous people in the school, he and she belonged together. He deserved her. His crush on her had gone on for so long he never said anything any more, but he didn't believe she didn't want him, he never had. It was just a question of how long he was prepared to wait.

2
the incredible journey

Three nights later, Dino strolled across the room of the Strawberry Hill Youth Club with just the slightest backward glance to check that Jon and Ben were following. He leaned on the wall next to the Coke machine and began a lively conversation with two girls who came up to use it. One of them bought him a Coke. Dino smiled with pleasure, like a lamp slowly lighting up, and the girl shone straight back.

Jon leaned across to Ben.

'The rustling of nipples stiffening against the poly-cotton pads of a thousand Wonderbras. The gentle hiss of a roomful of drenching gussets,' he said.

'Shut up,' said Ben.

'Sorry.'

The Youth Club wasn't the sort of the place where the boys usually hung out. Dino had persuaded his friends to come along because Jackie was there. Jackie came to fence. She'd been there the whole time, getting togged up, and now she came into view in the big hall at the other end of the room. Dino knew her at once, even covered as she was with protective clothing and the wire mask. She began making passes with the rapier, her hand poised in the air behind her head. He was hoping for a snog later on. No chance. Jackie was right: Dino was a prat. He was even too big a prat to understand he had no chance, despite any number of very clear messages about it.

Dino was unfazed. Jackie obviously didn't understand something. He had right on his side – his good looks, a sudden smile that could charm the knickers off a supermodel and a disarming openness that took you by surprise over and over again. And the voice. Dino had a voice like a lecherous teddy bear. It was magic.

And he was It. That's what really counted.

'Tonight's the night,' he said.

'No chance,' said Ben. 'I told you. She thinks you're a prat.'

'And you *are* a prat too,' observed Jonathon.

Dino laughed, then sighed. 'I'm scared,' he confessed, and swigged his Coke. The girl who had bought it for him, who had been waiting by his side uncomfortably being ignored for five minutes, walked off in a huff. Dino watched her go, his mind on other things.

'Perhaps you ought to give it a miss,' suggested Jonathon.

Dino scowled. 'You're supposed to be helping here, not letting me down,' he said. 'Thanks, friend.'

Jon was immediately mortified. 'I didn't mean it like that . . .'

Dino rolled his eyes and snorted, but he let it drop. Jon

and Ben exchanged a wry glance. Dino walked through life like a blind man on the edge of a cliff, but angels guided his steps and he never fell or tripped. It was just a matter of time. Surely, that time was now.

One reason why Jackie despised Dino so very much was because she was It, too. She'd been It since she was little, just like Dino. Unlike Dino, she'd put such childishness behind her. She knew that she thought far too much of herself, and didn't like herself for it, but she couldn't avoid the conclusions that she was far more mature than most of her fellow students – certainly far more than any of the boys, who were mere children. That didn't stop them from wanting her, of course. They knew she would, they knew she had, they knew she *did* – but not with the likes of them. To get anywhere with Jackie, you had to be so grown up you were almost old. Her boyfriend, Simon, was eight years older than she was. He occasionally picked her up after school in his car. He had his own flat where she often stayed over, with her parents' consent. They trusted him. By his side, Dino was a foolish boy-child. There was no reason on earth for her to swap.

She only snogged him that night out of curiosity. The club held its monthly disco that evening. People let their hair down a bit, had a few slow dances, got into a clinch or two, a bit of a grope. Jackie had been going out with Simon for two years, she was very faithful but she was starting to feel that she was missing out on this kind of thing. Perhaps that was why, when Dino came up and asked her to dance, instead of rolling her eyes and telling him 'NO!' again, she shrugged and let him hold her close and waltz around the room with her. She allowed him to manoeuvre his thigh between hers, felt him swell against her stomach and felt – tickled. Tickled enough to allow him to kiss her as the track was ending. Just out of curiosity.

The kiss went further than she intended. She ground herself against him. Her legs went. When he pulled back, she still hadn't finished and hung around his neck, eyes half closed, dazed. She felt like a leech prematurely pulled away from its host. Dino looked into her eyes and exclaimed, 'God!' passionately, before he pressed her to him again and murmured over her head, 'That makes me so happy!'

Jackie started to think, What a crap line! But even as she did she knew it wasn't a line. It was *true*. He meant it. She'd made him happy. She tried to stand up and her legs twitched. Her pelvic floor clenched involuntarily. She panted three times. Dino was a popsicle; she could lick him all up. He pulled back to look at her again as if he couldn't believe what she was doing to him. His face was shining. It was as if he had just handed her the glowing ball of his happiness, and could she let it drop?

He rested one hand against the side of her face in a way that made her feel both slightly threatened and vulnerable. 'Come out with me. For a walk or something. Tomorrow afternoon?' he begged. 'Please?'

'Oh. OK.'

'Thanks.' Dino squeezed her tight again and his heart beat against her like a bird. He didn't hang around. Some instinct made him leave her and go home before she changed her mind. Suddenly abandoned, Jackie staggered back to her little group of friends.

'Enjoy?' someone asked.

'Don't get it myself,' she replied coolly, but her heart had already begun the incredible, traitorous journey down to you-know-where. And once her heart had lodged in you-know-what, she was doomed. There is no fate more humiliating than falling in love with a lust object as arrogant and as charming as Dino the Lozenge.

'See?' said Dino, as they walked home.

'But how?' wondered Jonathon. He was amazed. He had been positively scared of the damage to Dino's fragile but massive ego when Jackie inevitably spurned him. Instead, here he was, beaming like a lighthouse, still licking the taste of her off his lips.

'She let me feel her tits as well,' he confided.

'Really? What are they like?' asked Jonathon.

'She has nice tits,' Dino replied.

'How does he do it?' demanded Jonathon. 'Do you think she forgot who he was? Do you think she suffered a temporary hallucination and thought he was Brad Pitt?'

'I think she wants his body,' said Ben.

'Wow.' Jonathon could only wonder at the luck of having a girl want you for your body, let alone someone like Jackie.

'Well, he has the personality of a doof, what else can it be?' asked Ben.

'Don't be stupid,' said Dino. He felt like a lion. If he'd been on his own, he would have roared.

By the time she got home, Jackie still hadn't realised what was happening to her, but she was concerned enough to ring up her best friend Sue.

'You snogged Dino?' repeated Sue incredulously. 'You have a date with *Dino*?'

'It's not a date,' insisted Jackie.

'You snog a boy and then arrange to meet him and it's not a date?'

'Don't be such an old hen, nothing's going to happen.'

'So why go?'

'So why not?'

Sue began to feel anxious on her friend's behalf. 'You don't like him, remember? What's the point of going out with a boy you don't like?'

'Just because. Why not?'

'Stop saying why not! WHY?'

'What's up with you?' asked Jackie, and Sue replied,

'I. Smell. Trouble.'

Jackie just laughed. She felt mildly giddy. Look at Sue going all mumsy just because she let herself do something crazy for once! Sue giving *her* advice. It was always her who advised Sue. Sue had the lousiest taste in boys in the world – hopeless. She just couldn't help herself.

'I'm curious,' insisted Jackie, and to her annoyance, Sue laughed at her.

'Listen to me, dolly,' said Sue. 'Blokes like Dino, they're like some sort of horrible addiction. You always think you can handle it, that you're the one who can try them out just to see what they're like. Then you're hooked, and your whole life becomes ridiculous.'

'*You're* being ridiculous,' snapped Jackie. She refused the advice on principle, and went to the park to spite her friend as much as anything.

They walked along. He tried to hold her hand and she didn't let him, but he didn't seem put out. In fact, he was smiling his head off – at her, at the grass, at the dogs, at the people, at himself.

'You look happy,' she said.

Dino glanced around as if they were being spied on, then leaned across and whispered huskily close to her ear. 'You're beautiful, I expect people tell you that all the time. You could be in one of those magazines. I just think . . . I just feel . . . I don't know what to say! It's you. You make me so *happy*!'

It was part ridiculous – like a girl in one of those magazines! – and part nonsense, and part pathetic; but it was all gorgeous. The words sent a shiver all the way up and down her insides. Dino adored her. He couldn't believe his luck. Where was his caution? Here he was, handing her his heart on a plate, just like that, before her very eyes, even though she had spent the past ten years telling him to get lost. He meant every word he said. He was as open as the sky.

Then he sort of tugged her off into the shrubbery for another snog and she let him.

Afterwards, Jackie thought, In the *shrubbery*? She had a boyfriend, he had a flat they could go to. What for? But at the time she didn't even think about it. Maybe she didn't even want to do it, but suddenly there she was leaning up against a tree with Dino's hand down her knickers, just like she'd been planning on it all week long. It was just the most intoxicating thing she'd ever done. She was hanging round his neck moaning, 'Dino . . . oh. Oh. Oh. Dino!' in a little surprised voice. Saying his name like that turned her on even more. They were at it for ages. In the end he had to stop because his wrist was getting cramp. They were very tight jeans. They staggered out into the day, blinking at the light, and she was in such a dazed, hormone-sodden state that she agreed to a date at the cinema mid-week.

Jackie couldn't work out if she spent the next few days in a dream or a nightmare. Dino was still a prat, only now, she realised, he was a mind-meltingly delicious prat. She kept picking up the phone to cancel the date and then putting it down without ringing. She was thinking, I could just go along for the ride . . . and then she'd think – What ride? She couldn't get him out of her mind. Like Sue said . . .

'Good-looking, horny and arrogant. Irresistible, huh?'

'It's awful. Am I in love?'

'This is lust, babe. Enjoy!'

'But you can't fancy someone you don't even like!' insisted Jackie.

Sue shrugged. 'I think they're supposed to happen at the same time but I'm not sure it always works like that,' she said.

'What am I going to do?' begged Jackie, feeling suddenly tearful.

'What about Simon? You're supposed to be in love with *him*.'

'I *am* in love with him,' she told her.

'Then forget Dino.'

'I don't need you to give me advice,' she snapped.

'You've got it bad,' said Sue.

'No I haven't. I'll just do the date and then tell him I don't want to see him again.'

'Why not tell him now? Why didn't you do it yesterday before it was too late?'

'It isn't too late, that's silly.'

'How often do you think about him?'

'All the time,' she confessed. 'The things we did in the park. And he's such a wanker. It's just gross.'

Sue laughed. 'He sounds just like my sort of boy. Tell you what, leave Dino to me. I've had loads of them. He'll make me unhappy and I'll shag his brains out. When you see what's left you won't want it.'

It was true, Sue ate Dinos for breakfast, even though they gave her severe indigestion. But there was no way.

'Don't you dare!' snapped Jackie, and they both wet themselves laughing, although it wasn't in the least bit funny.

So she went to the film and it was the most fantastic experience of her life. They never watched a second of it. When she undressed that night, she had little bits of sticky popcorn all over her, which must have worked their way under her clothes while he kept feeling her all over. She felt like a drawer that had been thoroughly rummaged through. Dino was over the moon, he couldn't leave her alone. When he kissed her, she

could feel his heart not beating in his chest but literally fluttering. After the film they walked the streets and he talked.
He confessed all his secrets to her and she felt as if she was being
showered with jewels. He made her feel as if she was the only
person in the world that mattered to him, that he was giving
her everything he had. He made her walk with him for hours,
because he couldn't bear this to stop and he was so anxious
that in the morning the magic would be gone and never come
back. She got home at half one the next morning, to be roared
at by her dad for being so late without ringing. Only as she
stood in the shower rinsing away the popcorn, did she realise
that in five hours she had barely said a word to him about
herself, and he hadn't even asked.

'Oh, shit,' she murmured, but she didn't care. It was too
late. Her heart had burrowed its way down and made a cosy
little nest for itself just below her womb, where it snuggled
in and pulsed and glowed and purred happily. It wasn't coming
out of there for love nor money. She was going to have to tear
it to little pieces and chuck them away one by one to shift it.
She'd fallen in lust.

3
the secret history

As he caught the bus away from school that Tuesday afternoon, Ben felt like a man with a chest full of treasure. Hot wet jewels. Palpitating doubloons. Warm golden breath and silver shivers going up and down, up and down. Riches beyond all measure.

That didn't stop him feeling anxious as he rode on the top deck and watched the houses and gardens flick past. Treasure can be lost or stolen. What if it isn't yours? What if it's so seductive and dangerous that you shouldn't be playing with it in the first place? What if it was cursed?

It was just great; if you didn't have it you were worried about getting it and if you did have it you were worried about losing it. Whatever, it was perfectly certain that if he was ever caught running his fingers, his face, his tongue or anything else through the contents of this particular box, all hell would blow up around him. It was bound to happen. He felt as if he was muttering a dark enchantment under his breath, which one day was suddenly going to work and release every demon God could dream up, scorching up out of hell towards him. And where would his soul – or his education – be after that?

But you know what? It was worth every hot, wet, little second of it. It was an education in itself, and while he was fairly certain he could get another crack at his A-levels, he wasn't sure how often this sort of chance came along.

The bus took him right to the outskirts of town until it was running past hedgerows and pasture. He got off and walked up the road a little way, then back the way he'd just gone. If a car went past he speeded up, as if he had somewhere to go. It was April, a wet, clean day. The nettles were out in soft clumps, there were little white flowers in the hedge, the hawthorns were covered in little green sprouts. Someone had told him they called it bread and cheese. He broke one off and nibbled it. What sort of bread, what sort of cheese? It tasted nothing like.

After about ten minutes, a yellow Renault came driving out of town and pulled up next to him.

'Hi.'

The young woman inside leaned over and opened the door for him. Ben climbed in and they drove off.

She was chatty today. Asking about the day at school and what he'd done at the weekend. Ali was a gossip. She told him a great story about Mr Haide (maths) whose wife was having a nervous breakdown. Apparently she'd started pruning the privet hedge outside their house at two in the morning because she was scared that the wind would whip the long branches against the windows and break them. As always, Ben was amazed. He couldn't even begin to relate to the home life of teachers. It's like something you might get on a natural history programme. Food-gathering and mating and what territories they have, that sort of thing. Mr Haide! Poor old sod. Haide was a miserable old wombat. Ben didn't want to feel sorry for him.

At her place she made coffee and they sat on the sofa drinking it in silence. Then she got up and pulled all the curtains, made him stand in the middle of the floor and undressed him.

She did that one most times. He often thought that one day he'd like to do it to her. She took everything off, one after another, as if she was unwrapping him, until there he was, stark bollock naked in the middle of the room with an erection on the front of him like a concrete pillar. In some ways, it was uncomfortable standing there like that with your teacher stalking round you, but what came next was so indescribably delicious, he could put up with just about anything for it. She took his erection in one warm hand and gave a long, deep kiss. He could have harpooned a walrus with it. He pulled up her blouse and slid his hands round to unhook her bra, and then she crouched down and took it in her mouth.

He was one lucky boy.

Ben's affair with Ali Young had been sown over three years ago when he was in Year Nine, involved in the school production for that year, *West Side Story*. Ben was helping with the lighting and sound engineering. She was very familiar right from the start, always trying to tease bits and pieces of information about the other students from him in exchange for titbits about the teachers while they were backstage sorting out gels and fixing the lights. Ben was flattered and enthralled, even though he felt a little uncomfortable with some of the information she gave him.

The headmaster had a hernia operation last May, and by all accounts was walking around for weeks beforehand with half his digestive system in his scrotum. Mr Collins (history) had a cat who shat in the house, and he left the turds there for three days before cleaning it up, on the grounds that it was easier to deal with when it was dry. Mr Collins' wife had died of cancer of the bowel the year before, did Ben think there was a connection? Mr Wells in maths had had an affair with Mrs Stanton in geography. And so on.

'That's just between us, Ben, OK?'

How could he disagree? It wasn't often that you got a truly adult peep into the world of school, especially from an attractive young woman. Ben fancied her something chronic. They all did. She was just out of college, this was her first job and she dressed like the girls he knew dressed when they were out of school. Over the weeks they got very relaxed together. There was a lot of talk and fooling around together. His friends teased him about it. He even had pleasant little fantasies in which the teasings were true.

Then came an incident which changed everything. She was up on a chair backstage fiddling with one of the lamps, when she tripped, fell over and rolled on her back with her legs in the air. Ben went rushing over to help, all excited and embarrassed because he'd seen her knickers. He embarrassed himself further by actually trying to brush her down. It seemed like a good excuse at the time. He knew what he was doing. He couldn't keep his hands off her.

'I can do that, thanks, Ben,' she said. He smiled self-consciously at her, going red at the same time, because he'd overstepped the mark by quite a bit. But she just smiled at him. 'Did you enjoy that?' she asked him.

'Sorry, Miss. I did, Miss, yes.'

'Then how about this . . .' And she did a silly little dance for him, lifting up her skirt and waggling her bum. It only lasted for a second, but Ben almost died. Her knickers were tiny. He was such a kid at the time. She flushed red with embarrassment as she realised what she'd done.

'. . . Oh God, I shouldn't have done that. Let's pretend I never did that,' she said, waving her hands in front of her face as if she could chase the previous seconds away.

'I won't tell, Miss.'

He kept his word: he never told a soul. Not Dino, not Jonathon, not no one. He was determined to be loyal, but the incident dented their relationship. The long conversations about lighting and sound, as well as the gossip, came to an abrupt halt. Ben understood. She was a teacher and she'd showed him her underwear. It was magic, but it was also an amazingly stupid thing to do. Imagine if she'd done it to Dino or Jonathon – it would have been all over the school in hours. She could have lost her job. She'd put herself in his power, and from then on, the relationship waned. She'd overstepped the mark and now she put a distance between them to get things back on track.

Ben was sad but he admired her enormously for being so spontaneous. She wasn't like the others – she regarded the students as people, not as a bunch of sausages to process. For years afterwards, the image of her bum waggling at him in those tiny low-line knickers drove him mad with lust. It kept him supplied with fantasies for years.

Ben knew all about fantasies – he kept a stack of them heaped up in a wicker basket in his bedroom – and they all had one thing in common. Whether it was the just-possible ones, like falling on top of her by accident into a costume basket in the wings offstage and her closing the lid, or meeting her in a pub and having a few drinks and then ho-ho; or the middling ones, like her inviting him to peel the knickers off that pert bottom she was sticking out to him, or the wholly unlikely ones, like him blackmailing her, or her deciding to become a nun but wanting to have a really filthy sex orgy with him before she said goodbye to the pleasures of the flesh for ever – the one thing you could say about them all was this: they weren't gonna happen. They were fantasies. That was the whole point.

Gradually the fantasies faded and new ones replaced them. He had little to do with her. The following year he didn't take part in the school production and she never asked why. But Ben kept faith. No one knew, no one was going to know; it was as simple as that. There were plenty of occasions when he might have told the story of how she lifted her skirt and wiggled her bum at him, but he never did. He would have loved to tell her that he was doing this for her, to reassure her that he had kept quiet, that he understood why she had withdrawn. He knew she was worried about it still, because he noticed her looking at him from time to time. She wasn't assessing his performance for a mark at drama, that was for sure. It was a lingering, appraising look. He had no way of knowing that it was nothing to do with anxiety; it was lust. Miss Young was having fantasies of her own.

Another year went by. Even the odd looks stopped. As the new school year began, he had offered his services again for the Christmas show. The bum dance was three years ago, a thing of childhood. He attended the first technical rehearsals, helping set things up backstage. Once again, those odd, lingering looks began and once again, he thought she was worrying about him.

Things changed for ever one afternoon when she had to go to the theatrical suppliers for gels. Ben went with her into town to help.

She made small talk for the first ten minutes or so, then fell silent. Ben reached down inside himself and picked up the courage to speak.

'I never told anyone, you know,' he told her.

She twitched in her seat. 'What? What did you say?'

'I never told anyone. None of my friends, no one. About that day you fell off the steps. I never told anyone.'

There was a pause while she just carried on driving. Ben ploughed on.

'I just wanted you to know because I thought you might be worried about it. So you don't have to be, because I never told anyone. OK?'

They drove on a bit further in silence. Ben was scared. Maybe he should have kept his mouth shut.

'I appreciate that, Ben. I appreciate you telling me that. I thought you must have told at least a few people.'

'Well, I didn't.'

'No one at all?'

'No one, not one.'

'Well, I believe you. Do you know why I believe you?'

'No,' said Ben.

'Because you brought it up. You told me without me asking. If I'd asked you if you'd told anyone, of course you'd have said no. You'd have to. So I know it's true. Do you see?'

'Yes, yes, I see,' said Ben nervously, although he wasn't really sure at all.

'You were worried about me worrying,' she said.

'I could tell you were worried by the way you were looking at me, that's why I said,' said Ben.

She laughed, he had no idea why. 'You're a very grown-up boy, you know that? Very grown-up. Very mature.'

'Thank you,' said Ben. He knew that. He was more mature than Dino or Jonathon, both of whom were just kids in one way or another. But it was nice to have someone say it for him.

'More mature than me in some ways,' she added.

'I don't know about that,' he said.

'Well, you never showed me your bum, did you?' she said, and then added, 'More's the pity.' She looked sideways at him and smiled. Ben smiled back and his heart started beating, beating, beating in his chest like some kind of alarm machine.

* * *

Miss Young was in a hurry at Straelers, the theatrical suppliers. She rushed through the choice of gels that they'd spent so long talking about earlier, and on the way back she suggested that since they were early, they could stop off at her place to have a cup of coffee.

Ben sat awkwardly on her sofa drinking the coffee she'd hastily made, while she continued to be impressed by his honesty and faithfulness.

'It's a question of trust,' she told him. 'You kept our little secret.'

Afterwards, Ben spent many, many hours trying to work out how many clues there had been to what was going to happen next. He decided that there were about six hundred thousand at least, but he was still surprised every single time it happened. She started talking about boys and girls, and then Ben and girls. Having discovered that he had no girlfriends, she wanted to know what sort of sexual experiences he'd had. Ben, by now hopelessly out of his depth, told her that surely this was private stuff, wasn't it? She nodded approvingly. Then she stood up, brushed down her little skirt and smiled at him.

'Sorry, but I've been wanting to do this for a long time. Ever since I showed you my knickers,' she added. Then she leaned down to him and gave him a dirty big snog. Ben responded with his tongue and she almost fell on top of him, running her hands over his face and up under his sweatshirt. Blinded by a sudden rush of hormones he put his hand on her hip, then let it slide down to the side of her bum. She pulled up her blouse, and Ben slid his hand up and cupped a breast. He thought he was going to faint with lust and had to sit up.

Miss Young – 'Call me Miss' – pulled him back onto the cushions and kissed him even more deeply, making little moaning noises deep in her throat as though she was eating something surprisingly delicious. Her hand caressed his thigh and stroked the bulge in his school trousers. Ben heard himself muttering, 'Jesus,' three times, one after the other. They carried on kissing. She unzipped him. Mad with lust but terrified by authority, Ben suddenly froze up and couldn't think what to do next, but that didn't seem to bother her.

'I guess I'm going to have to take the lead, aren't I?' she said. She reached behind and undid her bra, pulled her jumper up so that only the thin material of her blouse was covering her breasts. He could see the deeper colour of her nipples showing through. She took his hand and placed it on her breast.

'Go on,' she told him.

As he did as he was told, Ben found himself thinking that this was how young girls must feel when they are seduced by an older man. He was so bewildered and sexed up he could hardly think. There was no question of him having any choice about what was happening.

When she began to peel his trousers over his feet, he panicked.

'I've never done this before,' he told her. 'I don't think this is a good idea,' he said. 'Are you sure?' he asked. Or was it, 'Please, Miss?' He could never remember.

'Ben,' she said. 'I'm your teacher. Do as you're told.'

Ben did as he was told.

*   *   *

27

An hour later he found himself deposited back at school, fixing the new gels to the lamps while Ali, who had transformed herself back into Miss Young like some sort of dark fairy, sorted out a group of Year Sevens who needed to learn how to walk in step. He thought to himself, I just lost my virginity during school hours. To a teacher. He felt immensely proud and privileged. I sucked Miss's tits, he thought. I know what colour pubes she has. He wanted so bad to boast about it to someone, but he knew he never could, not for years and years, maybe even never. But who cared? Even though he'd just come three times in the previous hour he was still more horny than he had ever been before. OK, the whole thing had been awkward and embarrassing as well – but it was easily the nicest half an hour he'd ever had in his life. Fleshy, filthy and holy. It had everything.

You lucky bastard, he thought to himself. You lucky, lucky bastard.

4
dino

Going out with Jackie is the best thing that ever happened to me. The best. I knew it was going to happen. It felt right. By the time she said yes I felt like I'd been waiting for ever.

'It might be right for you but it certainly isn't right for me,' she said once before she realised, and there were her and her mates laughing away. But it can't be like that, can it? With those sorts of feelings, it can't be right for one person and not for the other. That would be wrong.

The main thing about Jackie is, she's gorgeous. People look at her all the time. When I'm walking along and she's holding onto my arm, she makes me feel like I'm on a red carpet in front of the world. As long as I can remember, she was always out there, growing up ahead of me. She was always the one everyone fancied, even at Primary School. And now here I am, watching her long fingers pop open the top button on her jeans for me while I stroke her tits in the rhododendron bushes down Crab Lane on the way home, and it makes me feel so fucking good.

'Not here, don't be daft,' she says in a little while, but both of us are panting like steam engines by then. Wow! I mean! I stood back and watched as she did up her zip and pushed the button back into place.

'You should wear a skirt,' I said. It felt like my blood had turned into boiling hot soup. That's what she does to me. I felt like a cow in the slaughterhouse with a bolt going through its head.

'More accessible,' she said.

I can be a bit of an arse sometimes. I admit it. I'm my own worst enemy. I couldn't help it. I stood there watching her zipping up, I was almost mad with lust and I was thinking how she never wore a skirt or a dress for me. I was thinking, This is how it's gonna go. We'll go home to my place, I'll strip her to the waist, we'll get our hands down each other's pants and spend about an hour writhing around like a pair of earthworms . . . and that's it. That's as far as it was going to go. Her jeans would not go below her hips.

You know? It's been a month now, a whole month and I'm still a virgin. I mean, it's practically like I was saving myself for her, because there's loads of other girls I could have had. You ask anyone, there's loads of girls would love to go out with me, they'd shag me tomorrow if I just went up and asked. It's like that. You get my point? And she won't. So what's that all about?

You don't know Jackie. She's as stubborn as a brick in a wall. She smiled at me and walked out of the bushes and onto the road, and I knew I should have kept my mouth shut but I just started before I even had time to think about it.

'I've got some contraceptives,' I said.

'No,' said Jackie. Then she added under her breath, 'Not this again.'

'But you want to, why not?' I asked. I slid my hand down her arse and tickled her crack.

'Get off me! Not here.' She wriggled away. 'I'm not a bloody dog or something.'

'What's up with you? You didn't mind a minute ago.'

'That was in there.'

'You'd sleep with me if you loved me.'

'Dino, stop it!'

'It's true.'

'What's love got to do with it? You don't love me.'

'I *do* love you,' I said.

'Dino!'

'I do!'

'You don't know what love is.'

That's how she goes on at me. Like I'm some sort of kid. As if I'm ten years old and she's about twenty-something.

'But don't you love me, then?' I said.

She looked at me closely. 'I like you very much.'

'Is that all? Like? Just *like*?'

'Anyway, even if I did love you, I wouldn't sleep with you.'

'What?'

'I don't want to talk about it.'

'I want to know. I'm interested,' I whined. I could hear myself whining, but I still couldn't stop myself. 'I just want to know. I mean, is it me? Is there something about me you don't like? Is there something wrong with me?'

'It just doesn't feel right.'

31

'It felt pretty good with Simon.'

'Leave it!'

'So what was so great about Simon? Why aren't you going out with him? What's the difference between him and me?'

'Well, he was eight years older than you for a start.'

'Oh, right. I'm too young, am I? Not mature enough for you?' I was really pissed off but I knew I shouldn't be going on like that, I was really blowing my chances. I just can't help it sometimes. 'I get it. I'm stupid. I'm just a kid. You're all so grown up and I'm not!'

'You're behaving like a kid,' said Jackie coldly.

'I don't behave like a kid – you do!' I yelled.

And that was it. She was off, pulling her coat around her and storming off down the road. I thought, Shit! Why do I do this? I mean, I don't mind having a row. I don't mind throwing tantrums and sulking – it was pretty bloody unreasonable of her not to sleep with me, after all. But why did I have to do it *then*?

I ran after her, shouting, 'Sorry – please don't go, don't go!'

But it was too late. She pulled her arm away from me and shouted, 'Just fuck off!'

I froze. I was furious. Shouting at me like that. Right in the middle of the street! I could see people looking.

Listen – no one tells me to fuck off.

'Fuck you too!' I yelled. I stood on the pavement watching her, furious with her and furious with myself too. I mean, all right, she won't shag but she'll do almost anything else. Almost anything else isn't shagging, but it isn't bad and now I wasn't even getting that. I'm such a dick! I just can't help it. She drives me mad. I just want – you know. I just want to do it with her so much.

As he walked sadly back home alone, Dino distracted himself by imagining that a mighty power-beam grew out of each of his temples, destroying everything they touched. All that lay behind his step was crushed by his passing. Trees, houses, lampposts, even small hills were all reduced to trash or broken neatly off where the beam struck them. If he stood on tiptoe, he could peer over the devastation. The world below his nose was a tangled mass of rubble and destruction.

He'd been doing this as he walked along ever since he was about six. It was very childish, but it passed the time and since no one in the world knew about it, who cared?

Slowly, he turned in a circle and cut a kilometre-wide circle in the surrounding houses. Rising up on tiptoes, he peered over the allotment fence tangled with ivy, over the cabbages and beans and the brown earth on this blue after-noon to where his own house stood, miraculously preserved amid the devastation. The house stared back out of the window on the second floor and said, 'You think it's gonna be fun? Do ya? Do ya?'

As he approached the front door Dino failed to notice the strange car, which had in any case been parked up the road as a precaution. He walked straight up to the door and just as he was about to put the key in the lock, he looked sideways and caught a beautiful view of his mum in a clinch with a man through the bay window. They were kissing passionately. Her blouse was open. She was wearing a red bra which hung loosely off her breasts. The man was slowly hitching her skirt up from behind.

'More accessible,' whispered Dino to himself.

He watched in slow motion as the skirt hitched up right above her bum and the man's hand began to ease its way down the back of her tights. Then, before they turned their heads and saw him he fell on the spot to his knees, bruising them painfully on the hard plastic shoe scraper. He suppressed a howl of agony into a choked grunt. He glanced behind him to make sure no one was watching from the street. Right in front of the window! How could they? The neighbours! But in fact they were behind the wall; it was only from his position by the front door that they could be seen. As he crouched, Dino realised that he hadn't looked at the man's face at all. All he had noticed was his mum's mouth moving hungrily on the strange lips. There had been a moustache, he felt. Somehow, the fact that his mum had been getting another man's facial hair in her mouth made it even worse.

Dino scuttled rapidly backwards so he could get out of sight, stood back up and walked boldly up to the door again, this time staring straight ahead as he noisily put his key in the hole and opened it up. He ignored the alarmed scurrying sounds from the front room and walked through to the kitchen to get a drink. He flung his bag on the floor with a thud.

'Who's that?' called his mother in a surprised voice from the front room.

'Mum?' said Dino, also in a surprised voice. 'It's me.'

'What are you doing home?' she asked. Her voice sounded heavy. Dino had a vision of her standing there doing her bra up.

'History was cancelled. What are you doing home?'

'English was cancelled,' said his mum, and laughed. Her laugh sounded like china dropping to the floor. Dino walked through and opened the front-room door. His mum was standing there on one side of the coffee table and on the other was Dave Short, a teacher at his mum's college. He was smoothing down – or perhaps wiping – his moustache. Dave taught technology, Dino remembered.

'Was technology cancelled too?' he asked. To his surprise, Dave Short blushed as pink as a boy. Dino blushed back.

Dino spent a lot of time that evening in his room trying to think of nice things like Jackie or football or a good film, but all his mind would show him was his mum sucking Dave Short's moustache, in vivid, spitty close-up. The image was ghastly beyond belief. What was going to happen? Was his family going to break up? Did his little brother Mat have any idea what was going on? His mother was old, how could anyone want to kiss her? Did he have to tell his father? Did his mother know that he knew, did she suspect – or had he fooled them both completely?

As for Dave Short – I could blackmail the bastard, thought Dino, and at once, he realised that he was on to a good thing. Dave Short was a balding man with a dense, badger-coloured moustache and a fair amount of badly placed fat on his stocky little frame; utterly repulsive, the last sort of man you'd want as a stepfather. So repulsive, in fact, that Dino couldn't believe that his mum actually wanted to be doing sex things with him at all. Probably *he* was blackmailing *her*! So that was it! Blackmail! The bastard!

His mother needed rescuing.

Then he thought about the way she'd kissed him. Perhaps she did want to be doing sex things with him after all.

That just meant he could get both of them. Why not? The bitch was trying to ruin his life. Just because she was his mother . . .

But first that bastard Short. He sat down at his desk and began to compose a blackmail note. He got through a couple of drafts before he was called down to tea.

Knives and forks rattled on the plates, but Dino was miles away, thinking about money. Soon he'd be rich. He'd be able to get a car, at least. Maybe life would be *better* because his mum was having an affair, not worse.

As the word 'affair' rebounded in his head he looked guiltily up. No one seemed to notice he was thinking the unthinkable. For a moment, he became acutely aware of his ability to think things with no one knowing what he was doing. Deliberately, he began to conjure up the filthiest thoughts he could manage about Jackie – and they really were pretty filthy. No one seemed to notice. It was bizarre that you could sit there innocently eating mash next to your little bruv while your head was immersed in the most depraved filth man could dream up. It was disturbing but fun, until his mind began, quite against his will, to imagine the same filthy thoughts about his mother.

Bad mistake. He felt ill with anxiety and disgust. At that very moment, Dave Short might be eating his dinner with his family and thinking the exact same kinds of things about his mum – and he'd be *enjoying* it! Even worse, maybe his mother was thinking filthy thoughts about Dave Short. Sitting there, all alone in the middle of his family, Dino blushed a bright, bright red.

'What's up with you, wet your pants?' asked Mat. Mat was only nine. Dino sneered at him and looked away.

He began thinking about all the money he was going to earn again, when his dad's voice interrupted him.

'. . . going away for the weekend.'

'What?'

'Me and your mum are going away for the weekend.'

'Where?'

'We don't know yet.'

'What for?' asked Dino.

His dad laughed. 'What do you mean, what for? To go away for the weekend, that's what for.'

'You're so dumb, Dodo,' sneered Mat.

'Mat,' said his mother mildly. 'We haven't been away together on our own for ages,' she explained. Dino stared at her. She smiled fondly at his dad. She looked like a woman with no secrets at all.

'Mat's going to stay with Gran . . .'

'No!' wailed Mat.

'You haven't been for ages. It'll be OK, she'll get some vids out.'

'It's boring!'

'So you'll be on your own, Dino. Do you reckon you can manage it? You *must* be old enough to be responsible now.'

'I'll be fine,' said Dino. 'Do I look like a baby? You go. Have a nice time.' He didn't mean it but it came out all sarcastic.

'What's that for?' his dad asked him.

'Nothing. Everything's fine, isn't it?' Dino glanced at his mum who smiled and – was it his imagination? – avoided his eye. Then, as if to prove him wrong, she turned and looked at him so directly that Dino almost started to blush again. But he didn't, he just smiled straight back. He thought, I can be as innocent as you can. It went on for too long, though, and they both looked away suddenly in confusion.

I could blackmail you, he thought, you bitch.

After dinner, as he was wiping the pots, Dino found himself staring down at his mother's back as she bent to the dishes in the dishwasher. He could see her bra strap through her blouse. It wasn't red any more, it was her usual off-white job. Built for comfort, she used to say. She was quite well stacked upfront.

As he looked down at her, a number of thoughts flashed through Dino's mind. One was the memory of a story she often told about him, how when he was about five or six he was curious about breast feeding and had apparently asked her if she had any milk in them now.

'No, not now,' she said.

'Perhaps we should have a try just to see,' he'd told her. She told the story now to make him blush. Another thought was that seeing your mum with nothing on would be like seeing someone stripped of their skin, some sort of carcass. The third was that he wished he'd stayed and lingered at the bay window for just a bit longer, to see if Mr Short was going to lift her bra up, so he could have caught a better look at her breasts. The fourth was, how nice if she'd talk to him about what he'd seen that afternoon. This was one secret he definitely didn't want.

Without thinking, he bent down and playfully snapped her bra strap.

'Twang!' he said.

His mother jumped upright, blazing at him. 'How dare you do that to me!' she demanded, glaring inches from his face. 'How dare you!' she repeated, brushing the hair out of her face.

'Sorry,' muttered Dino. He was amazed. He couldn't work out what the fuss was about.

'Don't you ever do that again!' she ordered. She turned and marched out of the room, but at the door she turned and looked back at him curiously.

'Sorry,' said Dino again, shrugging. 'It was just a joke.' His mum didn't say anything but stood there watching him carefully, examining his face, and he knew exactly what she was thinking. She was thinking, Did he see or didn't he? Does he know?

'What?' he asked. 'What?' And he pulled a grim, mirthless little smile. His mother turned and left the room. A little later, Dino went back upstairs. He was half expecting her to come up and talk to him, but she never did.

'Ah-ha! And you know what that means, don't you?' said Ben.

'Party!' said Jonathon. Yes. Dino had to have a party. He'd made Jonathon have a party when his parents went away, partly by insisting that's what he'd do. It'd be awful. Ray and Alan Wicks would turn up late and chuck bottles up and down the road. The stereo would get broken.

'It's not so bad,' said Jonathon. 'People help you clear up. Those girls can clear up like magic. My parents never even knew.'

'Until your mum tried on those shoes and found out they were full of puke.'

'I said that was me.'

'Did you tell them it was you pissed on the sofa in the conservatory too?'

'I did mention I had a few friends round in the end. OK, I got caught, but listen. It was a great party. It was worth it.'

And that was the truth.

'Anyway,' said Dino. 'There's another possibility. Like, Jackie.'

'Ah, right,' said Ben. 'Two days all alone in the house. Better than a party.'

'Parents out, Dino in. Yum yum,' said Jon.

'Except she doesn't, does she?'

'An empty house,' said Dino.

'Will it make any difference?' asked Ben. 'If she says it doesn't feel right, why should an empty house make any difference?'

'She's been stringing me along for weeks, it's not fair.' He appealed to them. 'It could be the perfect chance. Do you want me to stay a virgin for ever?'

He convinced Jon and Ben, but Jackie was another matter. When she heard about the empty house, she favoured the party. Dino stared sulkily at her.

'What?' she said.

'It's just, you know. An empty house. You and me.'

Jackie chewed her lips and looked at him. 'You stand more chance of getting a girl into bed if she's had a few drinks first,' she told him, and smiled.

'Party's on,' said Dino.

5
knickers on

Dino was discovering that despite living with them for over sixteen years, his parents were strangers to him. What did they think, what did they feel? Long ago they used to read stories to him and wipe away his tears and he'd tell them his secrets – but what were *their* secrets? They might have been secret balloonists or Welsh people putting on an English accent for all he knew. He had assumed that the whole of their emotional selves was tied up in him, his brother and each other, but that brief glimpse through the window of his mother snogging like a schoolgirl had blown that vision right out of the water. They weren't just parents. They were friends and lovers, betrayers and cheaters and fallers-in-love. There was a whole crowd of them in there.

Did they have a love life? What did they get up to? It could be anything. Did they get kinky? Did they watch in the mirror? Did they do oral? Of course, he'd wondered about such things before in a kind of shuddery, jokey sort of way. Now, to his disgust, he found himself actually turned on by the thought. Just because he had seen her getting felt up by another man, his mother had turned into a sexual object. It was horrible

42

but he couldn't stop it. It made him feel like some sort of a machine.

Whenever he'd thought of parents and sex before, the term 'making love' came into his mind – a comforting, elderly kind of union. But it hadn't looked as if that was what his mum had wanted with Dave Short. It looked more like she wanted a bloody good shag.

One afternoon that week, he crept into their bedroom to see if he could find any evidence. He went in the drawers and under the bed, looking for stockings and suspenders, vibrators, pornography, membership cards to swing clubs, nipple clamps, peek-a-boo bras, massage oil, anything. He found nothing, not even any contraception. His heart sank. It'd be separate beds next. He crept out feeling like a skunk.

On the other hand, so what if his mum was having an affair? It's what people did. Read the papers, watch the telly. They were all at it, banging away at each other like it was keeping the world turning. Who cared any more? On the third hand, though – how did he know for certain that anything had really happened in the first place? What if there had been some kind of misunderstanding? Maybe he had mis-seen what was going on in the front room, like they do in films. His mum could have been doing any number of innocent things with Dave Short. Showing him a piece of jewellery. Looking at a cut on his nose. Having him adjust her blouse. He'd been so horned up over Jacks that he'd hallucinated the snog, the breasts, the urgent hands. It was all a mistake. That would explain why his mum hadn't come to have a word with him about it.

The trouble with this theory was the images crowding round

his brain. It was almost a form of sexual harassment, by his own mother. He considered asking her about it, but that was impossible. He could talk to Jackie, perhaps, but he had no idea how to talk about it. She was coming round on Friday after his parents had left to help him sort the place out for the party. Maybe he'd have a word with her then – sort of drop it in accidentally. She'd know what was going on. He could imagine what she'd say . . .

'Well, obviously it was a rehearsal for the school play/she was showing him her brooch/blouse . . . her button fell off and he was helping her with it . . . And you actually thought they were kissing! You twat, Dino!'

Something like that.

But maybe she wouldn't.

His parents left after the rush hour on Friday. He helped his dad carry out the bags to the car.

'You expect me to help you pack for your dirty weekend?' asked Dino. His dad decided it was a joke and laughed.

'I should be so lucky,' he said.

'Is it just you two, or are you having someone else along? You know what they say – two's company, but three's fun,' he said.

'I should be so lucky,' said his dad. Too lazy to think of another reply. He opened the back of the car and put the bags inside.

'It might be a good idea,' advised Dino. 'Help perk up your sex life. Married for all those years. Maybe you need a bit of a booster pack.' His dad smiled wanly as his mum hurried out with her walking boots in her hand.

'All ready?' she said.

'Are you having an affair?' said Dino.

He said it so plainly. As soon as it was out of his mouth he nearly fainted. What on earth induced him to say that, of all things? He grinned maniacally, he would have started to laugh but he knew he'd sound like Doctor Strange.

His parents stopped in mid-movement to stare at him. His father looked just on the edge of getting cross for this over-familiarity; his mum looked horrified.

'I should be so . . .' began his dad.

'What?' said his mum.

'Ahhhh . . . are you having an affair? It's like the two of you are off for a dirty weekend. Ha ha!'

His mother laughed too loudly, and chucked him under the chin. 'If only you knew, boy,' she growled. Laughing anxiously, she and he climbed into the car and drove off. As his dad wound the steering wheel round, Dino watched once again as his mum watched him watching them with that curious expression on her face, like someone watching the arrest of the man who had gunned down her family. An incomprehensible look. Dino waved as they got to the end of the road, then rang Jacks.

When she got ready to go out that night, Jackie was only plan-ning on jeans and a T-shirt, but she got carried away. It started with brushing her hair. She had long hair which shone like copper when she brushed it, and as she watched it come to life in the mirror, she was inspired to spend a bit more time on her make-up. It was fun, but it was too much for the clothes she'd put on. She was going to take it off, but she had some spare time so she went to try on a few dresses and skirts. As she turned and twisted in front of the long mirror on her wall, she found she was getting excited. How much Dino loved it when she dressed up. The transformation from plain schoolgirl to the full vision with lippy and scent and tight T-shirt and a flash of tummy and leg made him go weak at the knees. So she kept it all on, just for fun – why take it off when she'd gone to so much trouble, and it would tickle Dino so much?

Self-consciously, she hid herself under her coat before she said goodbye to her mum and dad, but even so they spotted it at once.

'Wow – party time!' said her dad brightly, but her mum scowled.

'I thought you were staying in at Dino's tonight?' she asked suspiciously.

'We changed our minds, all right?' demanded Jackie. Then she had to invent a bar they were going to before she closed the door and stamped bad-naturedly out of the house.

'Get a taxi back if you're late. Ring us!' called her dad after her.

As she walked the half-mile to Dino's place, Jackie felt unaccountably furious. Her mum had probably seen right through her even before she had. She was ludicrously over-dressed for a night in. She was on the pull. Why had she worn a dress? More accessible, she thought. Maybe, tonight was the night that she was going to make Dino's dreams come true.

For a long time she'd tried, and managed, to enjoy the intox-icating effects of going so far and then stopping, but she had to admit, these days it gave her a severe headache.

Jackie wasn't entirely sure why she was so reluctant to go all the way with Dino. The official line was that she didn't feel sure of his feelings for her and that she was waiting for their relationship to grow, but her hormones had another, simpler plan, which involved getting carried away one night. Unbeknown to Dino, she'd had a pack of condoms sitting accusingly in her handbag for weeks in case the night was now.

'This is a nightmare,' said a knowing voice in the back of her head.

'Shut up,' said Jackie. She speeded up to try and drown out the dissenting voice, but it was no use. She looked like a million dollars and she was certain Dino was going to try and have her for a fiver.

But when the door opened, Dino beamed, he just beamed at her, she looked so beautiful. He took her in his arms, kissed her and leaned back on his heels, lifting her up into the air pressed tight against him. He rocked her from side to side on his pelvis.

'You're so beautiful!' he crooned. A warm, tickly glow spread out from her stomach into her arms and legs. And bless him, poor old Dino was so embarrassed at showing his enthusiasm that he blushed bright red behind his smile. Jackie rested her hands on his broad shoulders, looked into his big smiling face and felt she was going to melt away on the spot.

The poor sap had no idea why she was so touched. Dino was one of those people who thought the world of his bad points and was ashamed of all his good ones. He was perfectly unaware of how attractive his openness and his eagerness to please were, which just made Jackie love him all the more. Already he was beginning to scowl at his own embarrassment. She leaned forward from her perch on his pelvis and kissed him deeply until he melted back down.

Inside, Jackie took a bottle of Ice Head out of the fridge and started gabbling away. She felt like ripping his clothes to rags and riding him round the room but instead she ran to the CD player to pick out her favourite tracks, talking some nonsense about her mum while he stood there bemused, wondering what to do with his seething blood. As soon as she turned to fiddle with the CD Dino came up and held her from behind. He pulled her dress right up her back, nuzzling her neck and pushing himself into her.

'You're so amazing. I'd like to take your knickers off tonight,' he murmured. Jackie spun round and seized hold of his hands as if he was about to do it that moment.

'No, no, naughty boy, naughty,' she shrieked, sounding like some kind of maiden aunt even to her own ears. She leaned forward and pushed her mouth into his ear and breathed a tickly whisper right inside him. But why not? Why not let him take them off and every other scrap as well? Why not tonight?

She pushed him off. 'Come on, let's make a tart, I mean a start,' she said. She gestured at the plates Dino's mother had displayed on the wall. The house had to be made safe for the party, which was why she was supposed to be here. She put down her Ice Head. Dino grabbed her bum again as soon as she turned round and she had to waddle to the wall with him still stuck to her back, where she began removing the plates.

Dino felt like something she'd sat in.

'We can do all that tomorrow,' he complained. But Jackie just smiled at him over her shoulder.

'Go and get the newspaper,' she told him. After a brief pause, Dino went to do as he was told.

Dino's mother was always collecting things. She'd build up a good number of whatever it was, sell them all off and start again. It had been these plates, a 1940s series painted with characters from Dickens, for about a year now. Before that it had been hatpins, and before that, egg cups. The plates were worth quite a bit of money. Dino had never thought about them on the wall, but now, holding them in his hands, he realised how horribly fragile they were.

'Maybe this party isn't such a good idea,' he said anxiously, after they'd taken down and wrapped up the first few.

'It'll be OK. I know how to pack them up.' Jackie enjoyed the preparation. Soon all twenty-five plates, some as small as dinner plates, some great round chargers you could serve a swan on, were all wrapped up and coffined away in cardboard boxes ready to be taken upstairs and stowed away in the spare room.

That done, they pushed the furniture back to get an idea of what the place would look like empty. The room was knocked through; emptied, the space looked enormous.

'Wow, look at it . . . space,' said Jackie. Dino pressed the CD to get 'They Always Do', Jackie started to rock her hips and they jived about the living room. Dino was a poor dancer, and he felt better when a slow one came on. They cuddled up on the dance floor, big long slow kisses, and in a minute they were in a clinch on the sofa.

She kissed him deeply as he unbuttoned her dress and exposed her breasts. She could see him peeping down at them secretly, which just slayed her. She wriggled as he eased her dress right up above her tummy and ran his palm over her knickers, tiny low ones that barely covered her pubes. Dino ran his fingers inside the edges, and then began to roll them down, first this side, then the other. Jackie sighed and lifted her bum for him. It was going to happen, they were coming off – but then just as they were about to pass the point of no return, she suddenly sat up, entirely against her will, and lifted her finger.

'Knickers ON,' she snapped, and she leaned over to pick up her drink.

'Why not now?' he mewed. He couldn't understand it. They were alone. They were in lust. He didn't know that Jackie couldn't understand it either.

'I – don't feel right . . .' she began.

'It's never going to be right, is it? Is it?' said Dino between clenched teeth.

'Yes, it will,' shrilled Jackie, but she could have howled with frustration, because he was quite right. In some ways that was the most humiliating thing about it – that a dope like Dino, who knew nothing, was in a position to tell her, who was actually quite sorted, what was going on. She could have killed him for that. She got up and started rearranging her clothes.

'Tomorrow,' she said. 'After the party.'

'What about tonight?'

'I can't, Mum and Dad are expecting me back, but they think I'm staying over with Sue tomorrow. We'll have all night long. All night.' Jackie had no idea why she was making such a rash promise. Maybe she was just fed up with being put in the wrong all the time, maybe somewhere deep inside her, she'd decided that she'd waited long enough for things to work out right – she just had to do what she had to do.

'Me and you in the place on our own, after everyone's gone home,' she promised. 'We'll do it then. OK?' She felt as if she was withholding sweets from a child.

'I can easily find someone who will, you know. You're not the only fish in the sea.' Dino scowled slightly to himself. Had he really said that? The lovely, unexpected things he came out with now and then that Jackie loved so much were matched only by these astounding pieces of oafishness. He had no idea himself where they came from. He peered at her to see how out of order it was. She was staring at him with a thin little smile.

'Tomorrow's another day,' she said.

'Don't forget you promised.'

Dino looked suspiciously at her, then beamed. He was in love again. He was happy. He came to hold her in his arms, and pressed her tightly up against him.

'You don't know how happy that makes me,' he murmured in a thick voice.

Jackie could feel herself melting away like a jelly. With her chin on his shoulder, she grimaced resentfully.

'I know. I know, Dino. Honestly.' She'd made him happy and she loved him for it – but only for a bit.

I'm going to get hurt, she thought. But she already was.

6
jackie

Can you believe him? 'You're not the only fish in the sea.'
Who does he think he *is*? And me! Letting him. Well, that's
it. If he thinks I'm going to go to bed with him at his ridiculous party, he's living on another planet. It's not just what
he says – it's the way he wraps me round his little finger
afterwards. You know? Gives me a big hug and a smile and
thinks that makes everything all right. And the worst thing
is, it *does* make everything all right, for a bit anyway, just for
long enough to watch a bit of telly and walk back to my place,
and I'm getting angrier and angrier so that by the time we get
to my door I can hardly speak I'm so furious, and you know
what he says? 'What's the matter with you?' What's the matter
with *me*? Can you believe it?

I've got no excuse, I've known what he's like for years. There
was a time at Primary School, I remember, he brought in this
enormous cowboy hat – very appropriate – and he walked
around the playground with a crowd of other little boys all
begging him to let them have a go wearing it. It was huge, a
great big black thing with silver tassels all the way around the

52

edge. It was about three sizes too big even for his head, it looked ridiculous. If it had been any other kid, they'd have all teased him about it, but somehow Dino managed to make that stupid hat into something they were all just desperate to have on their heads.

I should have listened to Sue right at the start.

'Just use him,' she told me. 'Use his body and then fling it back. Why not? Simon will never know.' But did I do it? Did I hell! And do you know why? Because I'm not that sort of girl! How stupid is that? That's how I see myself. I would never shag someone just for sex and betray my boyfriend. Other girls might do that but not me, oh no – I have to have a decent relationship with them before you get down to that sort of thing. I have to like them and respect them and have them respect me – even if it's a total arse like Dino! He doesn't even know what respect is. All the time I thought I was safe because I was sensible, and sensible people only fall for other sensible people. Only idiots fall for idiots. But when a sensible person falls for an idiot, that's the person who really suffers, because a person who isn't sensible just does mad things and likes it, but a sensible one spends her whole time trying to make an impossible situation sensible. I am so useless!

I keep thinking he's going to get it. I keep kidding myself he's going to grow up. But why should he? He gets everything he wants by just being a wanker. Except me. He just waved goodbye to that.

The first time I chucked him was after we went to see a film together – I forget which one it was, we go to films quite a bit. We sit and snog all the way through. It's great. Anyway.

I was still seeing Simon as well at the time. After the film we went for a walk in the car park and I gave him – well – I don't want to say. Oh, God, I'm blushing. You know. A blow job. It was the first time I did that for him. It sounds horrible but it was really lovely, actually. I enjoyed doing it. It felt right somehow. Not sordid at all. I was floating on this lovely cushion of sex. And then on the way home, he started. He had a stiffie again immediately and he wanted to do a knee trembler in the car park but I wasn't into that, that would have felt horrible. He went on and on and on, and by the time I got home I wasn't feeling wonderful any more, I was feeling horrible and crabby and frustrated and pissed off. Trust him to spoil it. I was thinking I'd go to bed and have a diddle down there and think about all the things we did, but instead I had a shower and went to bed feeling ridiculous, as if crouching down and sucking him in the bloody car park was some sort of compromise that wasn't really good enough.

I thought, That's it. This bloke's just awful. I gave him a ring the next day and told him. I was furious. And he was devastated – everyone said so. He begged me to go back out with him and what did I do? I said yes! Why? For a couple of weeks, I juggled Dino and Simon, trying to decide what to do but in the end there was no way round it. I had to tell Simon I needed a break. He was really upset. He kept sending me letters. Every other morning for a fortnight I'd open them at breakfast and weep into my cornflakes. I rang him up a few times and told him it was just for a bit. I really thought I'd end up going back to him in a few weeks.

'I see,' said Sue. 'You shag Dino's brains out for a few weeks, give him the elbow and go back to Simon for a mature, lasting relationship. Wouldn't it be easier to just have an affair with Dino?'

'I'm not shagging him,' I told her.

'What do you mean, you're not shagging him?'

'Not until I'm sure it's the right thing.'

'Shagging him is the single possible reason for going out with Dino. If you don't shag him, why bother?'

'I'll give him a reasonable chance. If it's no go, I'll put him back on the shelf.'

Sue looked at me wearily. 'This is wrong,' she said. 'Prepare to get hurt.'

'I'm not like you, Sue,' I said. 'Either it's serious, or it's off.'

Sue looked at me like I was mad, but Dino has got his nice sides. He's a sweetheart. I know that doesn't sound like him, but he is. He blushes like a baby. And he's so open – really. You can see what's going on in there like a goldfish in a bowl, he just can't help himself. When he's not thinking about how cool he is, he's actually very charming.

It's not just that he's desperate to sleep with me. *I'm* desperate to sleep with *him*. Really. He makes me feel like – ooooh. Sometimes I feel like weeping with frustration. When we . . . well, I don't want to talk about that but you would not believe how horny I get. And I'm not going to do it unless I feel right, and how can you feel right when your boyfriend's so selfish? Isn't that stupid?

But . . . the thing is . . . you can't blame him. Maybe we deserve each other. I've been leading him on for ages. I'm either chucking him or preparing to sleep with him practically

55

every week, and every time I chuck him we get back together and every time I try to sleep with him I back out at the last minute. I guess I'm frightened of getting hurt. Which is totally stupid, because I'm getting hurt, anyway. And so's Dino.

Maybe if I did it . . . I mean, what if that's the problem? Poor boy, he must get so confused, he isn't really all that selfish inside, he's just not very good with feelings. That's the problem, really. If I did shag him, maybe it would make everything all right? If I made him feel secure like that? And I do want to.

Tomorrow. After the party. I'm going to do it. Even if it makes me feel like shit afterwards, I'll never be able to live with myself if I don't. I'll have a word with Sue about it in the morning. Yes! Oh, God. What am I like?

7
pressure

While Jackie and Dino were jumping on each other in the sitting room, Ben was outside the little row of shops just down the road from his place, on his mobile to Ali Young. They were having an almost argument.

'It's my birthday,' she was saying.

'It's your birthday *today*,' he told her.

'You know I've got to see my friends tonight.'

'Ah ha, well, I have to see mine tomorrow.'

There was a pause. Miss was not happy.

'You could make the effort.'

'What would I tell Dino? It's his party, he's my best friend. I can't tell him I can't come to his party because it's your birthday, can I?'

'Make an excuse.'

'I can't.'

'Of course you can. If you wanted.'

'I can't! Look, I'll see you Sunday . . .'

'Don't tell me when you'll see me,' said Ali sharply.

Ben took the phone from his ear and stared at it suspiciously.

He felt completely fazed every time, when she veered from lover Miss to school Miss in mid-sentence.

'All right,' he said. 'I'd like to see you on Sunday.'

Another pause.

'It's as if you're ashamed of me,' she complained.

Ben didn't know what to say. This was getting complicated.

'Well?' she said.

'Well what?'

'Are you? Ashamed of me?'

'It's not that! We can't exactly go public, can we? I mean, it's not like . . .'

'Like what?'

'Well. It's not quite the same as if you were my girlfriend, is it?'

There was another pause, so long this time that he got alarmed. He was just saying, 'Hello,' when she replied,

'I've got to go now, Ben, that's someone on the mobile, I'll see you on Sunday, then. And don't you dare go with anyone else – I'll find out, you know. Goodbye.' And she was gone.

Ben tucked his mobile back into his pocket and went into the newsagent to buy a chocolate bar. He was surprised at how pissed off the conversation had left him.

What did she want? He'd thought it was sex but now he wasn't sure. He was seventeen years old, and he wasn't sure he wanted anyone to want him for anything. Not yet. Not for a long time.

Shagging Miss had always been scary, but lately there were other worries beginning to creep in. It wasn't just the question of where it was all going. It seemed ungrateful, but he was missing girls of his own age. He sometimes actually felt jealous of Dino's problems with Jackie; it all seemed so sweet and innocent and sexy. Miss not only knew it all, she'd done it all and if there was anything she'd accidentally missed she was keen to try it out. Measured against such monumental stark bollock naked, spread open, rampant rudeness, having a snog and a grope in the shrubbery seemed like a childhood game, a lost pleasure like toy cars and pogo sticks.

Then again, what if his sex drive got worn out? What if some sweet, shy girl came along and offered herself to him and he had to get her to swing from the light fittings with a telescope up her fanny and pegs on her tits before he could get it up?

Stupid. He was getting greedy. He was the man with more treasure than he could count, and here he was jealous of their little coins. As if he had any need to feel bad about himself.

8
the party

The idea was to have the Hand Dogs banging it out as people came through the door.

Look at you with your thigh-boots on,
Oh yeaaaah.
Won't you let me dance with you?
Oh yeaaaah.
Stand up with you,
Lie down with you,
All over yoou-hooooo-hoooo.
Kirry-kirry oooooooo.

The trouble was, when *were* they going to arrive? Everything was set by five o'clock in the afternoon. Jackie had come round again in the morning to help get things ready, then disappeared for the afternoon to get her homework done and get ready. Ben turned up about lunch time, Jonathon at about three. They drank Coke and watched Dino check on his mobile to make sure everyone knew exactly what to do that evening: be there. Jonathon started nagging to open the beers and get stuck in.

'There's not enough as it is,' said Dino. 'We don't want to get too pissed before the party's even begun.'

'Don't we?' said Jonathon, who seemed genuinely surprised.

Ben wagged his finger at him. 'What about the girlies, Jon? We don't want to be out of action for them.'

Jonathon, uncomfortable with a subject he felt unequal to, nodded and shrugged and tried to look cool.

Fasil turned up at six to drop off his famous party tapes, and then incurred Dino's ire by clearing off to get on with his training and homework.

'You can't, I'm having a party,' explained Dino, but Fasil was unmoved.

'There's no such thing as a party at six o'clock in the evening,' he said. The door closed behind him, and the long wait began again.

'I'm scared,' admitted Dino an hour or so later, just after Jackie arrived. 'In fact,' he added about an hour after that, 'I'm terrified.'

'Calm down,' advised Ben. 'It's going to be a great party.'

'I'm having a good time already,' said Jonathon.

The rest of the gang from school arrived shortly afterwards, but Dino cheered up only briefly. The main bulk were surely going to turn up any second now; the party needed to get hot. He kept running in and out of the front room putting the Hand Dogs on in case the first guests turned up, but by the time it'd played about ten times everyone was begging him to take it off.

Dino was laughing and loafing about, but inside he felt sick. What if no one came? He'd have emptied the house for a handful of mates and they'd all feel sorry for him. At nine Fasil turned up and began DJ-ing. The party had been started so many times that Dino was getting attacks of *déjà vu* and had to go into the garden to calm down with Jacks.

They wandered up past the lawn towards the patch of garden where his father grew vegetables. The music sounded tinny at this distance, nothing to do with him, almost. They had a snog. Jackie stopped him mussing her hair and made promises for later on. After the music. After the dancing. After the drink and the smoke and the sweat. After the noise, there would be love. Dino began to feel better.

'Perhaps it'd be better to just wait out here until it gets going,' suggested Jackie, but Dino was anxious to watch the agony of his party's birth pangs.

By ten, he was in despair. He was in the kitchen talking to Jackie and Sue and pretending to be cool when two things happened. The music went off. There was a long, loud silence in which the doorbell rang.

Dino ran excitedly down the hall, looked out of the window and saw about six thousand people clutching bottles, standing there like snowmen outside an eerily silent door.

'Wait! Wait!' he hissed. 'Don't let them in . . .' He burst into the front room. The hardcore were all in there dancing like maniacs to no music.

'What's this, you freaks?' he screamed. 'What are you *on*?'

'Are you deaf?' sneered Snoops. Everyone started to make out that the CD player was on full blast and that Dino was the only one who couldn't hear it, yelling things at one another and pretending they could hardly make it out. And – this shows what a state Dino was in – for a second or two he was ready to believe them.

'Huh?' he said. 'Huh?' and he was staring at the player trying to work out how come he could hear them and not it. They all hooted at him like baboons and began pogoing to no noise again. Dino blushed his deepest, most crimson red. Behind him, someone opened the door and a long queue of people came in. Two or three of them stood and stared in amazement at the collection of freaks head-banging to the silence. Outside in the corridor, Dino could hear the others, their voices booming and squeaking in an embarrassed way in the silent house.

One look at the happy little faces of his friends proved anything he wanted to know. They were already off their heads. Useless! He'd issued instructions not to Not to NOT TO before the thing was going, but here they were, peaking like Linford Christie already.

'Can't anyone here even think?' he groaned. Then Fasil walked in, strutting about like he was the only one with a clue in the world and pressed the button. A deafening soup of thick, chunky noise hollered out. At last! Dino poked his head out down the corridor. Everyone was standing still, heads turned to the opened door that was suddenly bellowing music at them.

'Drink, drink, drink!' he instructed them. If he got them drunk or stoned or something no one would even know whether they were having a good time or not. He herded them along to the kitchen and as soon as he was wedged into the corridor, someone turned the music up. It was so loud he couldn't talk to his guests even a hallway and a room away. The bastards! His own mates! They'd reached two o'clock in the morning while everyone else was still at 5 p.m. Dino was furious. The crowd was so thick in the hallway he couldn't even get back to the dance room without a fight. It was awful. Hang your coats there, no, put them in the boxroom, drinks, smoke in the garden please. He was turning into someone's mother, for God's sake! People were milling about in little groups not knowing what to do, it was pathetic. He felt like screaming at them, What's wrong with you, don't you know how to have a good time? Do you need *lessons*?

Suddenly he'd had enough. He fled the kitchen – leave the bastards to it – and made a dive for his friends in the dance room. He hid in the thick wall of music, drank a bottle of Ice Head quick, had a toke on a spliff and tried to relax. It didn't work, so he rushed across the room, seized hold of Jackie and gave her a good snogging in a corner for ten minutes.

It was perfect. It silenced conversation utterly. No one likes to interrupt a good, hard snog. By the time he'd done, someone tapped him on the shoulder, he was feeling cool already. Jackie hung in his arms, her face turned up, ready for more – ready for anything by the looks of her. Dino answered the question about coats, and gave it to her again.

'Oh, *Dino*!' She pushed herself right up against him and stroked his face and whispered right in his ear, 'That was some kiss. Oo-oo-oo . . .' she panted, which made Dino feel very good indeed. The next time they came up for air again Dino was ready for a look around. It was getting there. The music was down so you could hear people if you screamed, the dance floor was moving, people were talking.

He'd done it. He'd survived by snogging with a good-looking girl in the corner of the dance floor. Cool or what? And now it was safe to go and mingle. Jackie had other ideas. She was thinking, Right, right. She could see Sue scowling and trying not to look at her over people's heads, but she'd made up her mind. Tonight was the night. She just had to shag Dino. She was going to do it right now. She'd take him upstairs and ride him like a . . .

'Come on,' she said, pulling him into her. But Dino was already turning away.

'Just a bit . . .'

'Dino! Where are you going?'

'Got to go see, Jacks. Won't be long.'

'Dino!'

But it was too late. Dino was out of the door and off to socialise. He had no idea how close he'd just got. Furious, Jackie looked over at Sue, who was talking loudly in a corner and refused to meet her eye.

Dino did the rounds, shaking hands, five high, five low, great do! How are you? Things were looking good.

'Welcome to the Guesthouse Dinoroso,' he whispered to himself, and imagined that he was walking on air and that everyone was looking at him shyly, out of the corners of their eyes. He elevated his power-beams to a foot above everyone's head so they had nothing to worry about. Fasil was doing great with the music – he didn't have to worry about that. He didn't have to worry about anything.

What did you expect? Yeah – Dino did a great party. He walked up the hall and around the kitchen. He snogged Grace by the back door – it was a party, it was what people did – and coolly resisted her suggestion to go for a walk. Back inside, as he passed down the hall, he met with Ben in the hall, staring at something on the stairway. As Dino came up to him he saw what it was, an amazing sight – Jonathon enjoying a feeding frenzy with Deborah Sanderson on the stairs.

Jonathon had no idea how it had happened. They'd been talking at the bottom of the stairs and it was bit embarrassing because every time someone went up or down they had to squeeze past and Deborah had to push right up against him. That was a bit obvious, Deborah being a bit of a plumper. Jonathon was embarrassed – partly for her, but mainly because he didn't want to be seen squashed up against her like that. He got teased enough about his friendship with her without that.

The kiss had come out of nowhere – he couldn't even remember how it started. He had wondered so often how you actually knew when it was right to kiss a girl, that even as he was doing it, he was trying to work out what had happened so he could use it next time with someone he really fancied. Then, once it had started, it just went on. Deborah sighed, closed her eyes, pulled him almost on top of her and let him sink into her. Immediately, he was overtaken with a rage of hormones. Deborah felt his erection against her stomach and smiled up at him. She grabbed hold of his bum and moved him gently from side to side so that it rocked against her, twitching like Frankenstein's monster in an electric storm. He let his hands creep round her to cuddle a breast. They half fell, half walked a couple of steps up the stairs and collapsed. Jonathon slid his hand under her top and stroked her bra.

Not having known how it started, he had no idea how to stop it, either, even though he was embarrassed to be snogging a fat girl on the stairs where everyone could not only see but had to squeeze past in order to get up and down. Under her loose clothes he felt her all over – every bit that he could get to, anyway. Only when he began to ferret under her knickers did she open her eyes and whisper, 'Not here.' She smiled a languid, warm smile at him and her eyes drifted up to the landing. Terrified, Jonathon closed his eyes and kissed her again, more deeply than ever. He didn't want to be doing this. Or did he? Traitorously, his penis had turned to super-hard concrete in his jeans. Deborah was surreptitiously rubbing it with the back of her hand and he felt so good, he thought he could happily die.

'But I don't fancy her!' Jonathon tried unconsciously to explain, but Mr Knobby Knobster grinned his woozy little hard man's smile and said, 'Yeah? But I do.'

It seemed to go on for hours. He was curled up almost on top of her and they were taking big, long, syrupy slurps of each other's face. A steady stream of people were squeezing past on their way up and down the stairs. In the course of half an hour or so, everyone there would have seen what he was up to, and who it was with. He was feeling more and more uncomfortable, but he had no idea how to extricate himself.

'Jonathon. I see you're having a good party.'

He opened his eyes and saw Dino and Ben standing at the bottom of the stairs watching him. Dino was smiling like a flint. Ben was staring at Deborah, fascinated by this sudden glimpse of the woman sunk in a sexual trance. Deborah's face hung beneath him, her eyes closed, her lips wet, half open, relaxed, hungry. She opened her eyes and looked sideways at Ben. Ben smiled, made a 'Hi,' face, but she just smiled slightly at him before closing her eyes and held her face back under Jonathon's to be kissed. Lowering his, he began to feed. When he peeked out again a moment later, they were gone.

Jonathon came to a sudden decision.

'I need a wee,' he said, and immediately panicked at the thought that she might want to come with him up the stairs. 'Out in the garden, the queue's too long,' he finished quickly. He leaped off her; the image came into his mind of a small raptor leaping off the carcass of a dead sauropod. Wincing, he jumped down the stairs and ran out into the kitchen.

Behind him, Deborah got up and rearranged her clothes. She fancied Jonathon something rotten but never thought she stood a chance. They had so much in common. She and Jon spent ages happily chatting together at school but they'd never seen each other out of it. She'd dreamed that something might happen at the party, but never thought it would. The way he'd leaped on her! She'd actually gasped with surprise. It might have been just a party snog, but he'd been so enthusiastic – it had to mean something. No one had ever told her that a stiff knob means a stiff knob and no more.

'It was just a snog,' Jonathon told Dino in the kitchen a little later.

Dino pulled a face. 'I don't know how you could do it, that's just gross,' he said.

'What?'

'Gross.'

'What's gross about it?'

'She's fat.'

'She's not that fat,' he said, and Dino replied,

'Fat enough.'

Jonathon tried to be dismissive. 'A snog's a snog, so what?' he said. He thought of suggesting she had nice tits – something he'd heard people say dismissively about a girl they'd been with they didn't fancy – but he just couldn't do that to her.

'She still has feelings you know,' said Ben severely. 'Just because she's overweight . . .'

'Fat,' said Dino. 'She's fat.'

'She's plump,' said Ben. 'Some people find that very attractive.'

'People like Jonathon,' said Dino, and Ben snorted in amusement.

'Better than Jackie the beanpole,' said Jonathon.

Dino rolled his eyes. Who did he think he was kidding?

'She's a nice person and she's very fond of you, just don't hurt her, that's all,' said Ben.

'Fat's fat. That's all there is to it,' pointed out Dino.

'She has feelings.'

'Just fat feelings, though,' said Jonathon, who was utterly unable to resist a joke; and then felt awful the way both of them looked at him. His head was whirling. At that moment Jackie and Sue emerged meaningfully out of the crowd and cornered him.

'Are you serious about Debs?' asked Sue.

'What?'

'Are you serious about her?'

'What?'

'Don't keep saying "What!"'

'Do you really fancy her?' asked Jackie severely.

Jonathon was horrified. Part of him refused to give Dino the pleasure of thinking that he didn't fancy Debs merely because she was fat; part of him was scared of Ben and the girls thinking he was just using her; and part of him genuinely liked Deborah and didn't want to hurt her. He just didn't fancy her, but he wasn't sure he had any right not to.

'Well? Do you?'

'You're being a bit quick, aren't you?' said Ben.

'She's really fond of you, do you know that? She really likes you,' said Sue. 'You don't know how lucky you are, she's such a nice person. You're not just stringing her along, are you?'

'No, of course I'm not . . .'

'Do you fancy her then?'

Jonathon writhed, caught between Dino, Ben and these fearsome young women. 'Well, yes of course I fancy her, I was kissing her, wasn't I?' On the tip of his tongue were the words, 'But that doesn't mean . . .' But somehow they couldn't emerge.

'Good.'

'You've done it now,' said Dino after they'd left. 'They've probably gone to tell her that you want to go out with her.'

'I didn't know you felt like that,' said Ben.

'Neither did I,' said Jon. He pushed his way through the crowd to escape. He was definitely not in control of the situation.

'So you like fat girls too, then,' Dino told Ben, leering at him. Ben smiled blandly and slipped away to the back door.

The fact was, Ben was jealous. Not of Deborah herself, although he liked her. He was jealous of the sort of relationship she and Jon could have together. They got on well together. He thought how comfortable they'd looked on the stairs. He wished them well.

Bollocks, he thought to himself, as he stuck his head out into the garden and gulped down the cool air. All these lovely girls. All those lucky boys getting off with them, snogging with them, sleeping with them, feeling them up – and he couldn't do it. As she'd said, Ali would find out somehow and give him hell. Ben was a popular and good-looking boy, there were any number of attractive girls who would have got into a clinch with him, but he didn't dare. There wasn't anyone he could talk to. Stupid though it was, for someone who was getting quality sex from an expert, he was feeling left out.

Oh well, he thought. One thing anyway, at least the old harpy can't come here. The thought made him shudder.

Apart from having to watch one of his friends kiss a fat girl, Dino had ordeals yet to come: he spotted Jackie snogging Fasil in the kitchen. Suddenly, all the feel-good drained away out of the hole in his bottom. Out of order, or what?

Dino didn't mess about; he interrupted.

Fasil did the right thing. He grinned meekly, abandoned all hopes of single number status for the rest of his life and scuttled off. But Jackie turned round and eyed him aggressively.

'My girlfriend. My party,' said Dino. 'You snog me.'

'I snog anyone I want.'

The thing that really pissed Dino off wasn't just that they'd snogged. It was that they'd snogged in public. There was his girlfriend snogging one of his friends in full view of everyone. It was all cut and dried. Except . . .

'You were snogging Grace, you two-faced bastard,' Jackie snarled. It was true. Dino blushed. He'd been a twat, but that just made him angrier than ever. The one thing he really couldn't bear was to feel like a twat.

He bent down and hissed in her ear, 'Shut up, will you? Everyone's going to think I'm a right twat.'

'Is that all you're worried about? *Looking* like a twat? You *are* a twat! Twat!' she bellowed, and off she shoved, leaving Dino standing there feeling more twat-like than he had ever done before.

Dino was furious. 'Slut,' he called after her. 'Slapper,' loud enough for everyone to hear.

She turned round all little girlie and squeaked in a stupid voice, 'Oh, Dino, I was only practising so I could kiss you better later on. Everyone knows you kiss sooooooooooo goooooooooood.' And she said this in such a way that indicated – can you believe this? – that Dino was a crap kisser. Then she flounced off.

He stood there like a bare arse. He could feel his cheeks flushing redder and redder. Everyone had heard the whole exchange. He began, 'Don't give me that bollocks, everyone knows I kiss like a . . .' And then he had to stop because now he was putting his foot in it very badly indeed. Boasting about how well you kiss! God, that was so childish.

Having no idea what else to do, he just turned round and walked out. Right out. Out of the room, out of the hall, out of the house. He was blind with rage and humiliation. Let them have fun! Let them enjoy themselves, the whole lot of them. He didn't want anything to do with any of them.

Dino got halfway home before he remembered that he'd been at home in the first place. There was nowhere else to go. For a moment he thought about going back to the party and throwing everyone out, but even as he thought it, he realised it was impossible. That would not be a very cool thing to do.

He walked back. From outside it sounded as if the party was going like a bomb. He lurked, wondering what to do. It was a while before he realised the way out. Thank God! He'd been in the wrong! All he had to do was admit it. Admitting you were in the wrong was a cool thing to do. It made you more human, somehow. He'd been snogging people, so had Jacks. So what was the problem? Of course, he'd much rather not have stormed out, or lost his cool; and he'd *very* much rather Jackie had never snogged with Fas. But what was done was done.

He hung around a bit longer, plucking up courage. He practised laughing at himself. Then he took the plunge and went to ring the doorbell. It really was pretty funny, after all.

'I went home,' Dino told Stu, and started laughing and laughing. 'Outta my head!' he howled. Stu grinned back, and Dino knew he was going to get away with it. Once he'd recovered laughing at how out of his head he'd been, he went to look for Jackie and apologised. She forgave him at once.

'OK?' he said and she said,

'OK.'

Dino leaned in and whispered, 'Sorry.'

'Yeah, so am I.'

'No more snogging other people, eh?'

'No more snogging other people.'

Dino thought, I'm still in. 'I'm still in? Later?' he said.

'Mmmmm . . . OK. If you're good.'

But it had been a close thing. He found Fasil and – this was really cool – had a chat with him about nothing much, just to show no hard feelings. But warned him off as well.

'I reckon I'm in with Jackie after,' he said.

'Mmm,' said Fasil.

Dino leaned up right close to his face and breathed, 'Virgin hole,' right in his face. Fasil moved his head back and stared at Dino with a horrified expression. Dino winked and leered.

The party went from quiet to friendly, to busy, to loud, to frantic. Dino had a few smokes and a couple more Ice Head beers and gradually a holy, rosy glow started to hover around him. It was a good party. He was a saint, really. All these people having such a good time, just because of him. His Holiness Pope Dino the First, he felt like, as he went from group to group, bestowing his benedictions upon them. The hardcore were like a bunch of apes by comparison, they were all jiggering about and shouting. They had indulged in something a bit stronger than a few spliffs. Dino himself declined. He didn't want to do anything that might interfere with his session with Jackie later on. That, after all, was the main event of the evening. He didn't want his vital parts shrivelled up like a frightened slug. He wanted big, stiff parts for that night's action.

People were rushing up and down the stairs shrieking. People were yelling in the kitchen and having fights over the limited quantities of alcohol. Couples had moved into the bedrooms, or, if the bedrooms were full, into the garden and under blankets in the downstairs room. A row of them were snogging up the stairs.

'What's this, the queue for the bedrooms?' bellowed Jonathon up at them. Standing in a group three metres and about fifty people away, Deborah looked at him and laughed far too loud. Jonathon pretended he hadn't noticed. A crowd in the sitting room discovered that if they all danced up and down hard enough they could make the piano next to the door advance on them. It looked threatening and stupid at the same time, and someone christened it Dino's Dad, because it looked like it was coming to chuck them all out.

A girl called Sam made love in Dino's parents' bed with a boy called Robby, who was sick on the sheets next to her as soon as he'd finished. They covered it up with the duvet and went home. Next door in the boxroom a kid called Simon Tiptree pretended to pass out on top of a pile of coats. When he was left alone, he began systematically to go through all the pockets and bags, looking for money and valuables. At about the same time downstairs in the kitchen, a thin girl in a tiny pink dress was opening the fridge door. She stared rapturously inside. Treasure! Cheese, pork pie, cold cooked sausages! Paradise. Cream cake! What comes next on the ladder up after cold sausage paradise? Cream cake paradise, of course. Without even pausing to moan in pleasure, she reached in and seized an oozing triangle of pleasure, and bit in.

At that moment Jonathon entered the kitchen, trying to duck out of sight of Deborah. It was getting severe. So what if he'd snogged her? Sod it, why couldn't he have a snog just because she was a tubber? Now she was following him. It was awful. And so public! Whenever he lifted his head, there she was, looking at him, walking towards him, eyeing him sideways, craning her neck in between people to try and spot him. Jonathon was being hunted. By good fortune he turned up as the slight girl was opening the fridge door, just in time to duck behind it out of Deborah's sight. The thought, 'Never hide from a fat girl in the fridge', crossed his mind, but there was nowhere else to go. He lowered his head as if to peer inside.

'Yum,' he said to the girl standing next to him. She waved a wedge of cream cake at him.

'No' bad,' said the girl thickly. The little pink dress was so short she showed her knickers every time she bent over or lifted her arms; a pussy pelmet, as his dad would have called it. It occurred to Jonathon that it would be a good thing if Deborah saw him in close-up with a pretty girl like this. She might get the message.

'I'm Jonathon,' he told her, moving in, something he'd never have dared to do unless he had another reason other than to get close.

'Zoë,' she said thickly. She waved her cake into the fridge, generously inviting Jonathon to help himself. Jonathon reached in and took out one of the cold cooked sausages lying on a plate inside. He held it between his fingers, and on a sudden impulse – 'May I?' – reached across and dipped the tip of the sausage into the cream of the girl's cake, wiping it along so it had a big dollop on the end. As he did it he had a nasty feeling he might regret it. He held the sausage up in his fingers and waited.

'You disgusting thing,' said Zoë, but even as she spoke she burst into laughter, snorting around her cake. Jonathon bobbed the sausage up and down like a little finger puppet.

'Mr Porky is wearing a white hat today,' he began. He was about to launch into a puppet show, but the girl laughed in surprise right through her mouthful of cream cake and sprayed all over the inside of the fridge. Everything was covered.

'Jesus, sick in the fridge,' said Jonathon. The girl was delighted with him, it was great. But at that inopportune moment, Fasil turned up.

'What is this? What are you doing?' he asked them. He looked in amazement at the sausage and then angrily at the girl's handful of cake. Then he saw what looked like sick sprayed all over the inside of the fridge. Despite being caught snogging Dino's girlfriend, Fasil was a man of principles.

'That's his fridge! That's his food. You can't do that!'

'Who's this?' asked the girl. 'Someone's dad?'

'What are you doing?' Fasil asked Jonathon.

Jonathon smiled weakly. 'It's just a sausage . . .'

'Look at that, she's got half his cream cake there,' complained Fasil. 'She's spat it all over the fridge and you're encouraging her.'

'Is this how you *party*?' the girl asked. 'Is this how you have *fun*?' Fasil was pulling the fridge door shut on them. Revealed to the kitchen, Jonathon looked round. Sure enough, Deborah was there, right there. Two steps and she was on him.

'Oooh,' she said. 'Sausage and cream. My favourite.' She reached forward, took the sausage off Jon and licked the cream off the end of it.

'I see,' said Jonathon.

Taking advantage of the distraction, the girl in the pink dress dodged out of sight, past Fasil, who was staring at Deborah and her sausage as if he'd just seen a cat lay an egg, and out into the hall, where she leaned against a wall and finished off the cream cake greedily.

Zoë had started out the night before in a bar called Kas the Wanderer, drinking Red Bull and vodka with a group of friends. She'd done a load of e at another party, stayed up all day watching TV at a friend's house before going to Dino's. One of her friends was going out with one of Jackie's, which was how they'd found out about it. The others had had enough fairly early on and gone home, but Zoë had nowhere better to go. She hung around in the hope of doing a bit of looting. She'd had nothing to eat all day and she was starving hungry and exhausted.

That guy with the sausage had been nice. She liked funny boys.

When she'd finished she picked up a drink someone had left on a windowsill and took a swig. Snakebite – cider and lager. She whacked down the glassful, pulled a face. She put a hand behind her to steady herself against the sill. Her head was swimming. She decided to have a look upstairs, see if she couldn't find a place to get her head down right now. The stairway was solid. The first room she found was the boxroom, where Simon Tiptree had to quickly pretend he'd passed out on his back on a pile of coats. Zoë watched him closely, staring at him for a full minute, listening to his breath, until she was sure he was asleep. She went up and prodded him with her foot. He didn't stir.

Satisfied that he really was out cold, Zoë began to go through the pockets of the coats heaped on the bed beside him. In his false sleep, Simon was outraged – a thief, standing there stealing while he was asleep! The awful thing was, there was nothing he could do about it. If he woke up and nabbed her, she might make a fuss, and then someone might come in and find his own bag full of their valuables. He just had to lie there and take it.

The girl was disappointed to find so little money. She went through the coats – nothing. Then the bags, but it wasn't until she opened an unpromising-looking nylon rucksack that she suddenly struck it rich. It rattled like a collection box with handfuls of loose change. Inside were watches, bits of jewellery, paper money. There must have been fifty or sixty pounds in cash there.

'Oh yeah,' she whispered. She stared intently at Simon, who lay on his back in fury, still trying to appear fast asleep. His face twitched slightly.

'Thanks, sweetheart,' she told him, and slipped out.

She knew she should leave right then. But she was truly exhausted. The slice of cream cake was about all she'd eaten for twelve hours or more, she was full of vodka and cider and needed to lie down. She poked her head next door into one of the bedrooms. There was a couple lying side by side on the double bed on top of the duvet. She couldn't tell if they were post coital or just past it, but there was a small sofa under the window with a candlewick cover lying on it. She got onto the sofa, pulled the cover on top of her, and went to sleep.

Next door, Simon was furious. After all the trouble he'd been to! He'd had plans for that money, it was important to him. But what could he do? As soon as she left the room, he sat up, groaned and held his head in his hands. The vile little bitch was so tiny! It was infuriating – a small person getting one over on him like that! The funny thing about it was, he felt so violated – he the thief – because he'd been robbed of his thievings. Frustrated and sullen, he jumped up and stamped downstairs with the idea of finding the girl, following her home and mugging her to get his money back. But he didn't see her again. He went home with a headache, empty-handed. But there was one lesson to be learned, he realised: if you're going to steal, steal from a thief. They are the least likely to report it.

At two, Ray and Alan Wicks started throwing bottles on the street outside the house – a sure sign that the party was over. There was nothing left to drink, the strangers had left;

acquaintances and semi-friends were already pulling on their coats. There was a flurry of fury when people discovered that their bags had been raided. A few of them had nothing to get home with and had to borrow from those who had been more careful with their things. Taxis turned up and ferried people away. There was a final clump of dedicated smokers getting happily stoned on the landing, who made Dino feel very uncool as he booted them out. The semi-hardcore hung about searching through the bottles for dregs, then left in a lump, leaving Jacks, Ben, Fas, Sue and her boyfriend Dave. And Jonathon. And Deborah.

There had been a weak attempt to begin the clearing up, but Jackie evidently had other things on her mind. People were drinking coffee, but she was sitting next to Dino on the sofa sighing and leaning her head on his shoulder. Whenever he turned to look at her, she kissed him.

'I guess it's time to go,' said Sue. She stood up and smiled at Jackie. 'Come on, let's go and get the coats for the dregs. Speed things up.' Jackie got up and they went upstairs together.

Jonathon leered. 'You don't have to boot us out, Dino,' he said. 'You don't need the whole house for that.' He smiled awkwardly at Deborah, who was sitting next to him clutching his hand.

'Yeah, yeah, yeah,' said Dino.

'Do you need the downstairs for some sort of overflow system?' said Jonathon. 'Is it your organ size? Do you need the extra room to manoeuvre it? Perhaps some of us could help with the positioning?'

'Shut yer trap,' said Dino. But he loved all this.

Upstairs, Sue and Jackie were in Dino's parents' bedroom.

'So this is the holy of holies.' Sue tested the bed by pressing down on it and bouncing it up and down. 'Plenty of give, should give a good return service . . .'

'Shut up!'

'Did you change the sheets?'

'Shut *up*!'

'There's nothing worse than waking up to the smell of his dad.'

'Yeah, I know, I made him do them yesterday.'

'Did you? Make *him* do it?'

'Yeah,' said Jackie. Which was a lie. She just thought she needed a bit more cred.

Sue sighed. 'So you're finally going to go through with it?'

'Yes.' Jackie's voice came out all high and funny, but she was determined this time. The thought of it made her squeak with excitement.

'Well. I'll be thinking of you. I'll get the coats. You get into bed, eh?'

Jackie burst out into a fit of nervous giggles, but she kicked off her shoes and started to unbutton her top. She paused when she noticed that Sue was still standing on the other side of the bed, smiling and watching her.

'Go away!' she scolded, turning her back.

'I hope he appreciates what he's getting,' said Sue, and she left to get the coats.

Jackie walked excitedly round the room a couple of times, anxious about getting in naked. She ran to the door to listen and make sure no one else was coming up, then she took all her clothes off. Naked, she looked at herself in the mirror. Her eyes weaved their way across to the bits she didn't like. Her hips, which seemed to stick out sideways like a set of lard shelves. Her buttocks quivered as she walked – disgusting! Her breasts looked fine when she was standing, but headed south for her armpits as soon as she lay on her back, and when she stood up with her legs together, instead of her thighs touching each other on the way up to a neat triangle at the top, she had a slight bow in between her thighs which ended abruptly. These were secret faults, of course, only for lovers ever to see – which was of course precisely what she didn't want.

She scowled and tried to concentrate on her good points. She turned sideways, looked at her breasts and her tummy and her skin. Nothing's perfect but . . .

'Pretty good,' she told herself uncertainly.

She paused, unsure whether or not to wait up and give him a flash as he came in – she looked at her best standing, when gravity worked for her – or to get into bed and risk him finding he had to feel under armpits to find her boobs. She went to hover by the bed. She turned off the main light and put one of the bedside ones on. She decided to wait. She pulled on a gown she found on the back of the door. She'd slip it off as she heard him on the stairs and give him a second or two of full frontal as he came in, then she'd slip in between the sheets. She went to stand by the bed and pulled back the crumpled cover so she could jump in quick.

9
dino

Sue came back down with the coats. 'Time to go home,' she said.

'Mighta known, prefers his hole to his mates, typical,' groaned Jonathon, and I thought, Man! I am the One. I mean. They were going home and me – what was I gonna do? Me and Jacks. If you saw her, you'd know what you're missing.

I saw them out. They were all as jealous as a cat in a fish shop – or, put it another way – jealous as cats watching another cat in a fish shop, and that cat was me. I closed the door. I caught a glimpse of Jonathon turning to face Debs with a funny look on his face. Poor sod, I thought to myself, and Jacks is upstairs, all ready, in bed, probably with nothing on, waiting for me.

Up I went, up the stairs with a couple of bottles of Ice Head all ready to make it and what was waiting in the bed for me? You know what was there? A big heap of sick.

I think I nearly went mad for a moment. It was just lying there where she should be, and there was a definite second when I thought she'd actually been turned into a pile of squashed puke. Then I realised – she'd been ill! Just my luck – she's bloody drunk so much she's been sick and now the whole thing's off again!

I ran out to the landing and into the bathroom, but she wasn't there. I called, 'Jacks!' down the stairs, but there was no reply. Right then, I knew. In fact, I reckon I knew even before, as soon as I saw the puke. I started to think that maybe she was hiding from me, or maybe she'd passed out and was lying on the floor out of sight. I ran around the house checking behind all the chairs and things like that, but I knew she wasn't there.

The thing is, it was squashed sick. It was well slept on, that puke. I ran back up to check and tested the temperature of the vomit with the tip of my elbow – I know, it's mad, you have to remember what I was going through. I didn't want to touch it with my fingers. I had no idea of the cool rate of vomit, but this was stone cold.

'This is not my fault,' I hissed to myself. I'd even got her clean sheets to put on the bed! How could she do this to me! I stood there steaming, then I thought to look for her coat in the boxroom, ran through . . . It wasn't there. That was the final proof. The bitch had sneaked out without even telling me. I ran to the front door to shout after her, but I didn't dare to shout very loud; it was too humiliating. There was no answer.

Can you believe that? Why me? Just a few minutes before, I was about the happiest bloke on earth. It was so perfect, showing your friends out of the front door, while your beautiful girlfriend is sliding all naked and gorgeous and ready and waiting into the sheets upstairs. And now look! It's all just . . . a pile of puke.

I walked back along the hallway and I suddenly realised

what a horrible fucking mess everything was. There were crumpled plastic cups everywhere. Some of them had spilt, some of them were full of dog ends and other crap. I couldn't bear to go back into the living room, I just went straight up the stairs, but I could feel the presence of the mess in every corner of the house, like a haunting. Stinking beer and dog ends, ash, mud and puke on the carpets and in the beds. I remembered now that someone had been sick actually *in the fridge*. Even along the landing it was filthy. There were dark puddles on the carpet. Someone had rubbed the black rubber of their shoes along the skirting boards. There was broken glass on the top few stairs. There was a row of dog ends standing like a little fence on the little table by my bedroom door. Some of them had fallen down and charred the wood.

And I was still a virgin.

I went back into my parents' bedroom to have another look at the sick, like it might not be there this time, or it'd turned back into Jackie. It was really well ground in. I stared at it for a minute. I thought to myself, If I shag the sick instead of Jackie will I still be a virgin? . . . because just then I'd have done anything on the planet not to be a virgin. I'd destroyed my parents' house and it hadn't worked. What did I have to do? I took a deep breath into the depths of my lungs and I screamed, 'AHHHHHHHHHHHHHHHHHHHHHHHHHHHHHHHHHHH-HHHHHHHHHHHHH!' as loud as I could, and someone right next to me screamed back so loud I think I died briefly as I jumped about ten metres into the air.

10
jonathon

Dino closed the door and Sue and her bloke shot off home. It was Ben, Fas and Meandeborah. All I wanted was for it to be Ben and Fas and me and Deborah. Or even better Fas and Deborah and Ben and me. Or better still, Deborah, Ben, Fas and me on the other side of the whole fucking sentence, but there I was – Meandeborah. Help.

Ben was being very nice. He can be very . . . courteous, I suppose. Fasil was quiet, I knew he disapproved. Well, Ben disapproved too, but he disapproved because he thought I was going to hurt Debs. He was probably right. Fasil disapproved because he thought that going with a fat girl was morally reprehensible.

I was coming down. I felt like my nervous system had been wired up to some sort of fairground attraction. Have you ever had that feeling where everyone looks like machines? You know? Only pretending to be human beings? What do they want? What are they *up* to?

So this was hilarious, really. We'd just got to the T-junction on the main road when there was this low, moaning call.

It sounded like mating wombats lost in the drains or something.

'Was that *Dino*?' someone asked.

We all stopped and the call came again.

'Yaaaackeeee . . .' As if Dino, if indeed Dino it was, was scared of shouting too loud in case it punctured his status.

'Could be,' said Ben. We waited for a while, but there was no more noise, so we carried on a little way. Then, feet, clip-clopping down the road. It was like a movie. Like the camera crew and the lighting guys were going to come running backwards round the corner at any moment filming something coming towards us.

'I think it's coming towards us,' I hissed, and Deborah laughed too loudly. It was so late there were no cars about, everything was dead quiet. We all turned at once to watch the T-junction behind us, just as if we'd been told to.

Clop clop clop clop clop, they went. I turned to look at Ben to see if he was aware that we were in some sort of production; he just smiled at me sideways and raised his eyebrows.

Clop clop clop clop clop clop. It was like, will it be, won't it be, will it be . . . ?

It was. Jackie.

As soon as she saw us she stopped dead in her tracks and stared at us, before turning and heading fast up the road in the opposite direction.

'Jackie, where you going? Are you all right?' called Deborah. Jackie turned and looked at her, nodded, then shook her head and leaned her arm against the wall and rested her forehead on it. Deborah told me to wait for her and went clopping off herself to see to her, with Fasil, who fancies Jackie chronically, trailing behind her.

Ben looked at me and I looked at Ben – and we both just cracked up. Poor old Dino! After all that. We had to turn our backs so we couldn't be seen. He was so sure he was on to it tonight. And here she was running away! Poor old Jackie was obviously in a right state and we couldn't show her how hysterical we were. We didn't say a word, we just stood there with our backs to them, trying not to shake too hard.

Finally we got ourselves under control. Debs and Jacks were having a heart to heart with Fasil hanging around the edge, like he was looking for a spare bone. As if he didn't have enough bone already.

I was starting to move over towards them, but Ben hung back. He put his hands in his pockets and sort of rocked on his feet and said, 'Well, looks like there's enough gooseberries about. I think I'll go home.' And he smiled grimly at me.

'You bastard,' I hissed.

We looked across. Deborah was trying to listen sympathetically to Jackie and keep an eye on me at the same time.

'Make a run for it now?' suggested Ben.

There was a pause. He always scares me by lunging straight into things.

'It was just a snog,' I insisted.

'Not for her. She's smitten, I think,' he said. Then he looked at me and said, 'But it's nice to have someone who's smitten with you, isn't it?' I didn't say anything, so he asked me right out, 'Do you fancy her or not?'

'Yes,' I lied. 'Of course I do. But . . .'

'But?'

'I just don't want to go out with anyone at the moment.'

Ben smiled wryly. 'You'll just have to tell her then,' he said. He wagged a finger at me, and I could have strangled the bastard. I suppose he was only offering me a piece of advice but it felt like torture. He knew very well I couldn't bring myself to do that. Didn't he?

'See you,' said Ben, and he left, giving me a friendly little wave over his shoulder as he slid off.

So I sauntered over to see what was going on, like a puppet in a puppet show. Free will? Don't make me laugh.

Deborah looked as if she was having a good time. She has this gift, Deborah, she always manages to look as if she's having a good time. Maybe she is, who knows? – but on the other hand, maybe she was doing it for Jackie, who kept giggling and bursting into tears. Fasil was standing there staring at her like a weasel. He kept offering to walk her home every minute or so, until Debs snapped at him to shut up going on, couldn't he see she was upset?

So, of course Deborah had to offer to walk home with her. Which should have been great because I could have said, OK, see you later . . . What a pity! Just as we were getting to grips with each other, you have to rescue a friend! Oh well, I'll try not to be disappointed. Maybe another time (which will never come). But Deborah said, 'You can keep us company,' so I had to go along.

That bit was quite funny actually. Fas came along too, and we ended up walking behind, like a pair of shotgun riders or something. I tried to make conversation with him, but Fas, he gets so stoned, he could hardly say a word. He just kept staring at me with these big dopey eyes every time I said anything, so I shut up and we walked along in silence. Meanwhile, ahead of us, Deborah was being magnificent as usual. She was sorting Jackie out, no problem. They were laughing and talking, and Debs kept patting her and comforting her. She's just great like that.

Finally we got Jackie home. Goodbye goodbye goodbye. Fasil went off in one direction, Jackie flung her arms round Debs and went indoors and there it was, Meandeborah all on our own. She linked her arm through mine and smiled.

'I've been waiting to get you on your own all night,' she told me, and lifted her eyebrows up and gave me one of those big lovely smiles, so I knew what was in store. And of course Mr Knobby, the traitorous little fletch, stood up at the mere thought.

We walked along a bit, and then Deborah started cracking up, and had to tell me the story. See, Jackie had got herself all ready, all powdered and washed and lovely and naked and plumped up and ready in the bedroom, pulled back the covers to the bed to get in so she'd be like a nice tender, juicy little filling when Dino came up . . . and there under the sheets was this huge pile of cold puke lying there, all squidged up into the covers. And she was so offended, she put her clothes straight back on and left. Deborah just cracked up – it was pretty bloody funny. I mean, it wasn't even Dino's fault. She stormed out – very quietly by all accounts – and was halfway home before she realised she'd sabotaged her own shag.

'So why didn't she just go back?' I asked, and Deborah said,

'Because she didn't want to!' She thought this was priceless, Debs, she just kept bending over and roaring with laughter.

It was a real gas, that walk home, actually. We started pretending to be Jackie and Dino, with her dying to shag him and then panicking every time he took his knob out. I really lost it, actually. I started pretending I was Dino's knob in *disguise*, trying to look all friendly. I found some roses and sprinkled some petals on my head and ran around Deb with this crazy, knobby walk, wagging at her and promising all sorts of things if she'd just let me get in her. Deborah was killing herself. I was off my head – pretending to be Dino's knob! God, if he ever found out he'd never speak to me again. It was great. Then we got near to her place and I felt myself lose it again and got all quiet and anxious. We stood there holding hands. She moved up very close to me and said, 'Aren't you going to see if I run away screaming from yours?'

I said something, I don't know what it was. She came right up to me and kissed me and put her hand on it so it went up like a rocket inside my jeans.

'Yum,' she whispered.

So we stood hidden round the corner to where she lived, and we had this huge, magic, mammoth snog. It was just fantastic. And I felt her all over. It was like . . . well, how can you describe that? It was like drinking Fine Old Wine. I mean, not really – I've never drunk Fine Old Wine, only once, you know, and I didn't like it all that much. But it was like you'd imagine it might be. Or swimming in Fine Old Wine or something like that. Just rich and filling up all your senses and well – gorgeous and thick and loads of it.

I'd felt up other girls before, but Deborah was *womanly*. Tits and belly and bum. She smelt like a piece of fruit cake. I was really getting into it, and there was this little bit of my mind that was watching the whole thing, and another bit that was imagining someone else was watching us, which really turned me on. I got her jumper hoisted up and her tits out of her bra and right out into the air, and I kept turning her so that the street light was shining on her, and imagining that someone could see what was going on. She was breathing these deep, heavy breaths and staring up at me like she was stunned or something. She kept glancing up the road but I don't think she minded. I kept bending to kiss them and they got all wet. I kept trying to pull her knickers down too. I had this vision of her standing there with her tits out and her knickers round her knees that was making me go mad, but she wouldn't have it. And all the time she had Mr Knobby out in her hand, working away with him. She was having little looks at what she was doing. And finally – this was just so great – finally, she pulled away slightly to get a really big look, like it was a big treat for her, and stroked and pulled until I came all over her hand and on her skirt.

'Sorry,' I groaned, hanging onto the wall to stop falling down. It was all over her clothes. She roared with laughter.

'I enjoyed it,' she insisted.

'What about you?' I whispered, when I'd got my breath back. I'd spent the past ten minutes labouring away down there, with no success.

'I'll be all right,' she said. She paused and then added, 'I'll show you how another time.'

I stared down at her. She was looking up at me, her white teeth smiling in the dull light. I was thinking, Does that mean I don't know how? Yes, it does. And does it mean that she's expecting to see me again? Yes, it does.

And do I want to?

'You know what?' a little voice in my head said. 'I haven't got a clue.'

'I'd better go in now,' Deborah said.

'OK. Thanks.'

She laughed at me. 'You don't need to say thanks!' she gurgled.

'Did you really like it?'

'Yes!' she roared, as if that was a great joke too. It was beyond me what she got from it, but she seemed to be telling the truth.

'Are you helping clear up at Dino's tomorrow?' she asked.

'I said I would.'

'See you there then. About midday?' She reached up and kissed me. When she pulled back she put her hand on the side of my face for a moment, a very tender touch, then she turned and went inside. And I thought, That was so gorgeous.

Help!

11
party fairy

'AHHHHHHHHHHHHHHHHHHHHHHHHHHHH!'

What was it? A murderer? Jackie? The sick? Please, please not the sick shouting at him! He spun in a circle and landed facing the opposite way. The candlewick cover on the little settee under the window had opened up and inside it was a pale, grubby girl. Her bare arms made her look like a child. Her eyes were as big as saucers popping out from under her curly brown hair. She looked as terrified as he was. She was pretty. In the first fraction of a second, Dino had another mental illusion. As soon as he realised she wasn't the sick he wondered if she might be a fairy.

'Who are you? Jesus! What are you doing there?' Dino asked.

'I was asleep, sorry, sorry.'

'Jesus,' he said again. 'You look like a bloody fairy. What are doing there?'

'I fell asleep.' She looked around the room anxiously and tried to smile. 'A party fairy, that's me. Do you want three wishes?' As soon as she said it, she regretted it and blushed. Then she tried to smile as if she was being funny.

Dino thought, What? And then his heart went bang bang bang because there they were, alone in the bedroom, strangers – and she was offering three wishes. A shag, a blow job and a . . . He'd think of the other one later. He was so terrified by the thought that he hardly dared to look at her for a few seconds and walked round in a circle instead. Of course it was ridiculous – she was just saying it for a joke. But you never knew. When he looked back at her she was scowling.

'Do I really look like a fairy?' she asked suspiciously.

'Everyone's gone home,' he told her.

The girl stood up. She was wearing a tiny pink dress, which she tugged down over her thighs. She looked so bare standing there in her party dress that Dino thought again that she might be offering. Maybe she was waiting for him to ask. He remembered what someone had once said to him about girls: if you don't ask you don't get.

'What?' he said anxiously.

'Got a fag?' she asked.

'I don't smoke,' he told her. 'I expect there's some somewhere, though.'

'Hang on . . .' She walked to the side of the bed and bent down to pick up a packet of Marlborough Lights and a lighter lying on the floor by the bed. She shook it; the pack rattled. She took one out and lit it. She stood there smoking and looking sideways at Dino.

'Someone must've left 'em behind,' she said, shaking the packet at him.

'Yeah.' Then for some reason Dino looked at the bed. Her eyes followed his. Then they both looked at each other.

'I better go,' said the girl.

'Someone was sick,' said Dino. 'Look.' The girl looked at the bed again.

'Oh, yeah,' she said.

Dino began, 'My girl . . . I mean, this girl did that and walked out,' he said. 'Just now. Did you see her?'

'I was asleep.' said the girl, and she took a big hard drag on her fag. She looked pissed off, but she wasn't leaving, not so far. She was just standing there, looking all bare with her arms wrapped round herself, holding tight to her fag. Her legs were grubby too, he noticed. Actually, she looked like a bit of a tart. Make-up smudged all over the place, grubby legs – what did she have grubby legs for? She saw him staring and tugged at her dress again.

'Been a long party,' she said, and laughed.

'All night,' said Dino.

'Two bloody days I've been at it!'

'Oh . . . Well. Wow. You've had a good time, then.'

'Huh, yeah!'

She took another big drag on her fag and then she said, 'What's the time?'

'I dunno, maybe three.'

The girl sighed and said, 'Look, it's late, I don't like to ask, but can you put me up here?'

'My parents are back tomorrow evening.'

'I'll be gone by then, I won't be any trouble, I can sleep here.'

And Dino thought, Oh ho! But he was scared to ask her if she'd sleep with him, so he said, 'Will you help me clean up in the morning?' instead.

'Yeah!' She looked pleased about it. It was a deal. 'Yeah! All right. Thanks.'

'All right!'

'OK, then.' She nodded. 'Thanks.' Then she sat down on the settee and said, 'See you then.'

'No, you better . . .' Dino was about to be the host and say that she could sleep in a bed, but the word 'bed' froze on his lips. Then he thought, Sod this – she knows what I want. What sort of Wally would find a situation like this on their hands and then not try it on? What would he say to his mates? 'Nah, we just had a chat and then she went to bed . . .'

He said, 'Do you want a cup of tea.'

'Nah. I'll just sleep.'

He frowned. She knew what he wanted all right! There she was with her party dress up round her knickers . . . So he did it. He said,

'You can stay the night . . . So long as you stay with me.'

She didn't look at him at once. Her mouth opened slightly. Then she glanced up. Dino half smiled and took a step towards her. She didn't move when he sat there awkwardly next to her on the little settee. Dino knew, suddenly, without knowing why, that he could do anything he liked to this girl and she'd let him; he just knew.

He put an arm round her. Her shoulders were cold. He kissed her, she tasted sour and faggy. She shook her head and said, 'Don't.'

'Go on,' he told her. It was so obvious she wasn't going to

stop him, it was as clear as day. He pulled her backwards and sideways onto her back and looked down. Her little dress had ridden up and there was a little white triangle of knickers. He kissed her again and stuck his hand down there straight away, no messing. She wriggled slightly and turned her head away. He kissed her neck instead, nudged her legs apart and rubbed into her. He lifted his head to see her face and he was put out to see that her eyes were open as well. She was on her back looking away from him, staring at something on the other side of the room. Dino looked over in alarm. There was nothing there, just the wardrobe. But it put him off, her staring like that.

She said, 'I'm cold,' in a whiny little voice.

'We can use my bed,' he told her. He stood up and gave her his hand, which she took, and led her by the hand through to his room. Her expression looked so odd that he actually said to her,

'You don't mind.'

She shrugged, and he thought to himself it would be truer to say she didn't care. It was awkward, standing by the bed. He kissed her again to stop her mouth in case she complained. Then he pulled the pink dress over her head and there she was, with her knickers hardly covering her bush and her little titties out. Dino said, 'Oh, oh, oh.'

He pushed her gently to the bed, and she got in. He took his trousers off and got in after her. She asked him to turn the light off, but he took no notice. He peeled her knickers off and she lifted her legs to help him. And then . . . and then . . .

Dino began to lose it.

She was lying there, she felt all chilly under his hands as if she'd just come out of the fridge and he was trying to spread her on his bread. He kissed her again, hard, to try and stop his erection collapsing. Quickly, before it went altogether, he rolled on top of her and pushed her knees apart with his knees, giving himself a bit of a rub with one hand and holding himself up with the other. But by now the thing was almost hanging. He rubbed it between her legs and even gave an optimistic push, but it just bent. He kissed her again. He reached down and stroked her down there again, and began to nibble her breasts, but it did no good. He thought about getting cross with her because she just lay there like she didn't care, but it was too embarrassing. He rubbed his pubis on hers, but as his fear of failure grew, so his knob got softer and softer and now at last it was nothing but a felty slug hanging off him.

And that was it. It was over. It had just melted away. It was terrifying how easy it was for it to just melt away. The girl lay under him looking up with a half smile on her face, and Dino had never felt so alone as he did then, in bed with a girl and no erection.

'It's . . . I must be tired or something, I dunno. It's been ages.' Desperate for an excuse, Dino blurted, 'I've forgotten how, it's been a while since.' Then he stared at her in yet more horror. Had he really said that? Was she going to notice how ridiculous that was? The girl slipped sideways from under him and put her arms around him with her little white face pressed hard against his.

'Don't mind.' She giggled. It was a very pretty giggle, even Dino had to appreciate that. 'After all that,' she said, because he'd been so big and hard making her sleep with him and now he was all soft and pathetic and . . .

'Sweet,' she said. Then, bless her, she tickled him under the ribs, so of course he tickled her back. They had a little struggle in which the covers came off her and Dino got hard again. Quick as he could, before it disappeared again, he kissed her, very hard, suddenly. She said, 'Ouch!' because he banged her lips.

'Sorry, sorry,' he muttered. She watched his face curiously this time as he rubbed his hands over her everywhere, like a pirate running his hands through treasure. And it might have worked – Dino was sure it could have, although he was scared of the moment of penetration. But the girl suddenly lifted her hands, took his head between them and said, 'Don't. Please don't.'

'Sorry,' he said again.

'Don't worry,' she said. 'This is nice enough, isn't it?'

'Yeah,' said Dino miserably. She smiled.

'Are you gonna stay here with me?' she asked.

'Oh, yeah,' he said, thinking he might do it later on. The girl smiled again and cuddled up close to him. She looked really happy, lying there snuggled up with him. She put her face on his elbow and sighed.

'I've never done this before,' she said in muffled voice.

'What?'

'No, I mean, just cuddle up to someone all night, you know?'

'Oh, yeah,' said Dino.

'Like there's nothing to worry about. All cuddled up, here

101

in your arms,' she murmured. Dino lay there listening to his own heartbeat and to her breathing. Here in his arms. Nothing to worry about. It seemed to him such a curious thing to say, perfectly amazing, that she was so relaxed with him even though he'd almost . . . even though he'd been such an arse. He was flattered. She was safe in his arms. In about half a minute she was asleep. Dino thought, Poor little thing, she must be worn out. He stroked her hair. He felt bad now that he'd tried to blackmail her into staying with him. It was nice to let her have her wish and spend all night in his arms with nothing to worry about, and then he fell asleep as well.

He awoke in an eerie dawn light. He lay peacefully on his side for a moment wondering what had woken him up before he felt the warm body next to his and the memory hit him, and there he was, wide awake, wishing only that he was alone in his catastrophe. The girl lay sleeping peacefully up against his back, her breath on his shoulder. He didn't dare move for fear of waking her. Her skin was warm and heavy, her face relaxed and so peaceful that Dino, in his electrified state, thought she looked like an angel. First a fairy, then an angel. She smelled like nothing he had ever smelled, like nothing on earth. She was just an inconvenience to his misery.

I have a failure rate of One Hundred per cent, thought Dino to himself, even though he knew he was being unfair. What was really scary about it was he had no control over it at all. You can wink your eye, you can stretch your toes, you can waggle your tongue. Some people can even waggle their ears. But not your knob. You can flex any muscle but that one. It has to do it for you.

Dino knew he'd never be at peace with himself until he had managed a successful shag. Who knows how long that could be? Jackie had run away. He'd sworn anyway to chuck her if she didn't come up with the goods tonight, and she hadn't in a big way. This girl lying so peacefully by his side had been his final destruction. He watched her little pointy face half out of the duvet and he thought, She must be a right little slut to come to bed with me just like that. Dino wasn't all that familiar with sluts. The girls he hung around with were quite picky. There were some, particularly in the year below him, who let just about anyone feel them up but he doubted if even they'd go to a party and end up shagging someone they'd only known for five minutes just to get a place to sleep. What a slapper! He wondered if maybe it was her fault that he hadn't got it up. Maybe he needed a decent girl to turn him on. If she didn't care who stuck it up her, that was pretty off-putting.

But it was no good. Dino didn't want to get it up just for decent girls. He wanted to do it with slappers, slags and sluts as well. So long as they were good looking, who cared? The more the merrier.

None of these abusive thoughts about the girl felt true inside him. For one thing she was so lovely in her sleep. She'd been so pleased to just cuddle up. She'd stroked him and comforted him even though he'd bullied her. How could you say that someone was a slut if they were kind to you and happy to be with you?

Even so . . . There she was, lying stark bollock naked in bed next to him. He couldn't afford to let this night end without shagging her or he would suffer for weeks, months, maybe even years. He had to have her. He was thinking, all he had to do was wake her up and he could shag her. In fact, he probably didn't even have to do that – she wouldn't mind. She'd probably let him do anything to her he liked. And he bloody couldn't do it!

The girl rolled over. She was flat on her back, with her head tipped to one side and her mouth open. Slag or not, she really was very pretty. Very softly and quietly, Dino lifted the duvet up so that he could see down her body. He looked at the shadows on her body, her small breasts, the deep shadows around her stomach in the dull light. He could make out the dark rings of her nipples.

Ever so, ever so softly, Dino reached out with one arm and fumbled at the small bedside lamp on his table. At last it clicked on. The girl just lay there. Now he could see a lot more. Her nipples were pretty and pink, and there was the furry place down below. He could see his own body too, and his limp traitorous penis lying just inches away from this naked pleasure house; not a twitch. He looked from himself to her, but nothing stirred. Carefully, very softly, very gently so as not to wake her, Dino began to stroke himself under the covers, glancing from his own hand to her body in an attempt to get himself going. At first there was nothing, but then he started thinking dirty and gradually it began to move. It was so tatty, Peeping Tom on a girl in bed with you – but, oh, yes, things were stirring! Dino speeded up his tempo, beat,

beat, beat. The mattress moved slightly under him and her breasts moved gently with the rhythm; that was good. He thought, if he could get it nice and stiff he'd have another go, although in fact he was already nice and stiff. It was hard to stop though . . . just another little bit more . . .

'Mmm?'

Oh, God, no.

'What are you doing?'

'Eh?'

'What you doing?'

'Ah . . . Do you wanna cup of tea?' he said.

'What's the time?' The girl – whose name he didn't even know, he realised – sat up and pulled the covers up to her chin. She must think he was some sort of nutter, perving away at her like that. She was right.

Dino glanced at the clock. 'Five o'cock,' he replied, as his erection slipped into oblivion.

'Eh?'

'Do you wanna cup a tea?' he begged again.

She pulled a thoughtful face. 'I'm hungry,' she said.

'Cereal? Sandwich? I do a great egg sandwich.'

'Yeah!'

'What'll you have?'

'Both.'

12
dino

I went downstairs and put the gas on. It was endless! First Jackie disappears just when she's ready to open her legs, then there's sick in the bed, then my willy doesn't do it and now I've been caught wanking. From shagger to wanker to waiter in the space of about two hours. Being caught wanking is the worst thing that can happen to you. The only important thing now was to keep her away from my mates in case she told anyone.

It shows you what a state I was in, I was actually hoping she'd have done a runner by the time I got back. But there she was, sitting up in bed with her little pink party dress back on, waiting for me.

'S'great. Great!' she said when she saw the food. I put the tray on the bed in front of her and sat on the side of the bed feeling like her dad, and watched her eat it up. I was still trying to make my willy work. I was thinking, She's not got any knickers on under there, and trying to remember what her body looked like. But it wasn't working.

'Still here, then?' I asked her.

'What?'

'I thought you might be gone,' I said, and she said, 'Why?'

'I was a bit of a . . .' I was about to say tosser, but that might be giving the game away. I mean, maybe she hadn't seen what I was doing.

'Tosser?' she said.

I blushed. I hate blushing. It's my worst thing. 'I don't mean that,' I said. 'I mean, about last night. Making you stay like that. Making you sleep with me. I don't normally behave like that. I'm sorry.'

She shrugged her skinny little shoulders. 'I just wanted a bed for the night. Look, I just do anything, mate, I just do it. So don't come on all moral at me. At least I don't use other people. I just do what I want, right?'

'You didn't look all that happy when I told you you had to . . .'

'Yeah, well, no one likes being ordered around. I just wanted a bed for the night,' she said again, and she sank her teeth deep into her egg sandwich and dribbled ketchup on her chin.

There was a pause. 'I'm Dino,' I told her.

'I know, I heard people call you that last night.'

'And you?' I asked.

'Siobhan,' she said. 'Siobhan Carey.' She finished the sandwich and started on the cornflakes. 'Anyway, I know what you're really sorry about. You're sorry you couldn't get it up.'

'No!'

'Yeah.'

'Well, maybe,' I confessed. 'But that doesn't mean I'm not sorry about the other thing as well.'

'Don't worry about it. It'll come back. Dragging its tail . . .' she laughed.

I was blushing again. I felt so awful. She must have seen me blushing because she said, 'No, don't feel bad about it.'

All I could do was pull a face.

The girl looked curiously at me. 'I liked you for that, you know. I did – I liked you better for not getting it up than I did when you told me I had to shag you or get out.'

'I never said that!'

'That's what it meant, though, didn't it?'

'No,' I said, but she was right.

The girl was thinking about it. 'It made me feel safe,' she said. And when she said that, this weird thing happened. Her eyes filled with tears. I never realised that . . . I don't know what, I just never realised. I didn't know what it meant. I reached out and touched her shoulder. I'd have liked to hug her, but I didn't want her to think I was coming on.

'I wouldn't really have booted you out, you know,' I told her.

'You'd have gone on at me all night. Blokes do.' She finished her cornflakes and dusted her palms together. 'C'mere . . .' She leaned over her tray and put her arms around me. It was nice. After a couple of seconds she broke off, put the tray on the floor, and moved over so I could sit closer to her. We put our arms round each other and she pressed tight – making herself feel safe, I thought.

We sat on the bed hugging awkwardly until she said she was getting cold, then we got back together under the covers. She stroked the back of my head. By that time, I was feeling pretty safe myself, if you know what I mean, and I was thinking, Ho ho!

I kissed her and she kissed me back. She'd got her knickers back on, so they came off and up went the little pink dress. I pulled my stuff off. It was great, both of us naked. I had a raging erection. I put my hand . . . well, work it out for yourself. It was gorgeous. I pushed her legs apart really wide and she let me. And then I got on her . . . and down it went again. I could just feel the blood draining away like something had been turned off.

'Don't worry, you'll be able to do it in the morning, I expect,' she said, and that 'I expect' – the bottom just fell out of the whole world. That was it. Once it'd learned to go down, it was staying down, I was certain of it. I had a lifetime of impotence ahead.

We were lying half in the bed and half out. In one way, I was slightly relieved. Is that really weird? See, it meant I didn't have to try any more. I mean, it was such a bloody bother, it was just hard work really. You're better off wanking. Now I didn't have to bother. But I knew I wasn't going to be feeling like that for long.

But I did have another idea. OK, it was no sex life, no shagging. I was doomed to descend to about Number One Billion. Even Jonathon was better off than I was and he was with a fat girl. But, you know – it was still a pity to waste the chance.

'Can I have a look?' I said.

'What?'

'You know.' I nodded down the bed. Jackie used to let me touch but she was always scared to let me take her knickers off in case things went too far. I once tried to have a peek by pulling her knickers to one side, but she had her jeans on and couldn't open her legs. I wanted to see a proper spread.

'Have a look?' she repeated.

'Yeah. You know. I'd like to . . . see it.'

She giggled and grabbed hold of the bedclothes. 'I'm shy!' she screeched.

'Oh, right.' I backed off, but Siobhan seemed to be pleased for some reason. She was slapping out at me and screeching as if I was tickling her.

'No! Don't, don't!' she giggled, pushing me away, even though I wasn't doing anything, so of course I grabbed hold of the covers and tried to pull them down. 'Stop now!' she said, so I did. She held the covers tightly round her neck and thought about it. 'It's not very pretty,' she said.

'I don't mind.'

'What do you mean, you don't mind?' she scolded.

'I mean – I dunno.' I made as if to lift the covers at the bottom and she grabbed hold of my ears and screeched again.

'NO! I tell you what. Stop it. You can get – no, stop it. Stop! Under the bedclothes and have a look if you like,' she said.

'Can I?'

'Yeah. If you like.'

'I won't be able to see anything . . .' I began, but even as I spoke I found my eyes drifting across to the little bedside lamp.

'NO!' she howled, reaching out to grab my arm, but I fended her off.

'There's no point if I can't see!'

'No!'

'Yes!'

'But I'll be in the dark,' she complained.

'I won't.'

She let go of my ears and lay back in the bed. Down I went, under the covers. She didn't stop me when I pushed her legs apart and bent up her knees.

'All right?' she asked shyly. But I couldn't say anything. It was just . . . I mean, I'd seen pictures but they give you no idea, really. The real thing! It was bigger than I thought, and redder and hairier and it was just stunning. It had this amazing spicy, pee-y smell. It was pure sex. I pulled it open and my knob began pulsing like some sort of atomic weapon.

'Wow,' I said. It was awesome. The pictures don't tell you anything, really. Still staring, I wormed my hand out towards the bedroom table.

'What you doing?'

'Looking for a condom.'

She laughed at me, but I didn't care. It must have been really weird for her, with the light on her fanny and me under there examining her. But you know what? I think it turned her on. She found one and handed it down to me. I struggled under the covers to hold the lamp, put the condom on my vast, iron hard stiffie, and keep looking at it all at the same time.

I tented the covers and came up for air. 'I never saw anything like that before,' I told her. I held her and kissed her, hooking her leg up with one arm. She smiled up at me and reached down to guide me to the right place with her hand, and I just slid in.

13
ben

It was nearly eleven by the time I got out of bed, so I was late for starters. Had a shower. Couldn't face breakfast. Got my footie gear together. Her birthday present, a CD, 'The Handsome Cult'. I was planning on bringing something else for her – my old school uniform.

I'd got it all together. The blazer was at the back of my wardrobe – Mum had kept it in case my brother Neil ever needed it spare but he kicked up such a fuss about getting it second-hand, he never used it. The polo and sweatshirt were in Neil's cupboard – spares again, glad I'm not a younger brother – and so was a pair of trousers. I found the shoes right at the back of the cupboard in the end, all dried up. I'd cleaned them up a couple of nights before and they still fitted. I'd been kidding myself that I'd grown over the past year, but evidently not in the foot department anyhow.

But in the end I left it behind. I felt too ill. Just the thought – yuk. I just stuck my footie gear in my bag and cleared off.

'See you!'

'Where are you going?' yelled my dad.

'Footie.'

'Have you had breakfast, you need breakfast if you're playing sports,' yelled my mum.

'Yes,' I lied, and left the house. I felt sick, my head hurt. I just wanted to go back to bed.

That school uniform thing. She's always on at me about that. She put on a maid's uniform once. Sat me down in an armchair with a beer and waltzed around the flat doing the dusting, leaning over me so I could see down her top and bending over the table so this tiny little skirt rode up. No knickers. You know? Then I had to tell her off for missing bits. I was supposed to order her to do all sorts of jobs so I could get an eyeful but I wasn't very good at it. Too self-conscious. She didn't seem to care. She flitted around a bit, took all my clothes off, just the same as usual, except she called me 'Sir' as she did it. God knows what she'll get up to once she gets me dressed up like a schoolboy.

Kinky. I don't mind the uniform stuff and games and all that, but some of it really gives me the twitches. She does stuff at school – does that count as kinky as well? It wasn't too bad at first. She used to take me out to the store cupboard and give me a big snog and I'd feel her tits. That was pretty good actually, but it was still scary. There was this time she got me backstage, pulled up my top and her top, popped herself out of her bra and gave me this big, wet snog, skin to skin backstage with half the cast of *Toad of Toad Hall* just the other side of the curtains. I thought I was going to die. It was still pretty amazing though.

But it's getting out of hand. I think the thing is, she likes the risk. She always used to do things like grab my packet when I was standing behind her and there were other people in the room – you know, shielding me with her body so no one could see. Then she started giving me detentions so I had to stay behind after school. It was outrageous – right in front of the whole class. She said I was doing something stupid – I wasn't doing a thing. It was all so obvious. I thought she was going to make me shag her, but it was worse than that. She got me backstage behind the curtains, took my jeans down and gave me a blow job. The sick thing was, she made me face the curtains so I could peer through the curtains and see people in the hall coming and going.

'You'll have to keep an eye out in case people come,' she said. I tried to stop her but – I don't know, I just don't seem to be able to say no. She always gets it her own way. It's not fair.

14
mother love

At first he thought she hadn't heard the bell, but just as his finger was lifting towards the buzzer again he heard someone shuffling towards the door in such a way that set his heart beating fearfully, even though he knew that it wasn't, say, a wounded water buffalo or a starving tiger that was coming towards him, but Miss. She opened the door to reveal herself, hair in a rumpled mess on the back of her head, face a crumpled mess on the front. The air stank of stale drink, tobacco smoke and polish.

'Ben,' she groaned. She held her hand to her head and turned away. He followed her into the flat.

It was all wrong. For a moment he thought that he'd come by some impossible chance to the wrong flat and she happened to be in it – with a new lover . . . ? But it wasn't that. It was the flat itself that had gone crazy.

Miss's flat was always messy. She kept her clean clothes and her dirty clothes in separate heaps on the floor and didn't touch the washing up until there was enough to bother with. Dusting wasn't her thing, she was waiting to find a window cleaner, wiped the surfaces only when something sticky refused to dry out, and only did the kitchen floor when it stuck to the soles of her slippers. Every now and then she had a blitz, but what had happened here was something else. The place was spotless. More than spotless; it was sterile.

'What happened?' asked Ben, as she waved a despairing hand around, but he already knew the answer.

'My mother gate-crashed my birthday party. Put the kettle on,' she replied and shuffled back to the bedroom.

There are many different sorts of mothers depending on what they make you do or feel. There are love-mothers and hate-mothers, guilt-mothers and sad-mothers, rage-mothers, glad-mothers, sleep-mothers, mania-mothers, laughter-mothers, fear-mothers, hit-mothers, tear-mothers, bore-mothers, sick-mothers, work-mothers and safe-mothers, to name just a few. It works for dads too. Alison Young had a lobotomy-mother. Whenever her mother visited her she spent the rest of the day walking around like a narcoleptic zombie.

Ben had seen it before. He'd come round one Sunday a couple of months ago and found her like this, in bed with what seemed like a huge hangover because of her mother visiting. It looked at first as though she had a drunk-mother, but it wasn't that. Her mother made her feel like a great lump of shit.

He made his way into the kitchen to make coffee and found, just like last time, that the place had been totally rearranged.

'Where have the cups gone?' he asked.

'Wherever that fat bitch put them,' said Ali. So it was. The cups were where the tins had been, the tins were where the bowls had been, the bowls – who knew where the bowls were?

'She pretends she does it by accident,' murmured Ali, sipping her coffee a little later. 'She empties everything out so she can clean in the cupboards and then puts them back somewhere else *better*.' She leaked tears and leaned across for a tissue.

Ben already knew a whole host of stories about Mrs Young. How she'd convinced Ali to have a fourteenth birthday party, swore she'd keep out of the way and then stayed anyway and forced everyone to play party games.

'Blind Man's Bluff. Postman's Knock! Imagine being forced to play Postman's Knock when you're fourteen by your mother. Being locked in the cupboard like that . . .' raged Ali.

How, when Ali had her first period, her mother had taken her up to the bathroom to sort her out and then come back down and announced it to the whole family at tea. And for the week after, to anyone who happened to come into the house.

'"She's having her first period!" she'd say, and she'd point at my crotch. I swear it. And, of course, people would look down there for a second, just following her finger. I felt like they could see it!' wailed Ali.

This time, Mrs Young had travelled down to surprise her daughter on her birthday. Ali had had a few friends round. They'd gone out for drinks and then come back for more of the same.

Mrs Young marched in unannounced – Ali had no idea

she'd got keys cut for herself. She didn't look too happy, according to Ali, to find other people there, but she made the best of it by serving drinks and snacks. She didn't do small talk. She left the 'young people' to it and went into the kitchen to begin her ritualistic clean. After she'd emptied all the cupboards onto the floor and made the kitchen impassable, she changed her mind and came out to begin on the living room, starting quietly by vacuuming in the corners but gradually moving into the middle until she'd achieved her objective, and people made their excuses and left.

Ali had asked her if that was what she wanted and they'd had a huge, blazing row that she could bear for about five minutes before bursting into tears and rushing hysterically to her bedroom in tears while her mother mercilessly cleaned and shouted at her over the vacuum. It was so humiliating. Why couldn't she *stop* her? Why did it *get* to her so much? Wasn't she pathetic? Why did it have to happen to her?

Ben listened in sympathetic amazement. Part of him was appalled, part of him was amused. Ali seemed a pretty effective sort of person – why so helpless with her own mother? It seemed all wrong. After she'd drunk her coffee, she flung herself sideways in the bed, pulled the blankets up and buried her face on the pillow. Ben stood by the edge of the bed feeling awkward.

'Are you all right?'

'I'll be OK.' But she didn't look OK.

'Are you going back to sleep?' he asked hopefully.

She glanced up at him. 'You can give me a cuddle if you like.'

Ben hesitated a moment. He wanted to say he had things to do, but she knew he hadn't, so he slipped off his shoes and made to get into the bed.

'Not like that, I want some skin,' she complained. He pulled off his jeans and shirt and slid in next to her. She pushed her back up against him, and he put his arms round her and squeezed.

'Hmm,' she said. He wondered if he was supposed to make love to her. Although he'd felt exhausted on the way round and had wanted to get back to bed, he felt wide awake now. He felt like getting up and rushing busily around. In a minute she turned round and nestled her head on his shoulder. 'Mmm,' she said again, and closed her eyes with a sigh. As he lay watching her he noticed for the first time two very straight, white scars running neatly from one side of each of her wrists to the other. Then he fell asleep.

15
nemesis rising

The girl Dino knew as Siobhan was really called Zoë by doting parents whom she despised. When she woke up the night after the party in bed with Dino, she smiled with pleasure at the thought that she'd spent the night with a boy who thought she was someone else. Over breakfast, without thinking or caring why, she'd started to tell him more lies just to amuse herself.

Her dad was a vet who specialised in reptiles. She was seventeen years old, the youngest of five. An accident, her parents didn't want her. They hated and controlled her in equal measures. If they knew she was having sex they'd go mad. They'd probably kill the boy. It would be better for Dino never to call her at home.

Dino believed everything.

In fact, Zoë was only fourteen but she had for many years had an irresistible appetite for trouble. She loved it, lived it, was it. The imaginary father she conjured up for Dino wrestled with alligators with toothache and giant pythons with sore backs, trying to get them to take their medication. The real one supervised a production line in a yoghurt factory. He kept his hands so clean, the skin cracked through over-washing. He'd have run a mile at the sight of anything in scales. She thought of reptiles, partly because her father was one, but also because he'd gone ballistic only that weekend when she'd tried to sneak out of the house dressed only in a tank top and pair of skin-tight snakeskin pants.

'It looks like something's swallowed you,' he snarled, barring her way out of the front door.

Zoë had run back upstairs shouting, 'Is that rage or lust making your eyeballs bulge?' She changed into her pink party dress, came down and threw the hot pants onto the gas fire. 'I'll never wear them again,' she screamed. The hot pants shrivelled and stank and melted down the coals and Zoë zipped out of the door. Out on the street she ran down the road listening to her father's bellows retreat as she turned the corner. She was furious with herself for letting her dad catch her dressed to kill and for throwing her pants away like that. She was so full of red hot life and danger it surprised her she didn't just sizzle her way through the pavement all the way down to hell.

She'd liked Dino that morning. Once he'd stopped trying to throw his weight around he was undeniably sweet. And rather gorgeous. Dino was a looker all right, every bit of him was lovely, but she hadn't forgotten either that he *had* tried to throw his weight around, or that she had unaccountably let him. The whole time they spent in bed, she was wondering whether or not to bite it hard or kick him suddenly in the goolies. She was quite capable of doing either. One thing she did know: Dino was going to suffer, no matter how much she liked him. Telling him a huge pack of lies was an amusing form of revenge, but it wasn't enough. The poor boy thought he was using her. Sooner or later, he was going to find out differently.

In the meantime, she was enjoying herself. They spent the morning romping about in bed like a pair of kids on a bouncy castle. She would have been happy to stay all day – she had nowhere better to go, certainly not home – but as soon as she found out that Dino's friends were coming round to help him clean up, she remembered that she was going bowling. She jumped out of bed and was dressed before he really knew she was going. He just had time to make a date at the weekend with her before she was out of the door and gone.

Zoë caught a bus into town and dialled a number from a phone kiosk.

'Hi, Sam.'

'So how was the party?'

'I stayed all night.'

'Zoë!'

Zoë laughed at her friend's scandalised tone. 'I stayed with the guy whose house it was.'

'What's he like?'

'Gorgeous, very. You remember that one with the dark hair with little goldy bits in it?'

'Him? Ohhh, nice.'

'But stupid. I'm seeing him again. Or at least, he thinks I am!' She roared with laughter.

Sam roared too, uncertainly. 'You're a bad girl, Zoë Trent.'

'No, listen. I told him the most monstrous pack of lies. You wouldn't believe it. Wrong name, wrong age, wrong everything.'

'What did you do that for?'

'I don't know why, I don't know why, I just did it!' roared Zoë, who was certainly not going to admit that she'd been gate-crashed into sleeping with someone. 'He thinks my dad's a reptile doctor – no, really! He thinks my name is Siobhan. He thinks we have an indoor swimming pool and that my parents trust me so much, they let me have the house at weekends when they're away.' That wasn't all true – she hadn't actually told Dino the last two things, but the fact was, Zoë was an inventive and helpless liar. She just did it as she went along. 'Not only that,' she went on. 'Listen; I got a bag full of money.'

'Zoë!'

'About sixty pounds.'

'Where from?'

'Where'd you think?'

But Sam wasn't having it. 'Zoë, that's really tight, those people were at that party in good faith.'

'Oh, don't be such a whingebag. They're all fat soft kids, they've got families and homes, they won't miss it.'

'Fat soft kids. You're a fat soft kid!'

'Not fat, not soft, not a kid, either. D'you wanna help me spend it?'

123

'No.'

'Come on! Sixty quid!'

'I can't today. What do you want to do that for, Zoë? Anyway, I've got loads of homework.'

'Homework!'

'Yeah, well, some of us want to have a life, you know.'

'Sixty quid, Sam.'

Sam paused. 'Sixty quid, that's a lot of money.'

'Come on. We can spend it all. Every penny. Today. All in one go.'

'OK. Right!'

'Good girl! Down town. See you in Stred's in an hour?'

'I'm going to have to finish my homework first. I'll be a couple of hours at least.'

'Come on, Sam, I'm paying.'

'Two hours. OK?'

'OK,' agreed Zoë grudgingly. It wasn't fair. She was paying, wasn't she? She wasn't sure Sam had the right to say no, but that was Sam. She was prepared to be as mad as anyone, but only after she'd finished being sensible and only if she was certain she wasn't going to get found out. She was a master of disguise, was Sam.

Zoë put down the phone and stood looking up the streets. Two hours to kill. Boring. Boring boring boring! Why was life so boring?

It was gone eight o'clock on Sunday evening by the time Zoë got back home. They'd had a great time. There wasn't a penny left. They'd seen a film, gone bowling, eaten a mountain of crisps and sweets and bought a CD each. Zoë had to leave hers round at Sam's because her parents searched her room regularly. She hadn't been there since Friday evening.

Her parents popped out of the front room like a pair of armed badgers before she even had time to close the front door.

'You just don't care, do you?' yelled her dad. 'We've been worried sick and you don't even care.'

'I'll bet.'

'It's not fair!' he yelped.

'Darling, what makes you behave like this?' cried her mother, the waterworks already coming on. Her eyes glistened, but her father put out his hand to silence her.

'You have absolutely no regard for anyone else. You don't think about anyone else, you don't have any feelings for anyone else. It's just you you you all the time. Well?'

Well, what could she say? It was true, every word. The thing was – she didn't care. She really truly did not care. She felt like the princess in the fairy story who had been brought up by strangers. She just didn't fit. Her parents weren't so bad to her. They had their faults, sure. Her father was high-handed and obviously didn't like kids; her mother couldn't understand her and rather pathetically never gave up trying to. Even when Zoë was a little girl, her mum used to hide outside the door for hours listening to her playing dolls with her friends to try and work her strange, elfin daughter out. She'd tried, you had to give her that. No, it was quite clear, it was Zoë who was the problem and no one else. She made herself feel like shit, the way she went on. She just couldn't stop.

Her mother stood staring at her, flaunting her tears like the Crown Jewels, but Zoë refused guilt of any kind. Was it her fault she had caring parents? No. She stamped upstairs.

'I ought to have had a couple of thugs, you two are bloody wasted on me,' she shouted downstairs. She went into her bedroom, then came out again. 'Stop making me feel guilty!' she yelled.

'Zoë, all we ask is that you let us know where you are. You're only fourteen, we need to know you're all right. We're responsible . . .' said her mother.

'Yes, responsible, responsible, remember about being responsible?' bawled her dad. 'But I don't suppose that word means very much to you, does it?'

Zoë slammed the door. 'Weaklings,' she growled. It was true. Her father blustered and her mother wept, but neither of them had the slightest clue how to keep their daughter in check. Inside, she prowled around her room. Why did she have nowhere else to go? Why was she so abandoned and alone in her own home? Why didn't her father come up and knock her about the place, when she treated them like shit?

'Pants! Shit! Cunts!' she yelled downstairs at them, but answer came there none. She crept downstairs. Her parents were watching a quiz show on TV and eating nuts as if they didn't have a care in the world. Zoë wanted to murder them, but all she did was run upstairs and weep on her bed instead. She couldn't kill them, but someone was going to have to die, and soon. It was just a question of who.

16
happiness is a full binbag

Sex? No prob, bruv! He was a natural.

I'm good at that, thought Dino. That girl . . . he'd almost driven her mad with pleasure. Jackie didn't know what she was missing. He felt so pleased about it, he was almost willing to forgive her. In fact, he probably would have if it wasn't for the fact that he didn't have to. He had a new girlfriend now.

About half an hour after Siobhan left, Jackie rang him, full of apologies. She was horrified at herself. She couldn't understand how, or why she'd run off. That sick had just offended her so much, she was out of the house before she knew what she was doing.

'We need to talk,' she said.

'I don't think there's anything to say.'

'I do want to sleep with you.'

'Well, someone else did last night too, so just . . . don't bother,' he'd said, and he put down the phone.

Jackie was history.

Dino was so relieved at having successfully lost his virginity that he had no idea how unhappy this new situation made him for all sorts of reasons. For starters, he didn't trust Siobhan as far as he could throw her. His behaviour at blackmailing her into having sex with him had left a very nasty taste in his own mouth and badly dented his self-esteem. Jackie had rejected him yet again, which hurt very much indeed. Finally, even while he was busy congratulating himself on having chucked her, he was terrified at the thought of losing her.

He was in love with her and he didn't even know it.

After dismissing her, Dino went downstairs to eat some cereal. That had showed her. He tried to imagine doing the things he'd done with Siobhan with Jackie, but it made him feel queasy and odd. A little later he looked at the clock and saw with a shock that it had somehow become one o'clock. People were supposed to come round at midday! His parents . . . ! The house looked as if someone had thrown a party in it.

Dino's anxiety levels began to rise alarmingly. He rushed back to the phone and rang his friends one after the other, but every one of them was too busy lying in bed to speak to him. He began running around from room to room throwing rubbish into a binbag, but in half an hour nothing seemed to have changed. Already, he was very seriously regretting having told Jackie about Siobhan, richly though she deserved it. It wasn't until gone two that the doorbell rang. He rushed to open it; it was Deborah. She smiled beatifically at him.

'Is Jon here yet?' she asked.

'Quick,' he yelped. 'We have to clean up!'

To his amazement, Debs didn't seem to get the message. The first thing she did was try to ring Jon, but there was no answer from his phone and his mobile was switched off. Then she wanted to go round to wake him up, and Dino had to keep watching the front door in case she sneaked out. And the rest of them? Not one of the lying, cheating bastards had showed up. The house was a death pit of household destruction. Fag ends in the carpet, plastic cups ground underfoot in puddles of sour, stinking beer. There were all the breakables to unwrap and puddles of sick lurking in places that no one had as yet even discovered. His parents were due home in just a few hours and there was a week's work for twenty strong men still left to do.

By the time Ben came round at three, Dino didn't know whether to cuddle him or punch him for being so late.

'Where the fuck were you?' he whimpered.

'Hangover,' said Ben. 'Don't worry, we'll get it done. Where's Jackie?'

Half an hour later, there was another knock at the door. Both Deborah and Dino ran to open it. There stood Jackie and Sue.

'Deborah!' gasped Jackie. Was this who Dino had spent the night with? 'You!'

'Have you seen Jonathon?' demanded Deborah. 'What? What have I done?' she added, seeing Jackie's horrified face.

It took a while to sort it out. Deborah, who had just spent an hour on her own with Dino, had had enough, and left. Jackie, realising that she'd made a mistake, apologised to her and started trying to make it up with Dino, but he was too agitated about getting the house clean to realise that she was offering to sleep with him again. Shouting started. Sue was furious with herself for coming at all. Jackie had rung her at an hour of Sunday morning she didn't previously know existed. She had a bad hangover and this was not her problem. It was all cobblers, anyway. She hadn't believed Dino's story about sleeping with someone else for a second.

'There wasn't anyone else there, what did he do, ring an escort agency?' she'd asked when Jackie rang her on her mobile. How obvious was it that as soon as they got there, Jackie and Dino would stand and shout at each other while she'd be expected to run around and actually help with the housework?

It was a point of principle. Sue never helped with the housework.

'OK,' she snarled. 'I'll do *one* bedroom and then I'm going. I have homework to do.'

'You came to the party too,' yelled Dino. 'You enjoyed it!'

'It was a crap party,' she snapped, and stamped upstairs to the big bedroom only to find that she'd forgotten about the offending vomit.

Jackie thought she was going to go hysterical. 'We have to talk,' she blubbed as Sue thumped upstairs.

'We have to *clean*,' insisted Dino.

'How can I do housework when you spent the night with someone else?' she screamed.

One brief glimpse at Jackie's face was enough to tell Dino that if he stuck to his story, he was unlikely to get so much as a light dusting out of her. Even guilt at running out on him wasn't going to help her to see reason. His parents were due back in a few hours. Deborah had gone, Sue was unreliable, Ben was male. What could he do?

'I was lying,' he lied.

'You were *lying*?'

'Yeah.'

'You just wanted to hurt me!'

'Jacks, you ran out on me. You promised. And you promised to help get the place together and here it is, it's half past three and look at it, it's a shit hole. I'm sorry I told a fib but can we please, *please* get this place put together. Please?'

Jackie blinked through her tears at the chaos all around them. It was, after all, her who was in the wrong. He was a lying bastard, but at least he was lying about *not* having slept with someone rather than the other way round.

'OK,' she said. 'But after this, we have to talk. OK?'

'I love you!' cried Dino. He grabbed her, hugged her and kissed her. He was happy again, and the poor deluded girl smiled with pleasure. It was one of Dino's greatest gifts; he was infectious. He broadcast his feelings. If he felt bad, so did anyone near him. If he smiled, the world smiled with him. It was all so perfect. He'd lost his virginity! He wasn't going to chuck Jackie! She was going to help him clean! He put his arms round her and squeezed her and radiated pleasure. Jackie was swamped by it. She held her face up to him and felt his joy sparkle in her eyes and fizz and tingle in her spine and in her belly. Ben, standing at the back of the room with a binbag full of beer cans, laughed to see them. Upstairs, Sue scowled as pleasure fizzed up through her feet. She thought, Why? And Deborah, plodding on her way home trying not to cry, thought of Jonathon waking up in bed and getting anxious and confused about her, and she forgave him suddenly for no reason at all.

17
dino

It was like magic once Jacks got there. The whole place just cleaned itself. Man! Just like that. She even got Sue into it, they liked it. Sue was humming to herself as she vacuumed the landing. That's girls for you. I can't even work out how to keep my room clean.

As we worked, I started thinking about my position and you know . . . I started to think that maybe, it was a pretty good position. I mean, it could actually work out pretty well for everyone, but for me in particular. Siobhan's all very well, but I don't know if I fancy her as a girlfriend. You know what I mean? She's a bit of a slapper. Not like Jackie. On the other hand, Siobhan shags and Jackie doesn't and that shagging business – that's something I want to do a great deal more of.

What I'm saying is – why not both of them? I could go out with Jackie and shag Siobhan. Siobhan and me, that's not going to last, but what's to stop me seeing her a few more times without Jackie knowing anything about it? It's perfect. It'd take the pressure off Jacks to give out, and then when she does . . .

'Wow, Dino, if only I'd known! I'd have done it months ago . . .'

I'll have had loads of practice! Cool or what?

Seriously, though, it's true I won't be nagging her so much for sex because I'll be getting it elsewhere . . . and she'll think I'm being all sensitive and understanding! Nice, eh? Anyhow, what does she expect? She's been mucking me around for weeks, I'm bound to go looking for it somewhere else sooner or later.

I saw everyone out of the house by half four. Sue has a car, she went to drop off all the extra binbags at the dump – that was her idea. She's done this before. What would happen if Mum and Dad looked in the wheelie bin and found all those cups and fag ends and cans and so on, you know?

And I was on my own in a nice clean house waiting for Mum and Dad to come back.

But as soon as he was on his own, Dino's anxiety levels began to rise again. He started to get worried that they'd done the place too much. What had Ben been thinking of, polishing the table so well? That table never got polished, and now look – it shone like an advertisement. Jackie had sponged down the curtains where someone had spilled some beer on them and made a big clean patch right down one side. Sue had gone out and bought some shake 'n' vac and other smellies to cover up the old beer and fag end smell lingering around the place. Since when did the house smell like that? They'd know!

He rang Jacks on her mobile for advice but she'd turned it

off, the selfish cow. Gone back to bed probably, just when he needed her. He began to deconstruct the cleaning job. He sponged down the half of the curtain that was still dirty, then he got to work on the table, trying to take off that sharp shine and get it back to its natural dullness. He rubbed his sweaty hands on it, but that just made it look like a polished table that someone had wiped their hands on, so he got a little sausage grease out of the grill pan, put it on a J-cloth and rubbed it vigorously onto the shine. That made it look duller, but greasy.

Then there was the key in the door and his mum's voice cheerily calling out, 'We're home!'

In that very second Dino remembered in a blinding flash of darkness what he hadn't thought about for two whole days. He ran halfway up the stairs before they came in, trying to escape; but where to? His mum was having an affair with some wanky bloke from her school. He'd just lost his virginity, it should have been one of the best days of his life. He had not one but two girlfriends, things ought to be just brilliant, but did he feel great? No. And why? Because of his stupid fucking mother.

His parents came chattering up the hall like a pair of children. If only his dad knew what Dino knew – that'd wipe the smile off his face. They came to a stop at the bottom of the stairs looking up at him. Dino glared back down.

'Well, that's a fine greeting,' said his dad. Behind him, Dino's mum had stopped smiling. Dino was obviously a bit of a downer as far as she was concerned.

'Welcome home?' she said in a little voice. Dino sneered

and went upstairs. What shit! He was furious. What right had they to spoil this moment for him? Sick to death about his *parents'* sex life on the very day his had just begun! It couldn't be more awful. How selfish they were. How self-obsessed. This was HIS day, HIS moment, and instead of swaggering about feeling great he was sweating with anxiety.

He went to lie down on the bed and tried to remember what sex had been like – his hands on Siobhan's breasts, the hot feel of her moving underneath him – but all he could think about was Dave Short doing the same things to his mum.

He heard her coming up the stairs and his heart began to beat violently in his chest. She was going to talk about it! She knew he knew! She knocked, popped her head round the door and asked, how come the table smelled of sausages?

Dino was amazed. Was that it? Was that all she could say after a whole week of unacknowledged knowing? He waved her imperiously away from his door with a hand, and – can you believe this? The bitch got cross with him for being rude. She got cross with *him*! Suddenly, Dino was screaming at her and then his dad came up to have a go at him for speaking to his mother like that. Get that! Both of them at the end of the bed telling him how many different kinds of shit he was and all the time he was thinking, You people have no idea. If they had the slightest inkling of what he could do just by opening his mouth and uttering the secret words. He was a time bomb. He was a fucking Cruise Missile. He could not believe he was having to put up with this shit.

* * *

While his dad was out picking up Mat and his mum was getting tea, Dino decided that the only explanation had to be that it didn't matter. They'd obviously had a nice time away. They seemed to like one another. Why should he worry? All sorts of things could be going on. Maybe they had an open marriage. Or they'd decided that the marriage was over but they ought to stay together for the sake of the children. It could be that. They could be swingers! Well – it happened. Someone's mum and dad had to be swingers. Maybe it just happened to be his.

'Did you have a good time, then?' he asked them at dinner that evening. He gave his mum a little wink. She stared blankly at him.

'Great. Thanks for asking,' said his dad sarcastically.

'Just the two of you, was it?'

'It'd be rather difficult to have a romantic weekend with more than two, wouldn't it?' asked Dad.

'Dirty weekend, you mean,' corrected Mat, but everyone ignored him. Dino smirked. He wanted to let them know that he knew what was going on. He stared at his mum until he caught her eye and gave a leering kind of look.

'You look flushed,' his dad said to her.

'Yes! Must be the menopause or something, I expect!' said his mum, fanning herself with her hand frantically. Everyone stared at her.

'What's that?' asked Mat suspiciously.

'I can't say I'd noticed anything menopausal,' observed his dad.

Dino lost patience. It was like some stupid game they were all playing. Ridiculous. So he just said it straight out.

'So, did Dave Short go with you, then?' he asked, and even as he said it he knew he shouldn't have. His own jaw fell open with horror as the words fell out of his mouth.

His mother was still flushed from her blush; now the blood drained out of her face.

'Dave Short? Dave Short? Dave Short?' said his dad nervously. 'Dave Short?'

In desperation, Dino started to laugh as if he'd made a great joke. 'Ha, ha, ha!' he said. He sounded like a dog coughing. 'Oh – so you're not swingers then,' he said. Suddenly he desperately, desperately wanted to rescue his mum. He was trying so hard to laugh he began to choke. Then his mum started laughing as well, a hollow, amateur dramatics kind of thing . . . 'He he he he he he,' she said. Then Mat joined in, properly. Even though he had no idea what was going on he always found other people laughing funny. Perhaps it was hysteria, perhaps it was the sound of a true laugh against their own hollow impressions, but Mat started Dino and his mum laughing properly too, and that made if even funnier. Pretty soon they were all howling and wiping the tears off their faces. Only his dad sat there holding his knife and fork in his hands, staring at them all as if he was on his own in a crowd of strangers.

Later that evening, when Dino was in bed, the shouting started.

18
jonathon

'So, let's get this straight,' I said. 'Jackie threw up in your bed and then cleared off. Maybe it was some sort of hideous perversion. What do you called vomit perverts? Sickophilia? Is she a pukeophage?'

'Yeah, yeah, yeah,' said Dino, rolling his eyes.

'Not exactly what you were expecting,' said Ben.

'I thought it was party on, knickers off. Are you sure it wasn't a failed attempt at oral sex you don't want to tell us about?'

'I was upset about it,' said Dino grimly.

'Because if it was I don't blame her for throwing up. The mere thought . . .'

'Bloody shut up,' hissed Dino. And there it was: the look. It's not fair. I ought to be able to talk the pants off him but all he has to do is look at me and I just shrivel up.

'Sorry, Deen,' I snivelled, but it was too late: I had ceased to exist.

Ben wagged his finger at Dino and smiled fondly at him. 'You said this was her last chance.'

Dino pulled a face.

'You can't force someone to do sex with you,' I pointed out, but he ignored me.

'So?' Ben asked him.

'I don't know how much she really likes me,' Dino complained.

'I don't think there's much doubt that she's very much smitten,' I said. He half smiled at me. Flattery will get you everywhere with the Lozenge.

That's what I call him. Dino the Lozenge. I can't remember why. He must remind me of a cough sweet in some indefinable way.

'Jon's right,' said Ben; and Dino looked so pleased about it, Ben and I exchanged a fond glance. Funny, isn't it? Why on earth should we feel so happy because Dino is pleased about something?

He scowled lightly. 'Do you think I'd be a bit of wanker to go back out with her? After all that?'

'It all depends,' said Ben. 'How much do you like her?' There was a pause, in which Dino looked at him as if he'd just asked what unicorn he was wearing today.

'What do you *feel* for her?' I asked.

Dino looked all confused, and then he blushed. Ah! Bless.

'I've never thought about it,' he said coyly.

Was it possible? After all the dozens of times he'd talked to us about Jackie, and he'd never actually thought about what he *felt*?

'Not even once?' I asked.

'Well, of course I have,' snapped Dino, through his blush. 'But . . .'

'Ah, now,' said Ben. 'I think old Dino likes her more than he cares to admit.'

Dino smiled shyly. He nodded. 'It's true,' he said, colouring up again. 'She's lovely.'

Nice, isn't he nice? As well as being a bastard, of course.

'So you might as well keep on with her, unless you've got someone better to do,' I said. Which was just a joke to cover up his embarrassment, actually, but he looked at me as if I'd said some horrible blasphemy.

'No, of course not,' he snarled. So there I was back in the depths of the shit heap again, without really knowing why this time. And it was at that moment, just at the height of my confusion, that I looked up and saw her standing by the lockers.

DeborAGHHHHHHHHHHHH!

She was talking to Sue and Lesley. As I watched, she turned round, saw me, smiled and gave me a big wave. I looked away and pretended I hadn't seen her – much too late. Ouch – that must have hurt! Poor Debs. Out of the corner of my eye, I saw her turn away back to her friends.

'Do you want to talk about it?' said Ben. I looked at him. He was nodding over to Debs.

'No, no no no,' I said. Then, realising I was being far too emphatic, I shrugged casually. 'What's there to talk about? It was just a snog, that's all.'

'I bet they don't think so,' said Ben, nodding at the little huddle of girls by the lockers.

Dino leaned over to me. 'Your woman's nipples are shaking with anxiety,' he told me. I grinned weakly, but he terrified me. That was one of mine! I live in constant fear that someone is going to be as horrible to me as I am to them.

The thing is, poor old Debs is the butt of an awful lot of jokes and most of them are mine. She never gets to hear them, of course. No one – especially me – would ever dream of hurting her feelings. She's too well liked. It's just that, well, jokes are funny. You know? And I like a joke more than anyone.

For example. Deborah has wrap-round tits. Her nipples have ended up behind her head. She has more skin than a elephant. She had so many folds and flaps on her, it's difficult finding the right one without a map. If you melted Deborah down and poured her into a fat-powered vehicle, you could drive to London and back without a refill. Some said it wasn't her fault, she had a problem with her glands.

'Sure,' I liked to point out. 'Too many gland sandwiches.'

See? I really am vile. I'd be mortified if she ever got to hear any of these witticisms, of course – but behind her back, yes, I'm ruthless!

'So, what was it liked to be entombed between her mighty thighs, then?' asked Ben. See? That's one of mine too.

'Leave it out.'

'Have you wiped the grease marks off, yet?' said Dino, raising his voice so that although she never could hear, it *felt* as though she might. The bastard. That was one of mine too. If she ever got to hear any of it I'd die of shame.

And so it went on all morning. It was all over school. I was amazed – really amazed at some of the attitudes that came out. I mean, all right: I am unbearably cruel, I know that – but it's all for the sake of a laugh. I'm callous. I go too far.

I'm insensitive. But it's horribility by *accident*. Some of these guys really go for it. I'd always thought that the whole thing about fat girls was something you went on about because it was funny. It never occurred to me that some people actually seem to think that there's something morally wrong with it.

'Like sheep shagging or something,' said Snoops.

'Don't be ridiculous,' I snarled.

Snoops is a bastard, but even some of the nice guys like Fasil were all over the place on this one.

'Sorry, Jon, but I can't understand it . . . that sort of thing,' he said. That sort of thing? What does he mean by that? Even Ben, who's just about the nicest of us all.

'Not my personal cup of tea,' he said. 'But each to their own, eh, Jon?'

'Yeah, you stick by her,' said Dino.

'I shouldn't think it's all that easy to escape,' I said. Joke. Stick, fat, get stuck, see? Bastards! Even I was joining in. Oh, we were all having a great time at my expense.

I'm just as bad as they are. I've always taken the attitude that it doesn't actually matter what size and shape a girl is. It's the personality that counts. So how come I don't want Deborah? I like her. My glands obviously think she's great. Whenever I think about those twenty minutes outside the garage with the wind blowing around Mr Knobby Knobster and her tits out, I almost pull my trousers off from the inside. So what's my problem? Could it be that I've been kidding myself all the time, and that actually it's just that I'm *ashamed to be seen with her*?

Because let's face it, the humiliation would be endless. People would go on and on and on and on. It's so stupid. She isn't even that fat. She's chubby. It's just her bad luck that somewhere down the line she got appointed the school fat girl, and that's it.

But then, I always get like this. I mean – I like girls. I get on well with them. And I like sex. Not that I've had all that much experience of it – not with another person being in the room at the same time, anyway. I just can't somehow put the two together. I can be getting on really well with a girl but as soon as I get an inkling that there might be a chance of anything happening, I just freeze up. It's scary. Sex is . . . well it's so rude, isn't it? You wouldn't think girls would like sex. You'd think it's too rude for them. Doing sex with a girl, it's a bit like putting a frog down their backs or scaring them with dead mice or throwing worms at them. They're such sensible, grown-up sorts of people. And yet apparently even the nice ones like you sticking the rudest thing you have on your whole body up the exact, rudest part of their body that they have! It doesn't make a lot of sense to me.

The fact is, I can't put together the sort of feelings that I get when I'm having a dirty big wank together with the kind of feelings I get when I'm having a nice friendly chat with someone. It just doesn't work. But here's Deborah, who I get on very well with and she actually appears to want me to do those things. It sounds too good to be true, right? Even better, she wants to do them back to *me*. I mean. Saying no – it just seems so stupid.

Maybe I'm just scared. Maybe I need to bite the bullet and give her one and I'll feel better.

Nemesis came the next day. It was about the most embarrassing thing that ever happened to me.

I was talking about it to Ben and Dino, and a couple of others, the bastards. Ben was telling me off.

'You shouldn't have raised her hopes,' he said.

'She can't help being fat,' pointed out Fasil. 'Do you think she likes it? You've encouraged her to think that it doesn't matter.'

'But it *doesn't* matter,' I snarled. 'Some people *like* fat girls.'

'Ugh, there, I knew it,' said Snoops. 'That means you do fancy her. Gross.'

'I don't! I'm talking about other people. Christ!'

'You looked like you were having a good time to me,' said Dino.

I suppose I should have noticed that they'd started looking over my shoulder. Later, Ben said he tried to indicate what was going on with his chin. I'm not sure I believe him. He could have said, 'Oh, hi, Sue, Jenna and Jackie, how's it going?' instead of just doing odd things with his chin. So these three harpies emerged over my shoulder just in time to hear me come out with this prime piece of bullshit . . .

'I was doing her a favour,' I said.

I didn't even mean it. It was a joke. Try explaining that to them.

'You bastard!' shrieked Jenna in my ear.

I leaped round. I think I might have briefly fainted in mid-air.

'You're disgusting,' hissed Sue. 'She was doing you a favour, if only you knew.'

'I didn't mean I was doing her a favour, that sounded all wrong. I meant – Jesus! It was just a snog! It wouldn't matter if it was anyone else I'd snogged.'

'Yuk. All that flesh,' said Snoops.

'Shut up,' I said.

'Don't tell him to shut up, you're as bad as he is,' said Sue.

'You lot are the prejudiced ones,' I told them, wildly going onto the attack. 'If it was a thin person I'd snogged, no one could care less.'

'You made her think she was in with a chance, that's what's wrong with it,' said Fas piously.

'You *all* make me sick,' barked Sue. 'She's "in with a chance" with lots of people. She had a boyfriend, just recently. And *she* finished with *him*, what's more!'

'See?' I said.

'She's upset,' said Jackie seriously. She nodded across the common room. I looked sideways across. Debs was sitting at a table, half turned away. She must know they were talking about her. How could she bear it? Did she know all we were talking about was her weight?

'I was only joking about doing her a favour,' I repeated pathetically.

'You have to speak to her. You owe her that much.'

'All right. OK. I'll have a word with her, OK?' I begged. And all three girls answered as one:

'When?'

I am blessed among mortals. I know it's hard to believe just looking at me, I expect I seem just your average geek to you. Don't laugh. It's embarrassing. See, I have a small flock of invisible magical helpers to do my every bidding.

I know it's ludicrous. I'm obviously mad. But – just imagine. Suppose it's true. You don't know. You can't prove anything really. It's a question of faith. It's just the same with bloody old God, isn't it? He's no different, you can't see him either. You don't know if he's there or not. God, magic helpers – they all basically have a big credibility problem. Something to do with moving in mysterious ways, or being invisible as I like to call it.

There's all these stupid rules these beings have. They're so *moral*, which cuts out most of the stuff I want for starters. And they're so touchy about it. If for instance, you asked them to bring you the Taj Mahal, or give you a twelve-inch knob or turn you into a millionaire or something like that, something really desirable and useful, they wouldn't do it, even though they easily could if they wanted to. It'd be too obvious for them. It'd be like you were asking them to prove their existence to you, which would mean that you didn't really believe in them properly . . . and if they get the slightest sense that you don't believe in them properly, they go all stroppy and start sulking. What you have to do is ask them to do things that are within the realms of possibility. Things that mean *you never know for sure* if they've been brought about by chance, or by magic. Things like, for instance: *Please make Deborah stop fancying me.*

It's just exactly the sort of thing my magic helpers could help with. All I have to do is work out what exactly they want me to ask them.

But please stop Deborah fancying me won't work because that would mean asking them to interfere in another human being's feelings, and they'd never do that. That's immoral. So

how about this? *Please please please make Deborah* **thin** . . .
but with big tits, so that I'd still have those wonderful bazookas
to play with, but no one would sneer at me for going out
with a fat girl.

Nice thought, but that wouldn't work either, because you
can't just make someone change shape to suit you. Making
their body change is just as bad as making their minds change.
That would make my magic helpers all huffy and disappointed
for sure. Even if she wanted to be thin with big tits – and
there's a fair chance she does – it would still be immoral
because it would be cheating. My magic helpers would expect
her to go on a diet like everyone else.

So how about – *Make* **me** fancy her! What do you think?
Maybe they already have. Mr Knobby certainly thinks so. But
in that case, why does doing sex things with her make me feel
so panicky? It's nice at the time – it's brilliant at the time –
but thinking about it makes me feel awful. What's going on
there? And anyhow, that's immoral too. Most things are, I
find, when you start thinking about it. It's as wrong to change
yourself to suit somebody else as it is to change someone else
to suit you. Almost.

So what about this?

*Please give me the courage to tell her that I like her very very
much, but I just don't fancy her.*

But they won't touch that one either because, of course, I
could do it perfectly well myself. Magic is only for things you
can't do yourself. And I'm certainly not going to do it as I
am, and you know why? Because I'm a coward, that's why. So
I'm shafted.

It makes you wonder. What use are they? They won't do anything to make it easier for me, and the difficult things they insist I do for myself.

I couldn't bear to hurt her feelings. Really, simply, couldn't bear it.

The easiest thing to do would be just to go out with her. Why not? For one thing, I am actually very fond of her. That's a start, isn't it? She's female for another. That counts for a lot. It means she has tits and a minge. Yes, I know, that's amazingly superficial of me, but there you go. Tits and minge are actually very important things to me in a girlfriend. In fact, they're just about the most important things I want in a girl. I dream about them. I think about them. I spend a lot of my spare time looking at them on my computer screen – tits and arses and minge till it comes out of my ears. And Deborah has them all. In fact, she has just about the best tits you can imagine. Big lovely womanly breasts with lovely big dark nipples and and . . . oooh, la, yum yum yum.

Maybe I should just be prepared to accept what comes my way. Beggars can't be choosers would be a bit harsh, but if I narrow my field down to the good-looking ones, I'm likely to stay a virgin for ever. It's something I've noticed. The good-looking ones don't tend to fancy me all that much. I'm just not one of the beautiful people. And she likes me. We're mates. She could be my best friend, and having a best friend who lets you do sex with them – having a best friend who *wants* you to do sex with them – is something really worth having, I reckon. Me and Debs. Why not? She's clever and funny. We like the same things. We share a sense of humour. We spend ages chatting about all sorts of stuff. She's talented. I ought to be flattered, really. She does these amazing cartoons of people. It takes her about a minute, she just sits down, looks at you, draws a few lines and there it is, a really funny caricature. It's like magic watching her. She laughs at my jokes and listens to my opinions. You know what? I think I make her happy. Isn't that something? She was smiling and smiling and smiling at me at the end of the party when we were on the sofa next to each other holding hands. Isn't that worth having?

And then there's the tits and minge.

It wouldn't last, though. Once she got to know me she'd go off me dead quick. I mean, I'm pretty weird, really. I'm only ever nice to people because I want them to be nice to me. Pretty superficial, huh? I think much too much of myself. I'm quite good with words but that's about it, there's nothing else. School work – very patchy. People – I'm shy. Chatting girls up – hopeless. Knowing when to stop – can't do it. And that's not all. My head – you wouldn't believe the things that go through my head. My head is unbelievable, it's a quagmire in here. How could I have a relationship with someone when I have so many secrets? My wank life, for instance. All the time! I'm like a monkey. And my magic helpers. Childish or what? And other things. The thoughts that fill my head! Sometimes I lie in bed and I spend hours thinking the most deliberately horrible things I can. The worst curses. The most violent acts, the most uncharitable thoughts, the most disgusting perversions. You just would not believe.

But – the fact is, she seems to like me. She's clever and sweet and thoughtful, and she likes me.

But *Deborah*! As a friend she's great but as a girlfriend she's a joke. Is that what makes my hair stands on end? Because she's overweight? I know I'm crap but that really would be too petty even for me. But why else? My knob likes her, I like her – but something just shrivels up and dies of embarrassment at the thought of doing it with her.

By seven o'clock that evening when he arrived at the War Memorial in Scofield Park, Jonathon still hadn't got a clue what to do.

She wasn't there yet. He kicked around the monument waiting and wishing and hoping, and dreading that she wouldn't come. The truth about wishes is, they can come true – but only if you wish for the right thing. The wish that can come true fits in like a piece of a jigsaw puzzle and everything falls into place. What was the right wish here?

He was walking around a bench muttering to himself when she suddenly appeared. He jumped. She smiled anxiously.

'I was scared you wouldn't come,' she said.

'I said I would.'

They stood looking at each other and smiling.

'Walk?' she said.

'OK.'

They headed across the grass and around by the rosebeds. She took his hand. They walked right round the little park talking about school, about Dino, about why on earth Ben didn't get off with anyone when they were literally queuing up for him. Neither of them said a word about . . . things.

When they got back to the monument, she leaned back against it and said, 'Kiss me.'

Jonathon put his arms around her and kissed her. She tasted of spices and winegums, which made him briefly want to giggle. Fat girl = winegums. He pressed his full weight right up against her, right down the length of her body and kissed her on the lips. She held him tight, her big bosoms pushed up against him. Mr Knobby rose up between them. Deborah pushed her tummy against it, and he pushed gently back.

'We get on so well together.'

'Yes.'

'So what's the problem?'

What could he say? Yes, I like you and I evidently do fancy you, but I can't bear the social humiliation of being seen out regularly with a fat girl? He shook his head and said, 'I don't know. I don't know. I'm . . . I need to think about it.'

Deborah looked away, then back at him. 'Is it my weight?' she asked.

'Good God, no! I don't care about that!'

She frowned. 'Then what?'

'I don't *know*,' insisted Jonathon.

'Look,' she said. 'I understand, you know.'

'What?' he asked, all panicky.

'You don't have to fancy me. I know I'm fat.'

'You're not fat!' insisted Jonathon furiously. 'Don't let them make you think that.'

Deborah laughed at his anger.

151

'You're not, you know you're not. Fat is – well, it's a lot bigger than you are.'

'Well, I'm chubby, then.'

'Plump, perhaps.'

'Plump,' she smiled.

'Don't you like being plump?'

She shrugged. 'No. But all the other girls' – she waved her hand over the park, the town, the world – 'they're all worried about being thin and the right shape and having the right boobs and the right everything. So I just think I'm not going to care about that. I'd like to be thin, I can't help that, but it's so stupid. Just fashion, isn't it? I don't go for fashion. It's like . . . being bullied, you know. I've decided to settle for being plump.'

'That's just so amazing. I think that's an amazing thing to do,' he told her fervently. Who else would think like that? Wasn't she something special? And she wanted to be his.

She smiled and wriggled her tum up against a grateful Mr Knobby.

'So don't you care what people think?' he asked her.

'Of course I do. I hate it. Of course I hate it. What did you think, that I was a fat jolly person?'

'No, no, not that. You always seemed so – I dunno. Well adjusted.'

'The way people look at me. All those jokes.'

He blushed. Did she know?

'The way no one wants to dance with me at school dances.'

'I danced with you.'

'You're different.'

'Ben danced with you.'

'He's nice.'

'Everyone likes you,' he reminded her.

'Who wants to be nice?' asked Deborah. 'Everyone likes me, but no one fancies me. Well,' she amended, 'that's not actually true. Outside school loads of people do. It's just you lot.' She looked Jonathon in the eye. 'And I don't care about any of them, actually. It's just you. I like you a lot.'

Jonathon smiled grimly. 'I like you,' he said. He was relieved to be able to say something true.

'So,' she said. 'What do you say?'

He just stood there. He had no idea what to say and no idea what he felt, except for this: he felt confused and scared.

'You don't have to make up your mind now,' she said. She took his hand again and looked sadly at him.

'Is that all right?' he asked.

'It's OK. It's just that it would have been nice if you wanted to straight away. But you can have a few days,' she said. 'Come on . . . I'll buy you an ice cream.'

She led the way across the park to where the ice-cream van waited underneath the poplar trees on the road outside. Jonathon tried to pay but she wouldn't let him. She smiled at him as they waited to be served. The ice cream came down in swirls onto their cones.

'Looks like a dog shitting,' he said.

Deborah howled. 'What are you like!' she screamed. It was great. She even liked his awful shit jokes.

They walked back into the park and sat on a bench, side by side, licking their ices. After the cones had gone, she stood up and brushed down her jeans. 'You'll have to let me know by the weekend,' she told him.

'Yes'm.'

'Kiss me again,' she commanded.

Obediently, Jonathon walked forward to kiss and be kissed. He felt so helpless. Once again, up came Mr Red Cap. Deborah reached down and held him in her hand. She drew back and looked closely up into his face. He was so horned up he could hardly focus. He heard her speak in a kind of dream.

'You make me so horny,' she was saying.

'What?'

'I want to be your lover. I want to do it with you – I want to do everything,' she said again. Then she let him go. She walked away, glancing over her shoulder at him without smiling.

Jonathon's penis had reached an ebony-like degree of hardness that was positively uncomfortable. It felt as if someone had injected a litre of testosterone directly into it. He staggered around the bench, concussed by desire.

'You traitorous bastard,' he told Mr Knobby, but he wanted to shake hands so much that he had to walk swiftly home to relieve himself of the pressure. How could someone he didn't fancy turn him on so much? Was it possible? He was ravaged by hormones. He seemed to be bobbing upside down in them, just one more ingredient in a thick soup of lust. At home, he had to see to Mr Knobby three times, one after the other. Afterwards, he lay back and gazed at the fatal organ.

'You don't know when to start and you don't know when to stop,' he said severely.

Mr Knobby grinned back. 'Who cares about all that?' he said. 'You heard what she said.'

'She said, Everything. She wants to do everything.'

'And you know what they say.'

'Fat Girls Are Grateful For It,' said Jonathon dutifully. 'Fat Girls Will Do *Anything*.'

'It's the chance of a lifetime,' said Mr Knobby Knobster.

19

sue

That's Jackie's big problem: she has to be right. If you disagree with her it's like some big insult. She goes on about it for hours and hours and in the end I just say, OK, OK. You're right, I'm wrong, but I don't care, I'm gonna do it/wear it/try it anyhow. What's wrong with being wrong? You get more done.

You'd have thought she had it all going for her. That's how it's supposed to be, isn't it? Be sensible, work hard, plan ahead and there it all is – good grades, good job, good kids, good husband. And then – Dino! What's that all about? All those years of getting it right, and then what? I mean, be irresponsible if you have to. But *Dino*?!

After the party, I thought even she'd be able to see what was going on. If she wanted any more proof that deep down inside she really did NOT want to sleep with him, then running away from his bed at two o'clock in the morning had to be it. I got her round to my place, sat her down in the lounge, told my mum we needed some space, and had another go.

I did it very carefully, very simply. Emotions by numbers. I pointed out all the things that mattered to her which her relationship with Dino was screwing up. Her work was suffering. She hates that. Jackie is the original top girl. She was making a fool of herself. Horrible! She was losing her self-confidence. That made her wince. She always used to be in charge; now she was like a puppet on a string. And finally – and this was the so-so clever bit, see – I told her she was *using* Dino.

She looked like I'd just slapped her round the face. See, Jackie's not only sensible – she's nice.

'Dino's a boy,' I explained to her. She seemed to have forgotten this vital fact. Some people do. They think boys are like girls with knobs on. They're not.

'So what?' she asked belligerently.

'He wants a shag, right? But it's more than that. His feelings are all contained in the end of his knob. Try and imagine that that's where his heart is. Well, Dino wants to *give you his heart.*'

She scowled suspiciously, but I ploughed on.

'All this leading him on, Jackie – it's not fair. You're not just stopping him having a shag, you're rejecting him. How do you think that makes him feel?'

She didn't like that. 'Why all this concern for Dino suddenly?' she snapped.

'I don't give a shit about Dino, but since you can't do anything for yourself, maybe you can do it for him.'

'You want me to chuck Dino for *his* sake?'

'No, listen. The thing is, we've been talking about Dino as

if he's just a selfish lump of meat who wants a shag. But it's more than that. He cares for you. You can't just treat him like he can turn it on and off like some sort of switch.'

'You've changed your tune,' she told me. 'According to you, Dino's never given a shit about any living thing except himself.'

I shrugged. 'Maybe he's human after all.'

For a second I thought I'd gone too far, but she seemed to be prepared to believe anything. She began to nod slowly.

'So what you have to do, right? – is just deal with him straight. You have to try being honest with him.' I could see her bristle at that, but it was true. 'It's obvious you're not ready to sleep with him. Right? So, put it to him. Be truthful. Tell him, you want to go out with him – but no sex.'

'But that's what I've been doing!'

'No, you haven't. You've been *going* to have sex. That's different. It's been sex tomorrow, sex next week. You've been holding out jam for him. It's time to put the jam away.'

Jackie thought about it.

'He'll chuck me,' she said.

'You owe it to yourself, and you owe it to him,' I said. 'I mean, say yes or no, Jackie, but not like this, it's not fair.'

Just for a second I thought she was going to tell me to piss off, but suddenly she started to weep instead. It was amazing, actually. You know how plans like that, they never work? And here was this one all falling into place – it was like magic. For once in my life I must have got it right. Or maybe Jackie was just desperate for a way out.

I went over to give her a hug and she sniffed onto my shoulder. 'You're right,' she said in a muffled voice. 'I have to be straight with him. I have to tell him. No sex.'

And I thought, Yes! Got her! That was it. No way was Dino going to go along with that.

20

ben

You know what heaven is? I'll tell you. You're lying across a big soft, king-size bed, so big you can stretch out in any direction without going over the edge. Everything's warm – the air's warm, your skin's warm, the sheets are warm and all rumpled up. There's an ice-cold beer on the bedside table and a packet of chocolate-covered raisins on the sheet next to you. There's a good film on the telly. Then the door opens and Ali Young comes in with a bowl of Frosties, stark naked except for a pair of white socks. You watch her tits jiggle as she comes across the room.

'Are you looking at my tits?' she says, and you say,

'Yes, miss.'

She puts the Frosties on the bed next to you, puts the backs of her hands underneath them and jiggles up and down. 'Jiggly-jiggly-jig-jig-jig,' she says, and then she bends over so they hang in your face like . . . well. Like a beautiful pair of tits.

'Mmmmnuh,' I say. And that's what heaven is.

'What?' she says.

'Just *gorgeous*,' I reply.

It was the week after Dino's party. She'd just about recovered from her mother and things were back to normal. Sometimes on a Tuesday evening she wants to grind her way around the sitting room – on the floor, on the table, you name it. Which is great, of course. But the thing I really like is just rolling about in her big bed, me on top, her on top, me behind. And then afterwards all shagged out with nothing on, titbits being carried to and fro, ready to start again any time you feel like it. It's the best thing.

Ali got into bed next to me and looked at the TV. It was a good movie – *Doubles* – but there were plenty more interesting things to do than watch a movie. I smiled fondly at her tits again and waited for her to look across and spot me doing it.

'One, two, one two,' she said, wiggling her chest.

'Yum yum yum,' I said. I leaned over and kissed them, and sighed happily.

'Stay over,' she said.

'If only,' I said, holding my head in my hand. In another hour or so I'd have to go back to parentland and sleep in my own narrow little bed, in my narrow little room, in a house full of people who felt like strangers just at that moment.

'Don't, then.'

'I've got to.'

'Why?'

'They expect me. You know?'

'Ring 'em up. Tell them you want to stay over with a friend.'

'They know all my friends. They'll want the number. They might ring back. Anyway, I never stay over on schooldays.'

161

'Ah, poor thing!' She smiled at me, a bit grimly I thought. 'Has iddle oodams got to be home on time, den? Come on, Ben, you're seventeen, they don't have to know where you are every second of the day.'

'Get off . . .' I muttered. I hate it when she comes on like that. It's bad enough as it is.

'Just ring them up and say. Tell them it's a new boy at school. Tell them it's a new girl!' She smiled at me. 'Are you allowed to have sex? Perhaps I should send a parental consent form home for you.'

'Don't be daft. Let's watch the movie.'

I could feel her looking at me, deciding whether or not to carry on with it. Just a moment ago it was drop-dead certain that I was going back in an hour or so, and now suddenly everything was all slippery. I felt like I was being dishonest in some way. She does that. She whips the ground from under your feet and you don't even know why.

And – well, let's be honest about it. I *wanted* to go home afterwards. I didn't want to spend the night in her bed. It made me feel uncomfortable.

'We should do this more often,' she said, snuggling down and holding onto my arm.

'Mmm.' I draped my arm over her shoulders.

'What about Thursdays?'

'Thursdays?'

'Why not? If you can't stay over?'

Maybe but . . . I didn't want to do that either. I suppose it sounds stupid. One minute it's heaven and the next I want to go back home to Mum and Dad. Maybe you think I was being a bastard, but it's an edgy business, having it off with Miss. I suppose I just wanted to keep it at arm's length. I lay there for a bit trying to think of a good reason not to come on Thursdays. I have footie practice, there's a good programme on TV, I have to stay in and do homework. No no no no.

'Can't really get away.'

'Why not?'

'They're always on at me. I'm always out. I'm out tonight, I'm out seeing me mates tomorrow, I'm out with you on Sundays. You know.'

There was a silence.

'I feel as though I'm having to beg,' she said at last.

It was new, all this. So far she'd been very keen about keeping it down to a couple of times a week, not seeing too much of one another. She could lose her job – in fact, she could lose her whole career if anyone ever found out about it. No one'd ever give her a job in teaching again if they knew she shagged the students.

Shagging the students. I used to say that to her but it always made her cross.

'I shag you,' she said. 'Just one, Ben, in case you thought I was having it off with the rest of the year. I'm not, for your information.'

'Sorry, Miss.'

But. So why the change?

'What's this about?' I asked her.

'What's what about?'

'You wanting to start seeing more of me?'

163

'I'm just trying to find a way of doing this more often,' she said, all huffy.

'Really?'

'You're so paranoid!'

'You just sound . . . I mean I thought we'd agreed it was the right thing to be careful and not see too much of each other.'

'Just because I like the idea of another evening?'

'Sorry,' I said.

'You're so paranoid.'

I looked at her. 'Well, you know, I'd love to do it more often, but it's really awkward.'

'Why?'

'It just is. At home. Getting out. You know? It's not that they don't let me, but it's just difficult. I have to talk to them and tell them what I'm up to. It's just awkward. Like having an affair, I suppose,' I said.

That seemed to make sense to her. She nodded and pulled a face. 'I suppose. We'll have to try and think of something.'

I didn't say anything. I sat up and picked up the Frosties and tried to watch the film. I was scared she was going to go all hurt, but it was OK. I drank the beer, watched the movie and we had a lovely big snog on the doorstep before I went home. Delicious. Going home afterwards was fairly delicious too.

21
six inches away from home

'Are you sure you're prepared to go through with this?' asked Sue.

'Go through it again.'

'You're very fond of him.'

'Right.'

'But for some reason' – Sue sighed impatiently – 'you can't bring yourself to sleep with him.'

'But I still want to go *out* with him.'

'Yes, but with no sex.'

'For now.'

'No, not for now! That sounds like maybe next week, same as usual. You don't want to even consider sex for the foreseeable future.'

'He'll chuck me!' wailed Jackie.

That's the plan, isn't it? hissed her friend silently to herself, but what she actually said was, 'Well, maybe, maybe not, who knows? Maybe it's like you say, he's more decent than you think. But if he loses interest just because of that, you don't want him. Right?'

Jackie pulled a face but she knew it was right. She couldn't keep on making promises about a sex life which, when it came down to it, she was unable to participate in.

'Either he's prepared to put up with it or he isn't. If he wants you for yourself, he'll say yes. And if he doesn't, that's that. And then perhaps we can stop having this conversation, and talk about something interesting. Like me, for instance,' she added hopefully.

Jackie rehearsed her lines, did her make-up, wept and did her make-up again. Sue soothed her and patted her and plied her with tissues and told her to be strong. She was fairly certain Dino would chuck her. It wouldn't last, of course, they'd be an item again within the week, but at least Jackie would gain a few Dino-free days. In the event, she didn't even manage that. At the time it was a complete surprise to Jackie the way things turned out and it was only in retrospect that she realised what a typically Dinoesque situation it was, the way he side-stepped her plans so effortlessly and manipulated her so blatantly, like a man working a complicated marionette puppet with one hand, while his real attention was taken up flicking through the TV channels with the other.

It started out so well. Her parents were out late that evening. Dino came round as arranged and they had a couple of hours ahead if necessary, although she wasn't expecting it to take anything like that long. She made him a cup of coffee and got straight on with it. She was very very fond of him but she didn't somehow feel confident enough of their relationship to sleep with him. Sleeping with someone, she explained, was a very special thing, a very close thing, a very intimate thing. Of course, she fancied him something chronic, she couldn't keep her hands off him; but something was holding her back. She wasn't sure what it was, but she had decided that she had to respect it and she wanted Dino to respect it too.

'Yeah. I think you're right,' said Dino.

'Pardon?'

'Right, I agree with you.'

'You agree?'

'Yeah. Let's give it a bit of time. There's no hurry. Maybe you have a problem in that department. Maybe there's some sort of experience you had once.'

'I don't think so, Dino,' she replied carefully.

'You must have covered it up. I dunno. But yes, you're right. Let's leave the sex for now. Is that what you wanted?' he added anxiously.

'Yes, yes, that's right,' exclaimed Jackie. Her hand was shaking so much she had to put her coffee carefully down on the table to avoid spilling it.

'God!' Dino clutched his chest. 'You gave me a fright. I thought you were chucking me there for a moment.'

'No no no.'

Dino shook his head. She really had scared him. He looked closely at her. 'You don't look very pleased,' he complained.

'Oh, I am. I really am.'

But the truth was, her first reaction was one of disappointment. She'd been thinking, that was it. No more worry and anxiety and fighting her better judgement. No more bullshit. Dino was going to behave like an arse and that was that. Instead, he was just terrified that she was going to chuck him.

'You're sure about this?' she asked.

'You *are* chucking me, aren't you!'

'No. But . . .'

'What?'

'It's just that, you know . . . I really thought you wouldn't want to know.'

'What do you think I am? Some sort of arse? No, if that's how you feel, sure. I mean, of course.'

'Oh, Dino!' The disappointment passed. She was so pleased she jumped up and wrapped herself round him. She'd underestimated him! He loved her after all! See? Suddenly they were in a clinch on the settee loosening one another's jeans.

'Ooooo, that's nice,' said Jackie. She was just so grateful, so happy that Sue had been wrong. She sort of let go. After a bit, someone knocked the coffee table and one of the cups slopped over. Jackie got up to clean things up and Dino came up behind her and seized her from behind. He pushed her forward until she jammed up against the back of the settee. Jackie bent over it and he began banging himself against her bum. He was looking down, trying to imagine that the thin layers of jeans and knickers were gone, but he was still a good six inches from where he wanted to be. Jackie lay there and soaked into her jeans. At the back of her mouth the words formed,

'Go on then – take them off.' She could feel the sentence moving inside her. She whispered it soundlessly just to see what it felt like and it felt just so gorgeous, so salty and sexy and true, that she wondered if, despite everything, she might actually say them.

'Go on then – take them off,' she heard herself saying.

Dino paused in his bangings. 'Are you sure?'

'Yes. Go on.'

She raised herself slightly off the settee while he felt underneath her for the zip. The zipper slid down with a growl. He tugged. Jeans and knickers came suddenly down and she felt the cool air on her bum.

'No!' she shrieked. She jumped up, spun round and tugged the jeans back up. 'Don't do that!' she snapped.

'But you said,' complained Dino.

For a second they both stood staring at one another.

'See?' she told him. 'I'm mad. I need looking after. Next time I tell you to do that – just don't, OK?'

'God,' said Dino. She put her hand to her mouth and started to shake with the giggles, while Dino stood watching her, lust vying with frustration vying with wanting to be sweet. Every time she looked at his face she laughed more. She kept expecting him to join in, but Dino just stood and stared at her with a wry smile on his face while she shook with hysterics. It went on for ages, until he got fed up with it and stalked out into the kitchen. Alone, she came suddenly to her senses, walked three times round the room and ran out to him to apologise. Amazingly, he was OK about it. More proof! She really had misjudged him.

They sat back down with their coffees. Jackie was delighted. He was sweet! He really was sweet. He hadn't a clue what she was going through, but he was respecting it because she'd asked him to. And here she was still being an arse! That was pretty bloody good, wasn't it? Her initial instinct had been right after all – there was more to him than met the eye. Under the bullshit was a kind, sweet boy.

Dino leaned back on the sofa, basking in her approval. On the spur of the moment, he told her all about his mum and Dave Short. He hadn't planned on it. He had no idea why. He just found himself saying it.

'I was just remembering,' he said. 'My mum's having an affair with someone from her school. I caught them at it the other day in the front room.'

'*What?*'

'You know . . .' He looked sideways at her. 'She's having an affair.' Dino smiled at her. He meant it to be amused, but his smile was a terrible grimace. Suddenly it sounded awful – exactly what he didn't want it to be. He stopped smiling and scowled at Jackie, daring her to be appalled.

Jackie scowled back. 'When did this happen?'

'Just before the party,' admitted Dino, closely watching her face.

'Why didn't you tell me?'

'I don't know. The party and everything. Anyway, it doesn't matter.'

'Doesn't matter?' Jackie was desperately trying to work it out. Had his unexpected compliance got anything to do with this? She stood up and pulled her jeans up, as if they were still on the way down. She sat down again. 'OK. Go on.'

'There's nothing to tell, really,' said Dino. And then he told her everything – everything, that is, except for the fact that he had been alternating between total amnesia and utter turmoil about it ever since.

'I don't think she even knows I saw them,' he lied.

'If she didn't, she does now. After what you said to your dad about Dave Short going away with them for the weekend.'

'That didn't mean anything,' insisted Dino irritably. It was so typical! He'd been so understanding and grown-up and now look. Far from reassuring him, she was trying to make out it was some sort of disaster.

Jackie decided to take it at face value and be outraged. 'Well, how could she do that to your dad? And to you! In your own house! And she hasn't even come to speak to you about it. Oh, Dino, you must feel awful.'

'Not really,' he told her coolly. 'It's their business, isn't it?'

'It's your business too! Well, if she won't talk to you about it, you'll have to talk to her about it.'

'Don't be stupid.'

'Can't you? How awful.'

'No. It isn't that bad.'

'Isn't it?' Jackie looked carefully at him. It was happening: he was getting upset *with her*. He was looking to one side, pulling a face, sneering at her concern. She could watch it happening. Dino was rushing into denial.

'Dino?'

'Bollocks,' he told her, and turned away.

Jackie grabbed him by the arm and swung him round to face her. This was important. He needed her, and here he was vanishing in front of her eyes.

'I care for you,' she hissed. 'How dare you just vanish on me. Dino! Look at me!'

Dino looked at her and began to sneer but before he finished it his eyes filled with tears. He was amazed. Tears? Where had they come from? What had he got to be upset about?

'Oh, Dino.' She put her hand gently on the side of his face. His whole face wobbled with sorrow and amazement. Then he took her in his arms, buried his face in her hair and sobbed.

An hour or so later, after she closed the door behind him, Jackie went to look at herself in the mirror in the front room. Her hair was still damp on one side where he had wept on it. Somewhere in the back of her mind a little voice – Sue's probably – was muttering away that there, see, he's done it again. Just as she thought he was being understanding and thoughtful it turned out he had an agenda of his own. Well, maybe – but Jackie didn't care. He'd clung tight like a big baby sobbing his heart out. He'd given her his bleeding heart. He needed her.

'I've never cried like that before,' he said to her afterwards. 'I don't think I could with anyone else.' And so he had wrapped her into his heart more tightly than ever.

Shortly after, the phone rang. It was Sue wanting to know how she got on.

'It was amazing,' said Jackie. 'He took it!'

'He what?' demanded Sue.

'He took it! He accepted the deal!'

'Are you sure?'

'Yes, of course I'm sure. He said he understood.'

'Understood?' asked Sue incredulously. Since when had Dino understood anything? 'What exactly did you say to him?'

'What we said. I told him. I said I needed more time to be sure of what we felt for each other, and he said that he agreed with me.'

'He *agreed*?'

'Yes,' insisted Jackie. 'He said he thought that we should just forget about sex for a while.'

'Dino said that?'

'Dino,' said Jackie.

'He's up to something.'

'Why do you have to be so suspicious?'

'Aren't you suspicious?'

'No,' said Jackie, in an offended voice. 'I mean, he's making all the right noises, isn't he? That was the deal, wasn't it?'

'I suppose the least you can say is, he knows the right noises to make. I wouldn't have even given him credit for that before.' Could it be that Dino was actually being clever? Surely not? But even that unlikely possibility was more believable than that he was being genuinely caring.

'He's up to something.'

'Don't be cynical. He was sweet.'

'It's better than his usual grunting, I suppose,' agreed Sue. 'But it's not like him, is it? Or are you going to give me some

173

crap about this being the real Dino, the Dino beneath who has been waiting to emerge?'

'Oh, don't be patronising,' snapped Jackie. But although she would never admit to anything so foolish, really she did hope that it might be so. She had no idea of the depths of deceit that Dino was prepared to stoop to.

Before she put the phone down, Jackie hesitated. There was more to tell, but she knew exactly what Sue would say if she ever found out that Dino's mum was having an affair and that Dino had more or less grassed her up at the dinner table the week before. She put the phone down, Dino's secret kept, but she could hear Sue's voice ringing in her ears even as she put the phone down.

'Sucker! Why are you doing this to yourself?'

He needs me, thought Jackie in reply. He was like a six-foot teddy bear, right down to the sexy little growl when he whispered in her ear. He needed her. But did she need him?

22
dino the destroyer

Back home, Dino went straight up to his room. He felt calm inside, but his whole body was vibrating as if a perfectly balanced mechanism was spinning rapidly inside him. One jolt and he'd blow to pieces. He was furious with Jackie for making such a fuss. Look at the state he was in!

Below, he heard his mother's step on the stairs. He'd been dying for her to talk to him about it, but what good did talking do? He'd just talked about it to Jackie and look at him now. Talking just made it worse.

Her foot sounded on the creaky steps. The creaking paused, then restarted. Then paused. Then with a firm tread, she came upstairs. A knock. Dino flung himself sideways on the bed and closed his eyes. The door opened.

'Dino?'

Pause.

'Dino? Are you awake?'

'Uh. What? Mum?'

'Did you have a good day?'

'Yeah. All right, why?'

'You look . . .'

'I'm tired.' He glanced over to her through screwed-up eyes as if he was unused to the light and saw her watching him as if he was something you could open up, a box, a purse, and she could just pick out and throw away the bits she didn't want in there.

'Do you . . . ? Is there anything . . . ?'

'No.'

'Anything bothering . . . ? Anything . . .'

'No.'

'. . . you want to talk about?' Dino suddenly couldn't work his mouth. He lay there and stared at her hopelessly until she gave in.

'Would you like a sandwich?' she asked.

'Yes!' That was more like it. Mother.

She smiled back at him, and for a second the two of them were complicitous in pretence, mother and son doing their mother and son stuff.

'Fried egg?'

'And ketchup.'

'Right.'

'Thanks, Mum!' he called after her. He meant it. He was so relieved, so pleased with her. All the business she had with him was a fried egg sandwich. He lay back down, exhausted.

'Things aren't as straightforward as they seem,' muttered Dino to himself. You ain't kidding. He closed his eyes and tried to blank everything out.

* * *

Ten minutes later, Kath Howther came upstairs, knocked gently on the door and went in with the fried egg sandwich on a small plate. Dino lay on his bed, fast asleep.

'Dino?' No answer. She went up close, put the plate down on the little table next to his bed and looked down into her son's pale face.

'Dino.' She said his name like a statement, as if she was testing to see if it still fitted this handsome, long man, who had been her baby son of just a few years ago. What was it like to be mother to a grown-up? How good would she be at it? She had thought it was going to be so much easier now, but look, she'd let go and thought of herself and here she was suddenly and hopelessly out of her depth. She had so much wanted the whole thing to work for them all – family, child-hood, Mum and Dad. She loved him so much and here he was, already passing beyond her and her own feelings were suddenly too big, too soon.

'I'm sorry,' she whispered. She tiptoed out. She waited outside his door listening to see if he was awake really, but there was no sound.

One of the worst things about the whole mess was not knowing how long it would go on for, but she found out the answer to that very soon, when Dino destroyed his family the next morning accidentally, like a man with a shotgun pointing it at someone's head and pulling the trigger whilst suffering from a temporary illusion that he was really holding a feather duster. It started with an outrageous argument with his mother. Afterwards, he couldn't remember what it was about until she told him, much later on. It was socks. He had no clean socks.

He called down asking where they were, and she yelled back up, 'Just a moment, Dino, I'm dealing with the cat.' Next thing, he was storming downstairs.

"Oh, the cat, the cat, the cat's all right, then. Always the bloody cat before anything else. You're mad about that bloody cat, I don't know why you don't marry it.' He burst into the kitchen, bleary-eyed and furious.

'Don't speak to your mother like that,' yelled his dad. First thing in the morning – not the time to start up. Before he could stop it, Dino's mouth opened and out it came.

'She might as well marry the cat, she's just a tart anyway. Come and get it, here it is. Pussy pussy pussy pussy pussy.'

In the silence that followed he watched his father's face change shape. He wasn't even conscious of being outrageous. It was true, wasn't it? His mother stood there with a tin of Katkins in her hand and her mouth open. Mat stared at him as if he was made of horror, a piece of toast halfway to his mouth.

'Just a tart,' Dino insisted in a squeaky voice. 'Pussy pussy,' he repeated. He couldn't understand what they were being so appalled about. His mother knew, his father knew – didn't he? They'd been arguing ever since he said that thing about Dave Short. The only person who was being kept in the dark was him. What did they expect?

His dad was rising to his feet and pushing the table out of the way. Dino was going to get hit. His mouth filled with wet, salty liquid. He smacked his lips, expecting to taste blood already. Now his father's mouth was opening and a stream of rage poured out of it.

'Fed on shit!' yelled Dino. He prepared to run for it, but then he remembered how small his father looked these days. He'd often had fantasies about beating the shit out of him. Well, maybe now was the time. He was fit and young; his father was a sad old bastard who couldn't even stop his wife shagging creeps like Dave Short in his own living room, probably in his own bed if Jackie was right and she usually was. Dino bent at the legs and moved his hands forward. His father was pushing the chairs out of the way. One went over. The milk spilled on the table. Mat jumped back.

It was all happening in slow motion but suddenly something broke out of the frame. His mother. It felt afterwards as if she'd jumped right over the table to get at him. She leaped on Dino, grabbed him tight, wrapped her arms round his neck and hugged him so hard it hurt.

Dino caught sight of his dad changing direction in midmurder, face popping, swinging his arms to keep his balance and stop himself from colliding with them. His mother kept her face deep into his neck, just like Jackie sometimes did. His dad ricocheted off the edge of the work surface and banged his fist violently into the breadbin. His mother lifted her face to Dino's ear and whispered right in there, in words that sent a shiver and a tickle down his side until he squirmed, 'Don't do this to me.'

'Ah, oh, all right,' he yelled, wriggling and jumping because of the tickle.

'I'll speak to you about Dave. OK?'

'Right,' he said in a quieter voice.

She let go of him.

The room had escaped by the skin of its teeth. Mat suddenly ran out of it and up the stairs. Chairs down, milk spilled, tea slopped out of the cups, toast and crumbs everywhere. The air was ashes. It was amazing how much damage you could do in just a few seconds if you stopped bothering not to knock things over. His mum was already straightening things on the table, but his dad just stood there. He looked older, more wrinkled, smaller and more useless than ever. He seemed to have shrunk and his mother seemed to have grown.

She brushed herself down and said, 'But first I'd better tell your dad, don't you think?'

'I thought he knew,' said Dino.

'Tell me what?' said his dad.

'You were right,' she told him. 'I'm sorry.'

He shook his head and added even as she spoke, 'Don't tell me, I can guess.' He sat down at the table, and to everyone's pity and shame, began to weep bleakly, his head in his hands, his elbows crunching up the toast crusts. 'I knew it, I knew it, and you just kept denying it. Why did you have to keep denying it?' he wept.

'I'm sorry,' she said. 'Can we get the children off to school first?'

'She's been shouting at me about my suspicious mind,' he explained to Dino, his eyes glistening, his voice wobbling. He stopped, wiping his eyes, and looked up at the clock. 'But I have to go. I have that meeting.' He stood up. 'An important meeting, God help me, I was looking forward to it. Now look. What timing!' He glared at his wife and then at Dino, trying to swallow the things he wanted to say.

He moved around the kitchen picking things up and getting his jacket on as he wept. Dino, watching from the table, thought he looked like a man in a movie.

'Do you have to go now?' asked Kath.

'You've had how long to tell me – how long? Weeks? Months? How long?'

'We'll talk later,' she said, looking away.

His dad looked at Dino. 'Dino. None of this is your fault. OK?'

'Why should it?' asked Dino, but it sounded rude so he added, 'OK, Dad.'

'OK like hell, eh? I've got to go. Christ, what timing!'

'Let's take the day off, Mike. We can talk now,' said Kath.

He stood in the kitchen considering. 'No,' he said. 'No. Not like that. Not because you say so right now after so many . . . so many lies. I'll take this afternoon off. See you here, OK?'

'The meeting too important for you, is it?'

'Don't be spiteful.'

'Sorry.' She looked away and bit her lip. 'Sorry.'

'See you later.' He clapped a hand on Dino's shoulder and walked out of the door.

Dino stood up. 'I'd better get going too,' he said.

'No. We need to talk.'

'School . . .'

'We'll take the morning off, both of us.'

'Sausages,' sneered Dino. He meant, she was treating him and his dad like sausages – him in the morning and his dad in the afternoon. But she knew what he meant.

181

'No, important people I've neglected too long,' she said. 'I won't be a minute, I'll just get Mat away. We have to talk.'

She went upstairs after Mat. Dino ignored her instructions. Why should he go through this shit? Everything was going to stop for her? Nothing was going to stop for her! He went upstairs to get his things ready and slipped out while she was in the kitchen packing Mat's bag. He walked halfway down the road before he realised that if he went, he'd have to wait all day before finding out what was going on. He felt sick with anticipation already. He turned round and went home to listen to his mother's music.

Kath came back from taking Mat to school, stood in the hall and called his name.

'I'm in the kitchen,' he told her.

'Be with you, I just need to pee.' She ran upstairs to her bedroom and stood in front of the mirror doing her face, as if her son was an interviewer, or a lover or someone she had to look good for. What was she going to say? Poor Dino didn't even know how to think about this sort of thing. It was going to be a question of what mood he was in.

Not fair to him, she thought.

How much had he seen? Ouch – she couldn't even think of that. What a mess. She hadn't got a clue how to go about it.

She patted her hair and went down.

* * *

'It's all wrong, I should be speaking to your dad first, not you,' she said.

'I'll go to school, shall I?' said Dino.

'No, no, please. Oh, God, Dino. I'm not very good at this, am I?'

'You looked pretty good at it in the living room the other day.'

'How much did you see?' she asked, before she had time to think about it.

'Enough,' he muttered, and turned his face away to avoid having to watch her blush.

She walked two or three times up and down the room, turned, and put the kettle on.

'Tea.'

'Thanks.' Suddenly impatient, he squirmed in his chair and said, 'What do you want to say to me? I should be at school.'

His mother rubbed her eyes. 'I should have spoken to you ages ago. I didn't know . . . I mean, I wasn't sure if you'd seen us.'

Dino shrugged.

'Although I suppose I knew you'd seen us by the way you were behaving. You made it pretty clear, actually, considering it's almost impossible to get you to talk about anything.'

Dino laughed.

'Thanks for waiting for me, anyway,' she said.

'OK.'

He watched her as she turned to make the tea. This was a woman; he hardly knew her. She was like a tiny box he had held in his hand all his life, and he had pressed a catch and she'd opened up and here she was, big as the sky. She was like the bloody Tardis. He felt a wave of resentment that she had so much life.

She turned round to face him. 'Sorry. That's what I want to say. Sorry for bringing Dave home here. Sorry for you catching us. Sorry I never spoke to you about it until it was too late. You know what, when it comes to affairs of the heart we're all just about sixteen years old. But really, really sorry.'

Dino cleared his throat, and to his own amazement asked the only relevant question left between them.

'And sorry about Mr Short as well?'

She looked away and then back. 'I'm sorry for practically everything, aren't I? But I don't think I am sorry about that.'

'Are you going to live with him?'

'God, no! No, I don't love him, Dino.'

'You don't love him and you're not even sorry?'

'Dino. God. Talking to you like this! But . . . No I don't love him. The trouble is, I don't love your dad either. He drives me mad. I don't hate him, but he's like . . . he's like . . .' She took a deep breath. 'He's like someone I can't live with any more.'

'Are you sure about that?'

'I'm sure.'

And having said it to her son, she was sure. She'd had enough. Kath Howther was out of there.

'I've known it for a long time,' she lied.

'Why didn't you go ages ago?'

'I was hoping things would change, I suppose.'

Dino shrugged. 'So leave,' he told her.

She gulped. *She* leave? *She* had to go?

'If that happens I don't know who would go, but there's one big problem at the moment.'

'What's that?'

'Money.' She shrugged. 'You know we don't have much at the moment.'

'You don't have much ever.'

'We can't afford two homes. Simple mathematics. The only trouble is, now it's out in the open, it might just become utterly unbearable.'

'So we all stay together, anyway.'

'I guess so.'

'So you'll just have to work it out?'

'I suppose . . .'

Dino felt a cloud lift off him. Everything was going to be all right. It wasn't his responsibility any more. He had no more power. Great! He smiled, then paused, wondering vaguely why his mother was glaring at him. 'Can I go to school now?' he asked.

'I guess so,' she said, and he had his bag on his shoulder and was off down the road before she could say another word.

23
this is me

The week after the party there was a youth club on at the school for Year Eleven and the sixth form. Dino, Ben, Jonathon and the other lads didn't very often go to these dos, but this time they were all meeting up.

Wood End School lay between two roads, one of them the main road leading into Wood End, and the other a busy A-road leading onto the motorway connections and nearby towns. Crab Lane connected the school with these two roads. It was a quiet road, blocked off at one end to stop it being used as a shortcut. The cracked tarmac was lined with old rhododendron trees, behind which stood a handful of big detached houses set back. Under cover of the rhododendrons were a number of nooks and crannies where generations of Wood End students had smoked their cigarettes and spliffs, drunk their beer, cider and alcopops and kissed and fondled their boyfriends and girlfriends. It was here that Dino had had his first serious kiss, and that he and Ben had seen their first fanny. It belonged to Julie Samuels in the year below theirs. It was a dark night, and Dino had lit up with a Zippo lighter, which he held so close Ben thought for a second he was going to set fire to it.

One of these hideaways, near the far end of the lane, had been formed from the space left by a couple of cypress trees, felled years before. One of the rhododendrons had snaked a long, low branch from one side of the space to the other, which made a bouncy seat, and the old stumps from the cypresses made another two. Dino, Ben and Jonathon went there to smoke some weed with Fasil before the dance. Dino and Fasil sat themselves down on the bouncing branch, while Ben and Jonathon crouched low on the sawn off-stumps on the dusty dry ground. It was early summer, still light, but the rhododendrons filtered most of it out and the boys sat in dusky silence as Fasil rolled up. His lighter flared and the red tip glowed like a coal.

'Nice stuff,' whispered Ben, wheezing on a lungful.

'It's skunk,' said Fasil.

Ben handed it on to Dino, who had his and handed it on to Jonathon.

'Skunk,' hissed Jonathon.

'It's skunk,' whispered Ben.

'Skunk,' said Dino.

'Skunk,' said Fasil.

All four of them laughed quietly down their noses, and then laughed again at the noise they were making. Jonathon handed the spliff back over to Fasil. The stump he was sitting on had speeded up. It was travelling at about seventy thousand miles an hour.

'Seeing Deborah tonight?' whispered Dino.

'Yeah.'

'How's it going?'

'Dunno.'

'Good luck with it, mate.'

'Thanks.' The spliff end flared up in the hushed darkness. They could just about see each other in outline. 'You seeing Jackie?'

'Yeah.'

'How's it going?'

'Great.'

'Great.'

'Hey,' whispered Jonathon a moment later. 'Look at these two. They're the two non-shaggers.'

'That's right, Fas and Ben the non-shaggers.'

'I'm shagging someone,' said Ben.

'Who?'

'Miss Young.'

Snorts of amusement went round the dark space.

'And me, I'm shagging someone too, I'm shagging everyone,' said Fasil, and he suddenly jumped up and started dancing around, swivelling on the dry dirt floor, hand jiving in front of his trousers. The other three cracked up laughing, holding their sides and wheezing helplessly into the darkness. Not being able to make a noise made it all the funnier. 'Me, yeah, I've 'ad 'em all. Look! This is me shagging everyone! This is me shagging the Queen, you know, man, I've done the Queen and I've done the Prime Minister's wife, me, I have. Cheree, baby!'

'Urrrgh,' they all wailed.

'Yeah, I've had anything, I have. I've had Carol Vorderman,

Geri and Posh, Zoë Ball. I've had all your sisters and your mums, everyone, man!' Fasil whirled round on his heels, poking and pushing in all directions like a demon, shagging half the kingdom. It was hilarious. Dino, Jonathon and Ben rolled off their seats and tried not to hoot out loud.

'Here . . . here, what's this!' Jonathon jumped up, stretched himself in a cup shape as if he was spread over the back of an elephant and began humping.

'What's this? What's this?' he hissed.

'What?'

'This is me shagging Deborah.'

They were in fits. Dino developed a stitch from too much laughing.

'Shut up!'

'Ssssh! Someone'll hear!'

'Shit, that's so funny!'

'Here – what's this?' Dino jumped up, put one hand behind his head and did more pelvic thrusts. 'This is me doing Jackie standing up!'

Howls of laughter. Dino collapsed onto his haunches and hands.

'What's this? What's this?' Ben jumped up and lay flat on the ground, hands rigid by his sides in the dark. 'This is me lying down staring up Miss Young's minge while she gives me a blow job.'

'You filthy bastard! That's sooooo filthy, you bastard!'

'What's this?' Dino got back up and did Jonathon staggering about with his head stuck up Deborah's fanny, but Jonathon objected.

'You're only allowed to do your own!' So Dino did himself, trying to kneel without getting his trousers dirty, thrusting and walking forward at the same time.

'This is me shagging Jackie from behind while she tries to crawl away! Come back here! Come back here! Come back here!' he hissed. Then Jonathon did doing Deborah first from the front, then behind, walking in a vast circle to do it; then Ben did being tied spread-eagled to the bed while Miss Young jumped about on top of him. Then Dino did shagging Jackie while he leaned on a tree eating a Twix bar. It was just so bad and so funny.

'You lot are sick. You're misogynists, that's what you are,' said Fasil.

'You started it!' objected Jonathon.

'Not with my own girlfriend! You ought to have more respect for your girlfriends. Look! This is me shagging all three of your girlfriends at the same time!' He jagged about to three points of the compass.

'You gotta do your own!' said Dino.

'No, that's not fair, he hasn't got one!'

'Ben hasn't got one either . . .'

'I'm only *imagining* shagging Miss Young,' said Fasil. 'It's the other two I'm really doing it to.'

'You leave Jackie out of it,' Dino told him, and they all stared at him to see if he was serious. He stared back at them, impassive in the half light.

'And you know what?' said Fasil. 'I'm gonna tell them too. I'm gonna say to them that you guys *watched* me shagging them and you didn't care!'

'But we wouldn't do it if they were here. Christ! Imagine if they were here!'

At the thought of them being here, all four cracked up and fell over again. They were convulsed.

'Anyway,' said Ben. 'You guys are disgusting. I agree with Fasil. You should show more respect.'

'Bastard,' said Dino.

'Let's go,' said someone, and then they were outside blinking at the light, saying hi to some friends on the road before they knew what was what.

Jonathon walked slowly around the dance floor. Deborah wasn't there yet. He sipped lager out of a Coke can and breathed slowly. His stomach had slowed down from 70,000 to a steady 300 or 400 mph.

'And . . . relax,' he said to himself.

The dance floor looked like a shadowy coral reef with brightly coloured fish swimming in and out of the sunlight. The teachers stalked about the edges like barracudas. The school was in fancy dress. Too many images! thought Jonathon, but he couldn't stop himself. Look at the girls! They were like a hundred species of exotic butterflies who had just emerged from the grub of their school-day selves. No more jumpers and jeans – it was low-cut tops and short skirts, make-up, glitter, everything beautiful and exotic. All that skin – he could see so much skin! He never knew that the girls in his class had so much skin! Whole parts of them were practically stark naked.

He hadn't realised it before but almost every single one of the girls he went to school with was utterly desirable. When had they become so gorgeous? Why? Was it just their idea of fun? Was it a trap? Could it be that they actually wanted some spotty boy – maybe even some spotty boy like him – to come up and dance with them? Or kiss them? Or touch them and run his hands over them and under them and . . .

Jonathon lurched across the floor and suddenly came face to face with Susan Mallary. She had broad shoulders and a deep bosom. Jonathon was just stopped dead in his tracks by her cleavage.

'Wow,' he breathed. 'Susan! I never knew. I mean – you look amazing. You don't normally look gorgeous. What have you done to yourself?'

Susan laughed and spread her arms and shook her chest to show herself off. Before she knew what was going on, Jonathon had stepped into her arms and pushed up against them. He froze, realising he might have been too forward.

'Dance?' he croaked.

'OK,' she replied. Fortunately it was a slow one. They began to waltz clumsily around each other. Jonathon was amazed that he had got himself so close to those big, beautiful breasts.

Christ, I've asked someone to dance, he thought. He'd never had the courage to do it before. He clung onto her and stepped cautiously around her feet.

Two tracks later, Jonathon still hadn't thought of anything to say. She extricated herself by saying, 'Can we dance further apart?' They jiggled about in front of each other for a while, but the attraction had disappeared. Jonathon excused himself and scurried away to try and remember what he had said, in case he was ever brave enough to ask someone to dance again. He went over to stand by a pillar and sighed deeply. That had been so nice, but he felt embarrassed that he'd had nothing to say.

Deborah appeared in front of him with a little smile.

'Oh, hi,' he said.

'I hear you've been unfaithful to me,' she told him.

'It was just a dance.'

He looked closely at her, but couldn't work out if she was displeased or just didn't mind. She stood and watched the dance floor with him for a minute or two and then said, too seriously, 'Come for a walk with me?'

'All right.'

'I'll just get my coat. See you in the foyer?'

Jonathon tried to sneak out without being spotted. He nearly made it too, but Ben was lurking by the doors.

'What are you doing here?' asked Jon.

'Just taking a rest. What about you?'

Jonathon paused, but Deborah materialised by his side.

'Oh, you're off?' Ben asked.

'Yeah.'

'OK, have a nice time.'

Deborah led the way out and Jonathon cast his friend such an anxious glance that Ben gestured with his hands . . . Go on, get on with it, go on, it's all right. Jonathon paused a moment longer to look back inside. It was hot and dark and bright. He could have gone staggering from girl to girl in a fever if only . . .

'Would you rather stay?'

'No, no, of course not.'

They stepped out together and disappeared into the darkness. Ben turned back into the building and cautiously picked his way towards the dance floor. He'd have liked to get a few dances in, but there was no chance of that. Miss was hanging about the edges with her radar turned up full, keeping an eye on him.

Deborah and Jonathon walked out of the school towards the rhododendron drive, with nothing to say. It was awful. Jonathon tried to rattle on about school, or friends, but it all fell dead between them. At last she turned round and asked him if he'd made up his mind yet.

'Nearly,' he said.

Deborah looked sadly at him. 'You're taking too long,' she said.

'I know, I know, I know.'

'I'd rather be just friends than this. If you don't want to just say so.'

'Yes, I know.'

'So what's the problem?'

In order to stop her talking as much as anything else, Jonathon kissed her. Deborah kissed him back, pushing herself into him. Mr Knobby rose up at once.

'He seems to like me,' she said.

'Oh, Mr Knobby says yes, all right.'

They walked on a bit further, until they came to another

little nest hidden away amongst the bushes. Jonathon guided her into it, pushed her gently up against a tree trunk and kissed her again, leaning into her. Once again, a flood of hormones rushed through him. It was like being hit on the back of the head with a frying pan. He stood back and looked at the ground.

'It's damp,' he said regretfully.

Deborah took off her little jacket and laid it down.

'We should use mine,' began Jonathon.

'I don't mind.' She took his hands and together they sat down on the coat and began to kiss again. Jonathon untucked her clothes. He fumbled with one hand at her bra strap, and she sat up and did it for him. Then, with a sigh, the two lovers lay down, half curled up on Deborah's jacket and kissed deeply.

'You're beautiful,' he whispered.

'In the dark.'

'My hands think you're beautiful,' he told her.

'That's a lovely thing to say,' she said. A little later she took his hand and pushed it down her tights.

'See if I'm beautiful down there too,' she whispered.

She was.

'Do you?' asked Jonathon.

'With you I do – but not here.'

'No, not here.'

'Somewhere comfortable . . . You still haven't told me your answer.'

'I think it must be yes, mustn't it?' Jonathon said. They kissed, slowly and luxuriously and there in the darkness, Jonathon felt himself relax.

'You sure?' she whispered.

'Yeah.'

'Sure sure?'

'Sure sure sure.'

'It took you a long time to make up your mind.'

'I just . . . I don't know if I want a girlfriend. Except now I've got one, I'm glad it's you.'

They kissed again. He tried to rush with his tongue, but she held his face and brushed her lips against his very slowly. 'When, then?' he croaked.

'Slow down, tiger,' she laughed. 'Somewhere soon. We'll see.'

'Kiss me again like that,' he begged.

'Like what?'

'Like this. Slow . . .'

It was so lovely, Jonathon would have liked that moment to last for ever, but they heard voices approaching and they froze, clinging together in the darkness.

'Oh, come on,' said a boy.

'I said no,' said a girl.

Inside their leafy cover, Debs and Jon looked at each other and smiled conspiratorially. It was Dino and Jackie.

'Why not?'

'Dino! I thought we'd put a stop to this.'

'That was shagging, I'm not talking about shagging. I want to . . .'

'We're not going to do that tonight.'

Dino laughed. Jackie was being crisp, but it wasn't clear whether he was teasing her or pushing her. Both probably.

'Come on, don't you want it?'

'I said no.'

'What about a bit of finger?'

'Don't be crude.'

'You like it normally.'

'I didn't say I didn't like it, I said I don't want to do it tonight.'

'Go on. Come here . . .'

There was a pause while Dino presumably kissed her. Then a bit more noise.

'I said, No.'

'Go on. Feel yer tits.'

'No.'

'Bit of finger.'

'No!'

'Just one.'

'No!' Jackie laughed at him. 'You dope.'

'Feel that,' said Dino. They could only guess in the dark. Jackie giggled at him.

'That's enough of that. Walk me up the lane and back. Just be together.'

The couple walked on. Jon and Deborah listened to the voices and footsteps disappearing and then began to kiss again. But Deborah was getting uncomfortable. They'd found a boggy bit.

'I'm getting damp,' she said. They got up. She dusted down her skirt and pulled on her jacket while Jonathon watched sadly.

'That was so nice. Can we do it again?' he asked.

'I'm a bit damp.'

'We can use my top this time.'

Deborah smiled. 'All right. Since we're going out together.'
He took off his top, laid it down for her in an exaggerated
gesture. She lay down and he snuggled in beside her and eased
himself half on her.

'Is that all right?'

'You're crushing me,' she giggled.

He moved a bit. 'Like that?'

'That's lovely.'

'Undo your bra like you did last time,' he begged.

'Like this.'

'Like that. And that other button . . .'

'That one?'

'Lovely. Lovely. Lovely.'

24
cool or what?

That weekend, Dino had his first date with Zoë. He was apprehensive about it – he hadn't said a word about her to anyone and he was worried about being seen. This two-timing business took a lot of nervous energy. He was looking forward to shagging her, of course, but in the end it didn't happen. Oddly, he wasn't sorry at all.

Zoë took what she wanted without a care what anyone else thought of it, but she had her pride. Dino had a few things to prove before she'd condescend to use him again. They met in town and Dino suggested a walk down the river. They walked hand in hand and kissed under Caversham Bridge. Dino's blood fizzed like champagne.

'Let's go somewhere. Let's do it,' he said.

'I don't think so,' she told him. 'Things went a bit too fast last time.' Dino grinned at her. She let him put his hand briefly up her top, but not down her jeans. At one point she almost gave in and let him fumble open the button, but then she took his hand away and got a little cross. Dino smiled happily. He was enjoying himself. He could wait – a bit.

'You're too much,' he growled in her ear. 'You don't know what you do to me!' Zoë hung around his neck and looked up at him blankly. Without even meaning to, he'd made her melt. She wasn't used to melting. If he'd put his hand down her jeans now, she wouldn't have stopped him.

They walked along the river and then back into town, where he bought her coffee and a pastry. He was sweating in his big coat. She teased him about his dress sense, without realising he'd only worn it so she had something to lie down on. All in all they had a really nice afternoon. He left her at the bus station with a kiss and went back for a date with Jackie after tea.

Two girlfriends. Was that cool or what? The way things turned out for him! It was like magic. He didn't have to think about it. He didn't even have to do anything. He just sort of hung out and it all fell into place. Which was, he supposed, the very essence of cool.

I ought to trust myself more, realised Dino.

Not only had he someone to shag, but he had taken the pressure off Jackie. She was going through a difficult patch for some reason and this gave him the opportunity to be understanding, to stand back a bit until she got herself together and at the same time give Zoë a taste of better things.

That last bit made him blush a little, but face it – it was true. You had to have the courage of your convictions. He was It. If there was a higher number than One, it'd be called Dino. Zoë was OK, but normally he'd be out of her class.

Even when he ballsed it up he got it right. Look for example at that business with his mum. At the time, blabbing in front of his dad had felt like a bad mistake, but now look. Result! The affair was out in the open. They were going to work it out. His mother had said so. The marriage was saved – thanks to him.

Even as Dino lay in bed that Sunday evening, congratulating himself on how he had saved his parents' marriage, they were downstairs doing a few sums. Things weren't as bad as Kath at first thought. There wasn't a lot of money but with some careful budgeting, renting a small flat was not impossible.

Kath smiled at the thought; Mike watched her coldly.

'Or we could work it out,' he said.

'Things have gone too far for that,' she said emphatically. 'It won't be so bad.'

'Don't tell me how bad it's not going to be,' snapped Mike. 'Bad for who? The one who stays here or the one who has to go and get the poky little flat and access every other weekend?'

'You agreed, Mat is too small, I have to stay with him.

Mike looked away. 'It'll take a few months to sort out,' he said.

'A few months? We could do this in weeks.'

Mike paused. 'I haven't agreed yet.'

'Yes, you bloody have, don't back out now!'

He glared at her. 'It's all right for you. What are you giving up? Your home? No. And don't say your marriage because you haven't wanted that for years.'

'And you have.'

'Yes, actually, I have.'

Kath looked at him. He'd had affairs in the past, one that she knew of, anyway. 'I wouldn't have guessed,' she said.

He pulled a face. 'What do you think love is, anyway, some sort of joint bank account? We all do stupid and selfish things over the years, me as well as you. People get through it.'

But she was determined. 'Well, we haven't.'

'It's not the only way. We could try to work it out.'

'No, Mike.'

'And there's the kids.'

'We can make it OK for them. It's better than the alternative.'

'Which is?'

'Living with parents who don't love one another,' said Kath, staring firmly into his eyes and uttering the magic mantra that all separating parents depend on.

'But I still love you.'

'But I don't love you. Sorry.'

He looked away, hurting. 'They've done pretty well out of it so far, despite the fact that you apparently haven't loved me for years, so please don't fool yourself into thinking this is for them. It's for you – just for you, Kath, and no one else.'

They both looked up to where, like bombs in their parents' hearts, Dino and Mat lay upstairs.

Dino was equally wrong with his assessment of how things were going with Jackie. Taking the pressure off? He was going on about it all the time. Of course, he didn't see it like that. He was just teasing her. Making light of it, really. He was barely able to let half an hour go by without some reference to how good he was being. There were endless little jokes about did she want a bit of dicky, or a few fingers, or how frigid she was, what a treat she had in store and so on. It was driving Jackie mad.

As for Zoë/Siobhan, Dino had no idea. Zoë was a beast with a very short attention span and he was safe only for as long as he could keep her amused, which was unlikely to be much longer than a few weeks. If he could hang on, she might just lose interest and simply allow him to drop off the edge of her attention. But one step wrong, and she'd pounce.

That weekend, Zoë had seen Dino at his best. For a few hours she'd been the centre of his universe. Whether it was because he wanted to shag her or hold her hand or make her laugh or stop her being cross with him, he hadn't thought about anyone or anything else all afternoon. He made her feel that he needed her. After the party he was some bloke who'd screwed her; that afternoon, she felt that she meant something to him. She was hooked. She was thinking, I was right. He really is a nice guy – and he adores me. Maybe I could actually go out with this one, who knows?

Zoë played it cool. She didn't rush things. She'd have liked to have rung him during the week but she didn't want to seem too eager, so she waited until the weekend as they'd agreed. It was a warm day in May. Dino didn't want to go into town so she suggested a picnic up the river. It was a very un-Zoë-like activity, but she looked forward to it. She even cut some sandwiches and bought some Scotch eggs – he'd said he liked Scotch eggs – and a bottle of stolen wine to drink. They had a brilliant time. He didn't take his eyes off her all day. They walked along the river holding hands in the sunshine and found a quiet spot to go swimming in. They stripped to their underwear. It was freezing. The sun went in as soon as they got out and they had to run around to warm up and dry off. After, they hid themselves down in the grass, their underwear still damp. The sun came back out and he pulled her damp bra up around her neck and her damp knickers halfway down her thighs, and she had him in her hand until he spurted all over her hip. They giggled and wiped her clean with dock leaves, and Dino looked so sad when it was time to go home.

There was another date during the week, at the cinema. They hardly saw any of the film. By the weekend, Zoë had forgotten completely about the blackmail any more. She was proud of herself. She'd held him at bay for three weeks even though she'd been practically barking for it. She'd also kept to a policy of two years' standing and not given him her address and telephone number and real name; but that weekend, if things went according to plan, she was going to bring him back to her place while her parents were out and make love to him on the settee in the sitting room.

And so it might have been if her friend Sam hadn't got her claws in. Zoë hadn't said a word to her or anyone else about the blackmail – that just wasn't the sort of thing that happened to her – but of course, her friend knew all about Dino. It had been one of Sam's other friends who had taken them to Dino's party in the first place. This friend knew about Jackie. It had to come.

'The bastard's two-timing you,' said Sam at school one morning.

'What do you mean?'

'She was at the party. He's been going out with her for ages. They keep getting together and splitting up.'

'Are you sure? Are they together now?'

'Yes. And they were together at the party. Apparently they almost split up after it, and you know why? Because she won't sleep with him. She keeps holding it out and holding it out, but never will do it.'

'How do you know all this?'

Sam explained her information route. It was impeccable.

'You can find out if you don't believe me. Give this Jackie a ring. I have her number right here.'

Zoë shook her head. Sam was certainly right, but she might have been a little gentler had she realised that Zoë was smitten.

'See what's going on? He's got a girlfriend, she won't sleep with him but you will. He's using you.'

Zoë turned pale around the throat.

'Are you going to chuck him?'

'Chuck him?' said Zoë. 'I'm going to fucking destroy him.'

25
ben

It's all getting a bit much. A lot much, actually. In fact, it was a bit much right from the start when I think about it, although that was half the fun of it, I suppose. But the final thing, where I thought, This is getting out of hand, came last Tuesday morning when I came down to breakfast and Dad was sitting at the table with a letter in his hand.

'What's all this?' he said waving the letter at me. 'Maths,' he said.

'What about Maths?'

He handed the letter over. It was from my maths teacher, Mr McGrath. Apparently I'd been falling behind. He was concerned. He suggested that I should stay in after school on Thursday to do extra maths and catch up in the areas I seemed to be having trouble with.

Since when have I been behind in maths? No one had said anything to me about it. But it was right. School notepaper, everything.

'But he got an A for his GCSE,' pointed out my mother. 'How come you got so far behind?'

'Mr McGrath didn't say anything about this to me.'

And then it clicked.

'This is . . .' I began; and then I stopped. What could I say? That it was a forgery?

'Ah . . . It's probably a mistake. Actually, I know what it is, it's a circular. The class in general has been falling behind, he wants us all to stay back. You know how they get . . .' I shrugged. 'League tables.'

'Wood End is very good on maths,' said Dad.

'Yeah, and they want to stay there. I'll talk to him about it. He may not mean me.' It was so stupid. Why pick maths, she knows I'm strong on maths. That's why I'm doing A-level, for God's sake.

I collared her in the corridor at lunch time.

'Maths tuition,' I said.

'Clever, eh?' she chortled. 'I'd love to have seen your face!'

'What if they checked up?'

'I'm sure you're equal to that, Ben, you're a born liar.' She raised her eyebrows and smiled. 'See you then, sweetie.' And she was off before I could say another word.

She's the liar. All this secrecy and plotting – I hate it. I think that's what she gets out of it. Maybe she actually wants to get caught, the risks she takes. Perhaps it turns her on, or something. She picked maths exactly because it's my strongest subject. More risk.

What about that business behind the curtains? Risky or what? She's always trying to get me into dodgy situations like that. She doesn't care, she likes it, but it does my head in. She made me shag her in the props cupboard last week. Sounds great? Don't you believe it. It felt like the whole school was listening outside the door. And then she gets really pissy when I try to stop her.

'What's up with you?' she hisses.

'I don't want to.'

'Yes you do, you're as stiff as a rolling pin. Here . . .'

'No!'

'Why?'

'Someone might come in.'

'There's no reason for anyone to come in.'

'They might not need a reason.'

She put a broom under the door handle.

'There.' And so she got what she wanted, as usual. I ought to just say no, but somehow . . . I mean, she's Miss, you know what I mean?

'I'd get expelled,' I told her.

'It's worse for me. No one would ever give me another job in teaching. That'd be it. Career, income, gone. I'd be practically a paedophile. I don't know what you're making a fuss about.'

Another thing. I've had four detentions in the past two weeks. Everyone sees how odd it is, they're always on about it, teasing me about shagging her. If only they knew! In one of them she even made me sit down and write lines. Lines! So what's that about then?

This. Has got. To stop.

Apart from it getting a lot too much, there's another reason. I mean, girls my own age. You know? Someone I can talk to. Someone I could really fall for. I mean, the sex with Ali is great but it's not like the real thing, is it? It's just porn with a pulse. I want to . . . you know. Well. I want to fall in love.

Does that sound stupid? Maybe that's asking a bit much. It's just that I can't be myself with Ali. It's like a big game. It's not real.

OK, to be honest, there is this one girl I really fancy, which is a bit stupid because I've not even spoken to her that much. She's called Marianne and I do actually think I fell in love with her, or I started to anyway. I can remember the exact moment. She was going out with this lad from our year, Toby. He was there too. He's a big tall lad – I'm quite short, and I thought they looked a bit mis-matched because she's quite short too, and he looked all over-sized and awkward standing next to her.

Anyway, we were all standing around talking, me and a few of the other lads and a couple of girls, and she was there with Toby, standing next to him and talking to someone opposite her. There was something about the way she stood there, close to Toby but listening to this other person. It was something about the way she was listening. She was holding some books up against her chest and she had her head to one side. I must have been staring at her because I saw her glance at me, and I smiled, and she gave me a little smile back.

Funny. She wasn't doing anything at all. I might even be making up all that stuff about her listening and standing protectively next to Toby to explain it, but I was really attracted to her. She's nice, that's all. And good-looking. Not in the usual way, like Jackie, but really pretty and neat.

I got embarrassed after that and I couldn't speak to her,

but I watched her whenever I saw her. She can be quite chatty and lively, but I think she does listen well. You quite often see her listening to people. I know how to listen too. A lot of people don't do that, you know?

She's pretty ordinary really – maybe that's what I want after Ali. Actually, thinking about it, I noticed her even before that during a gymnastics competition. That's pretty cheesy, isn't it? She was doing the dance on a mat – you know that thing they do. I think she came second or third, so she's fairly good at it. I thought she should have come first. She looked really good. She was flipping herself all over the place and running about, but she managed to look really serene and calm, as if it was no effort at all. It was only afterwards that she went red and sweaty, like she could hold it off until she wanted to, and I thought that was so great. I mean, that she was such a nice person and had such a great body as well.

That was last year. I mentioned it to Dino and Jon in the end.

'Ask her to go out with you,' said Dino.

'What if she says no?'

'Better than living in fear,' said Jonathon, as if you could miss out on something and ruin your life. It was a bit of cheek him saying that, because Jonathon would never dare ask a girl anything, but it made me think. So after a bit, I went and asked her. I got Jon and Dino to go along with me to her classroom for moral support, went in and asked her. She was very good about it. She said I was very nice and she was very flattered but she was going out with Toby at the time, and so she couldn't. I couldn't work out if it was an excuse or not.

And you know what? I was broken-hearted. But only for a bit, so it probably wasn't falling in love at all really.

I haven't had much to do with her since then, although we're at the same school. I was a bit shy of her, I suppose. Toby left and went to a sixth form college, but as far as I knew she was still seeing him. But the other day I came up behind her in the corridor. She was talking to some friends, and as I went past she gave me this big smile. It caught me unaware and I smiled back and went on. But I think it meant something, you know. Anyway, I asked around and apparently she and Toby stopped seeing each other a while ago. So maybe, I mean, under other circumstances, I could ask her again.

The lads are always on at me to get a girlfriend, they can't understand why I don't go out with someone. Dino was on about it the other day – did I still fancy Marianne? – and I had to say I didn't fancy her all that much any more.

I don't dare do anything about it. For one thing, I bet Ali would make Marianne's life a misery. I bet she would. She's doing drama for GCSE. Which shows that I don't think all that much of Miss, you know, because that would be a really shit thing to do. You know what I think? I think she'll do anything she can to get what she wants. I was thinking that the other day. About a year ago, I'd have given almost anything to have done all the things I've done with Miss Young. And I have to say, it was great, but it was only great because I wanted to do all those things so much. It didn't really have anything to do with who I was doing them with. And some of it, I don't think I actually wanted to do with anyone. All that risky places stuff – that's not my thing. I'm more straight-forward, I think.

If I ever manage to get rid of her and go out with Marianne, I'll go ever so slowly. I wouldn't try to sleep with her on the first dates. I'll try to kiss her and I may try to slip my hands under her top, but if she didn't want it, that'd be OK. And I'd keep it dead quiet, but not in the same way I keep it quiet about Ali. That's a secret because it's dirty and dangerous; this'd be a secret because it would be private. Some of my mates are really horrible, the way they go on about their girlfriends. Dino's the worst. He's always going on about Jackie – well, he used to anyway. I reckon I know as much about Jackie's body as he does. I know what size and shape her tits are, I know what colour her nipples are, how she plucks out the hairs around them with a pair of tweezers and goes yip! when she tugs them out. I know she hisses and whimpers when she comes. I even know that Dino can fit three fingers up her fanny but she doesn't like it much. That's personal stuff, man! You shouldn't say that stuff to anyone, not even your best friend! I bet poor Jackie would be pretty pissed off, I don't suppose she imagines that's going round the school. But then maybe she does, she's not an idiot.

Jonathon's different again. He's filthy, he's always been filthy, but it's just a show. I mean, he never says a word about him and Debs. Not a word. He's very discreet really. They're very different people, but I envy both of them because, at the end of it, I'd rather be kissing a girl and having her tell me to keep out of her pants, than spending hours and hours rolling around the floor with Miss, watching her trying to imagine new ways of doing the same thing over and over again. In school uniform. On the table. Over the sofa. It's like being trapped in a porn movie. I ought to grow a moustache. I ought to get rid of her. But I don't know how.

26
jonathon

So – onwards and upwards. And inwards. Deborah has Found an Opportunity. Her parents are going away the weekend after next. This is it. I get to lose my cherry.

Only it's not a cherry – it's a big, fat, juicy plum. I have it right here in my hand.

'Ho ho ho!' says Mr Knobby Knobster. 'This is what you've been after the whole time, isn't it, you filthy little stalk of gristle and engorged flesh?'

'Yep.'

So Mr Knobby is happy. He thinks, Right up to me ankles in hot meat. He thinks he's gonna have a good time. Well, don't say a word but there are things that Mr Knobby doesn't know. Secrets a knob would do better without. Hush! I'd hate him to get *worried*, you see. You understand me? Exactly. A worried knob is a limp knob.

Mr Knobby Knobster says: 'You fuck this up for me and I'll never forgive you.'

* * *

I have reason to believe that Mr Knobby is going to be very good at sex. You see, he *likes* it so much. Whenever there's a spare minute, there he is, asking for a hand. And since he's my best friend I'm always only too happy to oblige. In the bath, in bed. In front of the computer screen. I live in terror of the computer going wrong and someone sending it in to be fixed.

'Mr Green? Your computer. Upon delving into the hard drive we found a collection of filth which, quite apart from reflecting seriously on your morals also happens to be illegal. I realise that a great many of those women were doing those things to themselves – we expect to prosecute them as well. Your son, you say? You hardly ever use the computer? It's news to you? Ah. Now you understand why he kicked up such a fuss when you insisted on taking it in to get it fixed? Right, let's make that public knowledge as soon as possible . . .'

It will happen. I know it.

I'd like to put it on the record that a great deal of the porn I look at is only looked at for the sake of curiosity. The sight of someone chained up with a set of nipple clamps and a pregnant dog is not sexy to me. It just amazes me that it's out there and can be seen by perverts like me while they're looking for wholesome babes to drool over.

Oh, my God.

Hush! Mr Knobby Knobster is fast asleep. Lean closer. I can reveal that . . .

No. Not yet.

Secrets! I have thousands of them milling about in the black hole of my psyche, although nothing as awful as the one Mr

Knobby must never know. For instance, this is an interesting one, I bet loads of people have this one but never dare admit it. When I was fourteen and going out with my first girlfriend, I couldn't find her fanny. How about that? I know, I know – how is it possible to miss something like that? I mean, it's about two-foot long, when you get up close. Impossible to miss, you'd think. But I did. Her name was Lucy Small, in the same year as me, and she picked me up – the only thing I ever pick is my nose – on a school geology trip to Wales. Your first girlfriend and you met her in Wales – that's humiliating enough, surely? We went for a walk to post some letters, and then went to hide ourselves among the trees by the roadside for some Heavy Petting. She'd been after me for a while, but I was too shy. She'd been out with Alan Noble the night before, and he came back into the cabin and made us all sniff his finger to show that he'd been there. She only did it to make me jealous. So. I felt her tits – see, I'm not a complete goof, I knew where they were – and then she undid the button to her jeans, and I put my hand down and . . . it wasn't there. Nothing. I was amazed! What was going on? Was she deformed? Had I been unlucky enough to get a girlfriend with *no fanny*? Should I say something sympathetic – oh dear, no fanny, that's a stroke of bad luck. Or was I making some sort of mistake? That seemed the most likely, so I scratched about her bush, up down, all around, but there was no doubt about it: no fanny. Amazing.

That was obviously cobblers, even I could see that. What about Alan Noble's finger? Perhaps I'd found it already but it was completely different from what I had thought. Perhaps there was some secret way of opening it up. Open sesame! You know. Or a button or a flap or something. Whatever. There *had* to be some explanation.

I went back and let everyone sniff my finger in the vague hope that I'd somehow got it in there without actually realising it, but they all agreed. No way.

I wasn't all that worried, to be honest. It had to be something totally obvious that I just hadn't thought about. You know what I mean? Those patches of ignorance? You get them all the time. You just have to hang on and see what happens next. And then, of course, when the answer comes, it's so simple you can't believe you missed it, even though it was impossible to work out just the night before. This had to be one of those.

So, the next night, me and Lucy took another walk and went into the bushes, and . . . exactly the same. No fanny. I scratched around for ages. I couldn't ask her, could I? Excuse me, where's your fanny? I know you have one, Alan Noble made that very clear, but I need to know where it is. Not possible.

That's when I got dirty and started feeling around in a more adventurous fashion, further down. She didn't mind, somewhat to my surprise. I mean, that was bum territory, as far as I was concerned. I knew that girls were supposed to enjoy having their fannies felt, but even that seemed a bit doubtful – although I suppose if she didn't have a fanny then her bum might be the next best thing. So, anyway – I pushed further down and found – bits. Fleshy bits. I probed, I felt – and then suddenly, right down there, I mean right down there practically up her arse – there it was. She let out a little gasp as I found my way in. Bingo! I thought . . . Aaah, so that's where she keeps it! Amazing! And how embarrassing for those poor girls, having your private parts about half an inch away from your dirt box. Planning! I mean, who thought of that? It isn't even hygienic.

All those lessons in biology and no one ever told me that women keep their fannies practically halfway up their backs. I thought it was on the front. I mean, that's where your willy is, isn't it? Not right down between your legs. It sticks out in front. When blokes shag a girl, their bums go up and down, not to and fro. It was a logical assumption that fannies were in the same place.

Of course, looking back, it's obvious. I mean, those diagrams you get in biology – it's all down underneath her. But that's just diagrams – you can't take them seriously. I mean, if it was down to diagrams you wouldn't have a clue what a fanny actually looks like. All that red. And those bits. And it goes right from the back all the way up to their navels, practically. You don't get a real sense of the thing out of a diagram.

But it explained a lot. Like, for instance, why my willy stuck up in the air. Think about it; if fannies really were on the front, your knob ought to stick straight out. I used to worry about that too. I used to try bending it down so it stuck straight out, but of course it always just sprang back up again. That day with Lucy Small, I discovered the basic physiology of minge, and I've never looked back.

So now I know what it is, and I know where it is. All I have to do now is put Mr Knobby in it.

It's tragic really, but it's also unbelievably stupid. Only someone like me could ever get into such a mess about something so duh. So. Here it is. Ready? Well . . .

Hush now! It's a secret. Mr Knobby must never know. If he does – disaster. Total utter disaster. No Sex For Ever. It's because . . . Oh, my God, it's so stupid and embarrassing and awful at the same time.

Here goes. OK. Mr Knobby has . . . *I* have . . . cancer.

There you go. Look. Well, you can't see it now, while Mr Knobby is fast asleep, but when I get an erection, there it is, halfway up the shaft. A big, squashy lump. Cancer. It's obvious . . . What? . . . No, don't laugh, not so loud, he's waking up – don't mention the word, if he hears it'll destroy him. Whatever you do don't mention the word **CANCER**!

'What?'

'Nothing!'

'What!'

'Nothing!'

'Really nothing?'

'No nothing!'

'What was that about cancer?'

'Yes! Yes! It's true! I can't hide it from you any more. There, that lump. That's it!'

'**Ahhhhh!**'

'Yes!'

'I thought it was a vein. Take me to a doctor, quick!'

'No!'

'No? What do you mean, no?'

'Because if we go to a doctor and it *is* cancer . . .'

'Oh, my God!'

'Yes!'

'You mean . . .'

'They'll have to *chop you off*!'

That's it. I have cancer of the knob. Luckily it's been dormant up till now, but if I do anything silly like repeatedly sticking it in and out of Deborah for instance, the friction'll almost certainly set it off. And then . . . Well, then I'll have to make the worst choice any man has ever made. Death – or no knob.

I expect you think I'm joking. I'm not. It's stupid, you say? Oh, yes, I know that. The truth is obvious. It isn't cancer at all; it's a vein. Knobs are veiny kinds of things. That's why the lump gets bigger when I get wood. It swells up, same as the rest of it. Cancer wouldn't do that – *would it*? Ah, but who says? Who knows? You? Really? You know that? You're a knob expert? How sure are you? I mean, OK – *maybe* it would, but maybe it wouldn't. We don't know.

The obvious thing, of course, is to take Mr Knobby along to the doctor. And we all know what the doctor would say. He'd say, No, don't worry, this is just a vein, Jonathon, nothing to worry about, everything's fine. But. *But.* Although he almost certainly *would* say that, he might not. He might, even just a thousand to one chance, might take a long cool look at it and say,

'Hmm. Yes. A tumour of some sort, nothing to worry about, it's probably not malignant but just to be sure we'd better do a few tests . . .'

And then.

'I'm sorry, Mr Green, but I'm afraid you have a nasty case of knob cancer. Amputation is the only answer.'

So, OK, it's stupid, but it's got me. And the other thing is, it's so *embarrassing*. I mean, could you do it? Show another man your knob and ask him to examine it? Worse, I've been seeing that doctor for years. I could go in on an emergency appointment and get anyone who happens to be there to look at it. But that would be worse. It could be a woman.

That's where girls are so lucky. Doctors are always examining fannies. It's the first thing you do when you get a fanny, you take it down to the doctor and get it looked at. If you're a girl and you go down to the doctor with even a sore foot or something, the doctor looks at your foot and says, Fine, OK, ointment, bandages, whatever – Oh, and while you're here would you like me to look at your fanny? And the girl says, Yeah, sure, might as well, and off they go. It happens all the time. Girls are used to it. But willies are different. No one *ever* shows the doctor their willy. Name me one person. I bet you know loads of people who've had their fannies examined. You know, smear tests and things, they happen almost once a week. But name one single person who's shown their knob to the doctor. You can't, can you? There's even a profession dedicated entirely to looking at fannies, gynaecologists. Have you ever even heard of a single doctor who specialises in knobs? A knobologist? Doesn't exist. Now, see, if a man goes down the doctor's and says, I want you to check my knob out, you'd get thrown out of the surgery just like that. What do you mean, you pervert, you want to show me your knob? Right, nurse, ring the police. What's more, I'm going to put this down on your medical records . . . There. Tried to show me his knob. So that it'll go down in history for ever and ever for any doctor and his mates to see ever after. Tries to show people his knob. Not to work with women and children. And if it was a female doctor, it'd be even worse. You'd get done for indecent exposure. She'd start screaming, Put it away, help, help. And that'd be it. You spend the next ten years in prison, dying of knob cancer.

And anyhow. I'm shy.

It's a horrible trap, sprung on me by my own mind. The thing that truly amazes me about myself is that I'm actually more scared of being embarrassed than anything else. I'd rather die than get a doctor to look at my knob. Isn't that unbelievable? But can you imagine what life would be like with no knob? I'd have to have no friends, ever. They'd all be looking at me. See that lad over there? He's the one with no knob. Yes, I know. I saw it in the changing rooms. It was *horrible*. Even my family would be unbearable. My mother would be sickeningly sympathetic, my father wouldn't know what to say. I'd be a hideous freak.

I've been worried about it on and off for years now. I've developed a hand technique that avoids the cancerous area, avoided thinking about it, told myself it's nothing. For long periods I've managed to forget all about it. Then, every now and again it comes back, and I worry a bit, and then I forget again. But this time, now that it's actually time to shag, I can't think of anything else.

Please, please, *please* let me not have cancer of the knob.

Nah, won't work – too much like a miracle. How about, Let me stop worrying about my stupid vein. Or: Please let the cancer, if such it be, go away. Or: Let my vein get small again. Or finally, and I know this is the wish I need to wish, because it's the only possible one: Please, let me be brave enough to go down to the doctor's and get some decent medical opinion on the subject.

I'd rather die first.

27
dino

And then, of course, when everything is absolutely perfect it all falls to pieces around you. One minute, One and One makes Dino. The next, it makes the biggest heap of shit you ever saw in your life.

First thing was my mum and dad. The weird thing was, it all looked as if they were getting on with it. Everything was just like normal. Socks in the drawer, breakfast on the table. No, that sounds bad, but you know what I mean. Like, if you were rude to her he'd tell you off, that sort of thing. Normal. They went out for drinks, they kissed goodbye, they smiled and made jokes and teased each other, you know?

Except, looking back, there were these few things that happened – kind of isolated things that'd rear up their heads and then disappear again. There was the time I woke up in the middle of the night, in total darkness and there was this hysterical sobbing coming from the landing. It was horrible. I thought, Poor old Mum. I lay there and listened and then went back to sleep. But the worst thing about it was, when I got up in the morning, Mat whispered to me, 'Did you hear Dad crying last night?'

All the hairs on my back stood up on end. Really. I didn't even know I had hairs down the middle of my back, but they went all bristly then.

'What do you mean, Dad? It was Mum,' I said.

'Was it?' he asked, all hopeful.

'Yes,' I replied. But the thing was, I knew he was right. It had been Dad.

'Oh, I thought it was Dad,' he said, and he looked loads more cheerful, the little prick. Because, you know, it's bad enough to have your mum sobbing hysterically outside your door – but your dad? Sounding like your mum? Arghhh! And Mat had felt more miserable than me because he knew it was Dad, but now I knew it was Dad and he thought it was Mum, which meant he'd given all the extra misery to me. I was so cross, I kicked him, and he wailed and Mum came over.

'What was that for?' she hissed.

'For being a crud,' I told her, and stalked out of the kitchen with both of them yelling at me.

See what I mean? And then Dad comes down for breakfast all suited up and friendly and dadding about the kitchen, slurping his tea and teasing everyone and then dadding off out of the door as if nothing had happened. Just like normal. And they were normal that evening and normal the next day and normal the day after – it made me feel normal too.

Of course, they had to pick that particular Saturday morning just when everything else was about to fall to pieces. That's what really gets me – the way it all happened at once. They

225

got me just after breakfast. Mat had gone to play footie down at Beadles and they came into the room like a pair of coppers and sat me down in the living room around the coffee table.

'You know things have been difficult between me and your dad,' Mum began. Oh yeah? I thought. So whose fault's that, then?

'So?'

She glanced at Dad and he said, 'So we've decided, the best thing is for me to make a bit of space and . . . and move out. Just for a while.'

'How long for?' I asked. My heart was going away like mad.

'For as long as it takes to sort things out,' she said.

'Not too long, I hope,' said Dad, and he gave me this stupid little smile, and I thought, You idiot. Why should *he* go? I mean. Who was it shagging other people in the front room?

I just came straight out with it. 'Why should you go?' I said. 'She's the one who was being unfaithful.' I saw her scowl at me. Well, it was true, wasn't it? 'Why should you stay here and he gets booted out?' I asked her, and I saw him look at her and she nudged him with her elbow. You know? Like, go on, give him the line, ACT TOGETHER.

'It's our decision. A bit of space . . . time to think things through, clear the air . . .' he mumbled.

'What, do you want to go?'

'Of course not.'

'I don't see why he should go,' I told her. I was so pissed off! It was unfair.

'That's what we've decided,' she said crisply.

'That's what *you've* decided,' I told her. 'Why should he go? She's the one who was doing it with Dave Short . . .'

'Dino!'

'Don't speak about your mother like that!' he said.

'It's true, she did. That's what this is all about, isn't it? She fancies someone else, so Dad moves out? It's not fair. If you want some space, you should move out, not make him move out when he doesn't want to.'

'Dino, I have to go.'

'Then I'm going with you,' I said.

'You can't,' snapped my mum.

'You can't stop me,' I said.

'Tell him,' she told my dad, and he said,

'Well, we haven't talked about this yet, have we?'

'We didn't need to, we knew the children were staying here.'

'Why should he go? Why don't you go, you're the one who . . . mucked it up,' I told her.

'Dino, your father works full time . . .'

'Why should you get the house and both of us and everything?'

'Because your mother is the main carer,' said Dad. 'She does all the mum things.'

'You do all the dad things.'

'Yes, but . . .' And the poor twat looked at her to help him explain why he was being a twat.

'Dino, this isn't a discussion,' she went. 'We're telling you. We've talked it over and decided that this is the best thing. You're old enough to understand. These things happen, however difficult it may be. Our relationship . . . needs a break . . .'

'What about my relationship with Dad? What about Mat's? So why's your relationship with him so much more important than ours?'

'It's what we've *decided*. We're telling you before Mat because you're older and we thought you'd be able to understand better . . .'

'So,' I said, 'if it's just a break, how long for?'

'Not long,' said Dad.

'We don't know,' said Mum.

'Well, let's put a time limit on it, then,' I said.

'You can't put a time limit on these things . . .' began Mum, but I said,

'At least then we know it won't go on for ever. Put a time limit on it. So we know what's going on. So we can plan,' I said, which was a good one, because that's what my mum always says. You have to plan things. Yeah, sure. Unless it doesn't suit her.

She looked across at Dad.

'Why not?' he said. 'We could say, three months? That'd be long enough for you to . . . have some space. That's what you said.'

Mum glared. I'd got her.

'Six months,' she said crisply.

'Four,' I said, and Dad said, 'Four,' at the same time. So Mum pinched her lips together and nodded and I thought, Oh, yeah? See? I knew it was her all the time. She goes off shagging someone else and then tries to bully him into leaving home. And he's stupid enough to go along with it too.

I was furious with Dad too, though. Letting her push him

about like that. I mean, it's a bit pathetic having to have your son stand up to your wife, isn't it? But I was really pleased that I'd got a limit on it. If it was up to him he'd just go and do whatever she told him to do.

'OK, if that's the way it's going to be, but I don't like it,' I told them. I could see Mum glare at me as if to say, you know – like, what's it got to do with anything whether I like it or not? 'But I still want to go with my dad. OK?'

And my dad looked really pleased, and my mum looked so totally pissed off.

'Well,' he said. 'We'll talk about it.'

'We don't have enough money,' said Mum. 'You'd have to get enough room for him. Somewhere with two bedrooms and so on . . .'

'Oh? What exactly did you have in mind for me, then? A bedsit, was it?' he asked. And she didn't say anything, and he said, 'My God, it's right, isn't it? You want me out and in the cheapest little hole possible. What am I going to be eating in this hovel of mine? White bread and marge?'

'I didn't mean it like that.'

'Well, how did you mean it, then?'

'Well, there's not much point in . . .' She paused.' . . . in spending too much,' she finished, and she winced.

'Oh! Not much point in spending too much? So that you don't have to go without, is that it? So that the kids don't have to suffer getting a cheaper pair of trainers? So that . . .'

'Stop it, Mike!'

'Oh, stop it now, is it?' he ranted, and she began ranting back and . . .

229

I got up and left them to it.

So that was a shit start to the day. What a pair of dorks. It was only another year or so before I left home to go to Uni., they could have waited that long. It was for Mat, see. If it was just me she'd have bloody gone, but of course Mat had to have his bloody mummy. So she took her wishes into account and Mat's wishes into account, and me and Dad just had to trail along with it, and why? Because he's too weak to stand up to her.

I couldn't get out of there fast enough. It was shit, but I still had a life to get on with. I had a date with Siobhan.

28
set-up

They met in the Arndale Centre – the Aardvark Venture, Siobhan and Violet called it. Dino was feeling nervous. He'd heard a great deal about Siobhan's friend Violet. Siobhan evidently adored her.

They mooched about at the bottom of the escalator, something which Dino felt uncomfortable with, partly because he was worried about being seen with Siobhan, and partly because he was worried about being seen hanging around at the bottom of the escalator. That was for poor people. Siobhan was carrying an old plastic bag with some books and a couple of items of clothing in. Her parents, it seemed, gave her a clothing allowance, and she'd spent some of it before Dino turned up.

'What about the books?' he asked.

'Oh, they always like me reading books. If I spend the clothing allowance on books, they give the money back to me.'

Dino looked at the books. They were heavy, thick things. '*Picasso – A Visual Biography*,' he read. 'I didn't know you were interested in art.'

'I'm not. It's just, like, it's for free, innit?'

'Right.' He flipped to the back cover. '£32,' he read. 'Christ, they're generous, your parents, aren't they?'

'Vets earn quite a lot, especially when they do dangerous work for zoos and things,' said Siobhan. 'Dad did a job for Woburn the other day – taking the tonsils out of a hippo. It's tricky, you have to put your whole head inside and if the hippo yawns you can lose your life.'

'Don't they use anaesthetic?'

'Just local. Hippos react badly to going under.'

Dino picked out another of the books. '*Stalingrad*,' he read. 'Wow. Do you actually read this sort of thing?'

'I'm fascinated by war material. Hitler and all that. You know?'

'Wow.' Dino goggled. He hadn't realised how clever she was.

Siobhan and Violet burst out laughing. 'You dope – it's a present for my dad. It's his birthday next week.'

'Right.' Dino did his best to laugh at himself, but it came out rather hollow. He poked back in the bag and took out a CD.

'It's a present.'

'For who?'

'For you.'

'Really?' It was 'Spangles the Movie'. He'd been after that one. 'Wow, thanks, that's really generous.' Dino felt mean, because he was, after all, only in it for the shag. He put his arm round her and she pressed herself into him and wriggled in a way not really suited to a shopping mall.

'What are we doing today?' he whispered to her.

'Later.' She pulled away. 'We have some more shopping to do first.'

They rode up the escalator to the floor above and made their way to Debenhams. Dino was dismayed. He'd expected to have a good time. Instead he was going to get bored.

'Do we have to do this now? Can't you do it later? I thought we were going somewhere,' he complained, but Violet glared back at him so ferociously he sighed and shut up.

'She just wants to shop,' she hissed.

'It won't take long,' said Siobhan.

The girls went to the Miss Selfridge area and started raking their way through the clothes, while Dino lurked on the edges, feeling like a spare part. It went on for hours. Violet and Siobhan conferred, tried on a few things, conferred some more, asked Dino for his opinion, went back into the changing rooms, conferred some more. Dino thought he was going to go mad with boredom. At last they'd done – that's what he thought, anyway. They walked off together through the store, but in the perfumery, they told him what was going on.

'There's a great little top, I've got to have it, but I can't afford it.'

'How much is it?'

'Eighty quid.'

'Whoh!' said Dino. 'Sorry,' he added, getting the impression from the way they were looking at him that something was required of him. Eighty quid was not something he could do anything about.

'We're not going to buy it. You're going to nick it.'

'What? No way!' Dino started to laugh, but they weren't laughing back. 'Really? No way!' He began to back off. The girls followed him, scowling and pressing in.

'Come on – what's wrong with you?'

'Don't be a wimp,' hissed Violet.

'I'm not nicking anything.'

'Why not? Not scared, are you?'

'No. Yes. It's stupid. What if I get caught?'

'You won't get caught. Just do as we say.'

'If you're so good at shoplifting, you do it.'

'Oh . . . all right then. But I think it's mean of you,' said Siobhan.

'Are you really going to nick it?'

'Yeah, 'course we are. You can watch – see how it's done.'

'Er . . .'

'Perhaps it'd be better if he waits outside,' suggested Violet. 'I don't think he's much good at this sort of thing.'

'OK, then,' agreed Siobhan. 'Here.' She handed him her plastic bag. 'Take this for me and wait outside. We'll see you outside Marks, OK?'

'Right.' Gratefully, Dino took the plastic bag and moved quickly off. Those girls were crazy, man! Shoplifting! You always got caught sooner or later. Imagine the humiliation, the fuss, getting nabbed outside the store, the police, the court case, his parents finding out! Unbearable.

He hurried through the scattering of shoppers – it wasn't lunch time yet, there weren't many people about. The perfumery was quite close to the entrance. Dino moved fast. He didn't want to be anywhere near that store when Siobhan

234

and Violet came through the doors with the alarms ringing and the plain clothes men moving in.

He pushed through the doors and the alarms started ringing. He froze in his tracks – had they already worked out that he was an accomplice? – and someone took him by the arm.

'Excuse me, sir.'

?

'If I could just have a look in your bag, sir.'

Security guard. Big bloke. He took the bag from Dino's unresisting fingers. Another guard had appeared at Dino's other side and was standing close up. The first guard peered into the bag. Dino looked round. A number of other security guards had materialised around him.

'We'll have to ask you to step into the shop, please, sir. If you don't mind.'

No one was touching him at the moment, but Dino was surrounded. The guard stepped to one side and Dino walked back into the shop. As he went through the door he heard a voice – he wasn't sure whose it was, Siobhan or Violet or both – shouting out in the distance,

'Oh, Dino, you're so *sexy!*'

I've been set up, he realised.

'I've been set up,' he told the guards.

'That's what they all say, son,' said the guard.

After that, the endless humiliation. The humiliation of being walked through the store. Look! There he is! A shoplifter. The alarms went off and they got him. So that's what they look

235

like. The humiliation of being walked into the security manager's office and being searched. The items taken out of the bag one by one.

'My, you're a little sophisticate, aren't you?' The man held up a bra, black, frilly, edged with lace. Suspenders. 'Like a big of leg, do you?' The knickers, God help us, had a split crotch. 'Well, well.'

The CD. Then the books, one by one. '*Picasso. Stalingrad.* Educated too. Or are these for your dad?'

'They're not stolen, they're . . .' But he didn't even bother to finish the sentence, because they were stolen, weren't they? Bound to be.

'I guess we'd better give Waterstones and HMV a ring.'

The humiliation of the endless wait for the police. The underwear lay like a set of exposed genitals (his) on the desk, for everyone to see. Then, the police themselves. Their amused disbelief when he told them his absurd story. More poring over the underwear, the policeman looking at him curiously, as if he was making Dino a reference point for future perverts before he dropped them briskly back in the bag.

'This sort of thing is for old men, son.'

The humiliation of his parents being called in to see their erring son. The long, boring, frightened wait. Their faces as they came into the room where he was being kept, pale and scared as if it was them who had committed a crime. The shocked drive back home and the inevitable, awful interview at the end of it.

'Dino, is this about your father and me? Is that what it is?'

'I told you, I didn't do it.'

'Dino . . .'

'I didn't!'

'I know it's been very stressful. I know. But this sort of thing . . . It isn't going to help.'

'I didn't *do* it!'

'Denying it isn't going to make it go away.'

'Fucking hell.'

'Dino!'

'How dare you!'

'Oh, God. I'm sorry, but I didn't do it! I'm not upset about you and Dad. I mean, of course I was upset but I didn't do it. OK?'

A long pause. 'OK,' said his mother.

'What?' said his dad.

'No, if Dino is insisting, we have to go along with it. He's our son. He's old enough to know right from wrong.'

'No, he's not, he's a shoplifter, they just caught him in the act. He's upset. He's stressed. He's *disturbed*.'

'I'm not disturbed!'

'Well, you've never behaved like this before.'

'We have to trust him. We have to show him we can trust him.'

'Trust?'

'Yes, trust. Not something you're very good at,' snipped Kath.

'What?' Dino's dad looked as if he'd stung. 'Is that what this is about? Are you sure you're not talking about yourself here?'

'Don't be ridiculous!'

'Am I?'

'Yes!'

'Then what's all this about me not being good at trusting?'

Dino listened in disbelief. He'd just been through the most awful ordeal of his life and his parents had changed the subject already.

'You always have to give me ulterior motives for everything I do. This isn't about me. It's about Dino.'

'You get caught in the act and you want to be trusted and now he's been caught in the act and you want him to be trusted? I think a little honesty's the way forward here.'

'For God's sake, not everything I do has to do with me and Dave Short!'

'All right!' Dino leaped to his feet. 'I did do it! I admit it! OK? All right? Happy now? I've been doing it for months. Now just . . . leave me alone!'

Bursting to his horror into tears, Dino fled upstairs, his mother in pursuit. She stood outside the locked door banging it and asking to be let in, to no avail. She went back downstairs, where, shortly, recriminations and rage began to float up the stairs in suppressed whispers.

Siobhan wasn't finished with him yet.

After the shock had worn off a bit he thought about ringing Jackie for sympathy and realised in the same split-second that it was impossible. There was another landslide hovering above him. Jackie! What was he going to say to her? Look, Jacks, I've been two-timing you with this girl, and she framed me for shoplifting. No way. But – what if she never knew? His only hope was that it all remained a secret. Why not? It was possible. His mum and dad weren't going to blab. What if someone who knew him had seen him being marched into the shop with the security guards? Then he was dead – but if they hadn't? If it never got into the papers. If he never said a word about it to anyone. If his mum and dad kept quiet . . . then it was just possible that no one who mattered would ever know. Maybe it was even likely. He just had to bite his lip and hope for the best.

He had to see Jackie that evening round at her house. It must have been obvious something was wrong, because she kept asking him, 'What's up with you? Are you all right?' It was an ordeal, but somehow he got through it without anything dire happening. But when he got up on Sunday morning, there was a little note waiting for him on the doormat.

'That'll teach you to two-time me, you shit. And don't think Miss Jackie Atkins of 17, Canton Road is going to stay ignorant for long either. Fuck you. Siobhan. (Not my real name.)'

Dino stood there for a moment feeling it sink in. Jackie, he thought. Jackie, Jackie, Jackie. Please not Jackie.

He dashed up to his room and rang her on her mobile.

'Hi, oh, Dino.'

'How are you?' he asked.

'Fine. You sound a bit weird.'

'Have you checked your mail today?'

'What, on the PC, no, why?'

'No, snail mail. Letters.'

'Well, it's Sunday, isn't it?'

'Oh, right!' Just for a second he thought, Great! But then he realised – he'd had mail. No stamps. Hand delivered. She'd put the note through the door by hand. A similar note could be lying there on Jackie's doormat that very minute.

'Dino? Are you OK?'

'Yeah.'

There was a pause in which he tried to think of something to say. Just as he began asking her what homework she had to do that day, she began the investigation.

'Why should I check my post? Have you sent me something?'

'No! No, look . . .'

'Just a minute . . .'

'Don't go, don't go, no – listen, listen, I've got something important to say!'

'Dino, what's going on?'

It was there all right. It was there, lying on her doormat like a nasty little piece of life-threatening dog shit. He had to deal with it.

'I . . . got done for shoplifting yesterday.'

'Shoplifting? You?'

'I was set up.'

'Who by?'

'This girl.'

'What girl?'

'Just a girl. I met her down the Arndale.'

'What, just like that?'

'Well, no, not quite . . .'

'Well, how then? Why didn't you tell me yesterday?'

'I've been done for shoplifting and I didn't do it. What am I going to do?'

'But who's the girl?'

'It doesn't matter,' he begged. He tried to laugh, but it sounded evil.

There was a pause. 'Tell me what's going on, Dino.'

She wasn't even a little bit interested in the stuff about the shoplifting and Dino having a criminal record. All she wanted to know about was the girl. Who was she, why was he with her, did he know her from before? And then . . .

'Just a minute.'

'NOOO!' he bawled. But it was too late. He could hear her feet galloping down the stairs. There was a long pause. 'Please, please, please, please,' chanted Dino in a whisper. He didn't hear her come back up, but he did hear the crackle of paper as she picked up the phone.

'Jackie, listen to me, it isn't the way it seems, this girl is poisonous, she really is. She . . .'

'You two-timing bastard,' she hissed. 'All the time! No wonder you were being so understanding! Well, fuck. Fuck. Fuck fuck fuck fuck! Fuck you!'

'Jackie . . . !'

'Shit!'

'Why do you believe this crap, Jackie? Why do you believe her and not me?'

'Fuck you!'

'Please just trust me!'

'Fuck you!'

241

'And fuck you!' he yelled back at her, suddenly cracking up. He was so furious – everything was against him. 'And fuck everyone! And fuck everything!' he yelled, but she'd already gone.

Dino hung up and stood staring at the phone, daring himself to ring her back. But what could he say? The truth about Siobhan was as absurd and unlikely as any lie. It ought to be impossible to believe, but somehow it was stamped with the mark of truth. It just slotted into place so perfectly. There was no way he could explain this one away.

He sat down in the chair by the telephone and waited for something to happen. He was there for ages hardly moving at all, except to cross his legs and shift position slightly. He was there so long that everyone forgot where he was in the house, and his mum came into the room without knowing he was there. She stood in the doorway, completely unaware that she was being watched, and he got a good, long look at her face. She was thinking. She stuck her finger in her mouth and chewed the flesh on the edges around her nail, staring into space. It isn't often you see someone standing there thinking. He hardly thought of her as his mother at all. What was going on in there? What was she going to do? What was she going to change next?

Then she saw him and she jumped into the air.

'Christ! Dino! What are you doing there?'

'Just sitting.'

'Are you all right?'

'Fine,' he said. 'Just fine.' And he left her to it.

29

ben

'He's a shit,' said Sue.

'Yes, but he's a mate, as well,' I said.

'You should pick your friends better,' said Sue. Well. I've known Dino for years. I didn't pick him. It's just given. Jonathon started going on about how there was no point in cutting him off, how was he ever going to change if he was just left on his own and so on.

'He's not going to change,' sneered Sue. 'Why should he? He doesn't need to, he gets it all just the way he is.'

A couple of days ago, I'd have agreed with her. That's Dino. He's the original Teflon man. No matter how stupid he is, he never looks stupid. No one ever manages to tease him. Jon's a past master at teasing and he can't do it. He just makes himself look stupid. It's weird. But this time, something's changed. Dino looks pathetic. All the other times, he's behaved pathetically and looked cool, but now, suddenly, he's just an arse.

Not that anyone really knows what's going on. There are so many rumours going around, especially about this girl,

Siobhan or Violet or Zoë or whatever her name is. Dino says she's seventeen, everyone else says she's fourteen. Who knows? Dino isn't exactly trustworthy. Shagging her at the party? You're not trying to tell me he didn't make that up – but then there's the letter Jackie's supposed to have got. And shoplifting? Dino? You can't imagine Dino doing something like that. And his parents splitting up. And it's all public knowledge. Everyone knows everything.

Half the girls won't speak to him. Jackie won't even look at him. You can't blame her, although I don't see why the rest of them should be so down on him. He won't be the first one to two-time someone. It's his friends that really get me. It's like they say, you can really tell who your mates are at a time like this. Suddenly, he's a wanker. Suddenly, he was a wanker the whole time and everyone knew it.

Well, OK, it's true. Dino always was a wanker. You have to be a bit of a tosser to be that cool. How important is it to be admired? All that effort. And overnight he's turned into just some idiot with more problems than he can cope with, trying to look good and failing. You'd have thought he was the most popular guy in school last week and now all he's got is Jon and me. Bang! Gone, the lot of them.

'He's had it coming for a long time,' said Stu. 'Thinks he's It, doesn't he?'

'Poser,' said Snoops.

Fasil took the opportunity to give him a good old lecture. 'You don't know how to behave,' he kept saying.

Even Jonathon had a go, but not to his face of course.

'Those who the gods most wish to destroy, they first give

an ego as big as a small town,' he said. I had a word with him about that.

'Well, he wasn't there, he couldn't hear me,' he said.

'What if someone tells him?' I asked, and he looked horrified.

'Do you think they would?'

'Do you?' I asked.

You could see the light dawning. 'The bastards.'

'I think old Dino needs a bit of looking after,' I said. So me and Jonathon decided to do a bit of taking care. We go round to his place a few times a week, walk home with him, hang around with him at school when he looks as if he needs company, stay away when he doesn't. Go running over when one of the girls or the other blokes look as if they're about to start on him. We're a regular little emotional bodyguard, we are. Poor old Dino! Not that it changes anything, I guess, but it's nice to have your mates around you. And he's so grateful for it. You can read Dino like a book, he's so open. It makes you feel that . . . well, he appreciates you. And you know what? There he is up to his neck in shit but I still envy him in a funny way. I'm nowhere near as good on that front. Let's face it, I've got myself into a bit of a mess. I could do with a bit of problem sharing too.

Let's talk about secrets, shall we? Let's talk about talking. That's what Dino's got, even now when he's lost everything else. He can sit and tell you about what he did and what she did and what that makes him feel and how he thinks she feels till the cows come home. All right, a lot of it is self-centred crap. He tells loads of lies, I'm sure he does. And he gets embarrassed, he's blushing all the time when he's talking about it. But he does it anyway. I can't do that, neither can Jonathon. Look at all that stuff with Deborah. I mean, OK, I don't know, maybe he's having a good time and that's all there is to it. But what do you bet? Why does he look like he'd got a hot spike up his bum whenever her name comes up? I mean, what's going on there? Try asking him. He practically runs away from you.

There was this really touching thing with Dino the other day. He was in a right state. The rumours were at their height, everyone was treating him like a leper. This girl was thirteen, he'd date-raped her at the party by refusing to let her stay if she didn't sleep with him, she was on the run from some home, you name it. It was about the third day after Jackie chucked him and she was refusing to talk to him. He'd obviously decided that they had to talk, so he really tried to pin her down. She walked away like she usually does but this time he followed her, and she suddenly turned round and shouted at him to fuck off, right there in front of everyone. It was awful. Everyone turned round to look. I really thought he was going to cry. He made the best of it, you know, shrugged as if he didn't care and walked off, but his face had gone the colour of ash. I tried to have a word with him, but he couldn't even talk, he just ran off and hid in the bogs.

He really was looking awful, so after lunch me and Jon collared him and told him we were taking him out. He nearly jumped up and punched us.

'What the fuck are you on about?'

'Take it easy. We're your friends,' I told him.

'Some friends. Leave me alone.'

'Come on, Dino,' said Jon. 'You need a drink. Come on, we'll buy you a pint or something. We're your mates, remember?'

Dino stared at him wildly.

'You need it, mate,' said Jonathon, and he just gave in and came along with us.

He didn't fancy the pub, so we wandered down Crab Lane and ended up at my place. I cracked open some beers, we sat down at the kitchen table . . . and out it all came. The lot. His parents. There'd been rumours going around about that one, started by Jackie I suppose, but it was the first time he'd talked to us about it. That explained a lot. Siobhan, him, Jackie, everything, from beginning to end. It was awesome. Boy, he really was going through it. And halfway through it, he began to cry – really properly cry, big sobs. You don't see that very often. We just sat on either side of him with our arms around him. He'd have broken your heart.

'Is it Mr Blubberhead paying us a visit?' said Jon, and I could have kicked him because it's just the sort of thing Dino might get pissy about, but he just giggled and blew snot down his nose, so it was all right. It went on for ages, him telling us another bit and then cracking up and crying some more and then blushing because he was being so wet and then crying some more.

Afterwards, he walked back to his place on his own. We wanted to go with him but he said he wanted to be alone. It was just me and Jon. I looked at him and he looked at me.

'What about that, then?' I said.

'Well, it was a privilege,' said Jon, which was about right. We both loved him for that, for losing it so completely with us there. He tries so hard to be Mr Cool, Numero Uno, but underneath he's just a really nice guy. Somewhere. If only he knew it. I can't tell you how much I'd like to be able to do that – just to sit down and tell them everything that's happened, and then break down and let it all out, the whole filthy mess. Instead of having this bloody secret.

Secrets. What's the point? This one's doing my head in. If I did talk about it – that'd be telling, wouldn't it? She's always going on about it. 'Oh, you never told anyone, Ben, you never boasted, never said a word. That's so mature of you.' What's so grown-up about cutting yourself off from everyone else? It's not like it's illegal, I am over sixteen. I just want some advice. Jon or Dino or someone. A friend. The way she goes on, that'd be like high treason.

It's what people do with little kids, isn't it? *This is our secret, just you and me, you must never tell or awful things will happen.* So what's that all about?

Secrets are dangerous. They turn on you. You think it's all nice and snug, just you-and-me, our private place – and then suddenly you can't get out.

Do you want to hear the latest? She loves me. What about that? Lucky old me.

We'd just had this lovely big long session and we were dozing away, and she said, 'I love making love to you, Ben.'

That was a bit odd to start with, because it wasn't what I thought of as making love. It was shagging. There's a difference, isn't there? Now I come to think of it, we'd been doing less of the raunchy shaggy stuff and more of the slow sessions in bed sort of thing lately. Which was fine by me, I preferred it like that. In fact, it might have been all my fault because I think I might have suggested it. Anyhow, so then there's this pause and then she says,

'I love you. Do you know that?'

Everything went very still. Actually, perhaps it was me going very still. I suppose I didn't want her to know how shocked I was. I was scared. But at the same time I had this stupid urge to tell her that I loved her too. I almost did say it, which would have been a disaster because it's completely untrue. It was just like it was the polite thing to say. Do you think that happens in real life? Do you think people spend their whole lives pretending to be in love with someone just because it's good manners?

I waited a bit more, and then she said, 'Did you hear me? I said I love you.'

I said, 'Since when did love come into it?'

She sat up and looked at me with a crooked little smile. 'That's not the reaction I was hoping for.'

'What was?'

'I was hoping you might be flattered. Or even pleased,' she said. Then she folded her arms and looked cross.

'You never said you loved me before,' I said.

'Well, I'm saying it now. Just because I'm a teacher and you're a student doesn't change how I feel about you.'

'It's not that, it's . . .' And then I bit the bullet. 'It's . . . well. It's that I don't think I love you.'

I turned to look at her and she was staring at me as if

249

I'd slapped her. For a moment I thought she was going to flatten me, but she just looked away and slid back down into the bed.

'That's hard for me, then, isn't it?' she said.

There was a nasty silence. You know, when you hurt someone? It's horrible. I didn't want to hurt her.

I leaned forward in bed. 'It shouldn't have gone this far,' I said. I thought about it a bit and then I said, 'I think I'd better go.' I pulled back the sheet and got out of bed. She lay there with her back to me.

'You don't pick who you fall in love with, Ben. It just happens to you. I was just hoping it might have happened to you at the same time.'

'I'm really sorry, I'm really, really sorry,' I said. I got dressed, thinking to myself, Well, that's that. I mean, things had gone too far. We were going to have to call a halt to it, that much was obvious even to me. And you know what? I was pleased about it. My heart was going away like the clappers, but I was pleased. It was over. I was out of there.

She turned round to look at me. 'You don't have to go, you know,' she said.

'I think I should,' I replied.

She turned over to face the wall. Just as I was going to the door she said, 'See you on Tuesday, then.' I paused. My heart sank. I didn't want to see her on Tuesday! But I didn't say. I'd just hurt her once – how was I going to do it again right away? I just couldn't.

'OK,' I said. I waited a bit, then I let myself out. I felt awful. I didn't see her the next day at school, and I didn't see much of her on Tuesday either, but she did get in a wink in the corridor as I was going to a lesson. 'See you later,' she mouthed. She looked quite cheerful, which I thought was weird. Wasn't she supposed to have a broken heart or something . . . or maybe that's just me being romantic. It made me feel better, seeing her all cheerful. I hated hurting her. So I went round there and – it was OK. We had a bit of a heart to heart. She said she understood. She wouldn't put any pressure on me, I was still very young, all that sort of thing. She still wanted to see me. The annoying thing is, I went round there determined to say, Right, that's it, but when it came to it I couldn't. I don't know why, I always thought of myself as quite a straightforward sort of person. I think I was just so pleased she wasn't angry with me.

'I still want to see you,' she said.

'Even though I don't love you?' I asked.

'It'll happen,' she said. 'One day the penny will drop.' As if it was some kind of lesson I was being thick about.

She brushed her skirt down over her legs. 'Don't tell anyone about this, will you?' she said.

'Do I ever?' I said.

'I'm relying on you,' she said. Then she leaned over and kissed me.

I did get some advice the other day. Not from where you might think. In fact, it's embarrassing, it's such cobblers. Really cheesy. It's the sort of sad thing that happens if you don't have any real people to talk to. You remember that remark she made, about how falling in love was something that just happened to you, as if it was like a stone falling off a cliff, or a car accident, or being struck with lightning, you know? Shit happens. She was always saying those kinds of things. Like she'd had an abortion once, and that had just happened. I mean, how's that? She didn't want it, her boyfriend didn't want it, so it went, like she had no choice.

'You could have had it if you'd wanted it enough,' I said at the time.

'No one wanted it, you can't keep a baby no one wants, that's horrible,' she said. Which is true but it's not the point. I mean, she could have, couldn't she? If she'd wanted it. If she'd wanted to want it – you know what I mean? There is a choice. And doing drama was because she got on well with her drama teacher at school, and going out with me had been this spur of the moment thing. It was like her whole life was something that just happened to her, which didn't add up at all to me, because as far as I could see, she just does pretty well exactly what she likes. You try stopping her. So what's she got to feel so helpless about?

Right, so this is the embarrassing bit. I really hate this, but it's true, so there you go. It was my brother's birthday and I was in a shop getting a card for him. It was one of those big card shops, with gimmicks and mugs and loads of cards. There was a section with those signs you put on your wall. You know the sort of thing. 'You don't have to be mad to work here, but it helps.' Or, 'Just because you're paranoid it doesn't mean they're not out to get you.' Crap really, but sometimes there's a good one. Well, why not? I guess it doesn't cost any more to print something true than it does to print crap, except the market's probably smaller. Anyway, it went like this:

'Love isn't something that happens to you. It's a decision you make.'

What about that? It just caught me right between the eyes. I stood there staring at it. It felt so – well, I don't know if it was true or not but it fitted in so perfectly with what I was feeling about Miss at the time.

'It just happens,' she says – and there it was in black and white. No it doesn't. You *do* it. And – this is the thing – there was no way I was going to fall in love with her. No way. I'd have to be off my head to fall in love with her. But she'd *decided* to fall in love with me. You see? It didn't just happen. *She* was doing it. Not necessarily on purpose, I don't mean that. But she was doing it; and she hadn't done it *with* me. She'd done it to me.

Maybe that's fairly obvious, but it was like a revelation to me. It just shows what a state I was in. I hadn't realised I could say no.

See? I told you it was crap. No one to talk to, you start taking advice from greetings cards. That really is the pits.

'No,' I said to myself. It felt good. It felt great. I walked home saying it over to myself. 'Love is a decision that you make.' No, Miss Young. No, Alison. Oh, no. Thank you very much, but no.' It sounded so good.

She never asked me about anything, right from the start. I couldn't think of one single occasion when she'd been doing sex with me in those weird places, you know, the stockroom, backstage, in empty classrooms – not a single one of them where she asked me what I wanted.

'No,' I said again. Then I started to imagine saying it to her, and you know what? It already sounded a bit weak.

30
jonathon

It's the night before the big day. Mr Knobby's in fine form, polishing his head until it shines, arranging his shirt around his neck at a jaunty angle.

'You lucky, lucky boy,' he croons, looking at himself at various angles in the mirror. As Mr Knobby's personal trainer and physiotherapist, I'm giving him plenty of massage and exercise – not so much as to wear him out, of course – just enough to keep him on form, so to speak.

That's how it should be anyway.

It's begun to hurt. That should be the final proof, but of course it's no proof at all. The pain might be psychosomatic. I spend hours every day focusing on the afflicted area, trying to work out if the pain is real or not, which is actually the worst possible thing to do. Did you know that cancer is the final, terminal stage of neurosis? I read that somewhere. The mind and the body are one. If you feel good about yourself you get healthy. If you're depressed you get spots and colds and 'flu and things. And if you worry too much, that gives you problems too – heart attacks, ulcers – and cancer.

You see? The sheer neurotic force of concentrated anxiety for hour after hour on my willy will make it go cancerous in the end even if it wasn't in the first place! Yet another vicious twist to the trap. Every minute that I spend worrying about it is a step closer to malignancy.

I hardly dare even think about it any more. When I do, I try to concentrate on being positive but it's not easy. I've tried those visualisation things that people do – you know, you imagine that the stricken part of the body is being attacked by arrows and Cruise Missiles and things, or rays of calming, healing energy. But it doesn't work. It can't work because I'm neurotic, and as a neurotic my attention is about as healing as a bucketful of plutonium.

See? I worry about it even when I'm trying not to. I reckon all this worry these past few weeks has already made it go bad. Pretty soon it'll be so swollen with tumours I won't be able to get it out of my flies. And then – off with the whole dirty job, knobectomy, chemo, the lot. And they'll all be running around saying, 'Why didn't you *say*? Knob cancer is one of the most easily treatable cancers so long as you get an early diagnosis. If you'd only said a few weeks ago we could have saved your knob, your dignity and your life.'

It's at the point really where nothing else seems to matter. I just go through the motions. Deborah keeps asking me what's wrong and I can't tell her. I actually envy Dino – imagine that, envying the Lozenge! That shows how low I've sunk. All the time I'm trying to cheer Dino up I'm thinking, Caught shoplifting? Easy. Try having your knob cut off, mate – that's suffering. Parents split up? Piece of piss. Lost your girlfriend? Tough. Try losing your knob, see how that feels.

He's lucky. At least his problems are real. His girlfriend really has left him, his parents are actually splitting up. He has been done for shoplifting. Whereas with me, it's all in my imagination. Not only that, but I know exactly how to sort it out, and I can't do it. I'm literally dying of embarrassment. But it's just a vein! Can't you see that? Just the biggest little vein in the world.

And what about poor Debs? I'm going to have to dump her, it's no good. It's not fair to her. I could tell her I was gay or something – anything to avoid having to stick it in and make it go really malignant. Either that or she's going to chuck me. I really am pissing her off at the moment and you can't blame her. Just as I was getting to like having her as my girl-friend! Actually, I probably ought to chuck her for her own good. What if cancer is catching? When she gets some spunk on her skin, she might catch it. My spunk is bound to be terribly carcinogenic. Or in her mouth. She might get mouth cancer and it'll be all my fault. If I actually do manage to get it up, I could give her cancer of the minge. You see what a shit I am? I pretend to be supportive to Dino when really I don't care. I don't tell Debbie that she might already have the early stages of cancer – she's had enough of it on her in the past few weeks, that's for sure. And I don't even feel sorry for her. I feel sorry for me!

* * *

On the big day there was to be no forgetting. It was there when he woke and stayed all day until Deborah rang him at twelve to give him the all-clear.

He kept hoping. It was embarrassing going up the stairs and embarrassing again getting undressed and sitting side by side on the double bed, shivering slightly in the cool air. He wanted to look at her naked, but he was too scared. Mr Knobby vanished up inside him. Under the covers, he kissed her and pressed her up against him, and tried to remember how he wanted it to be like. He wanted to spread her and stroke her and bang her and roll her over and gobble her all up like the lovely big banquet she was. But there was no movement. Mr Knobby had gone into a coma, hanging down there like a piece of scrap meat discarded by a low-class butcher as being unworthy even of the cheapest sausages. All he could do was cling helplessly to her breasts like a shipwrecked sailor. After a little bit she fetched a blow heater to warm things up and gave him a massage to help him relax. After she'd done his back she did his stomach. Jonathon was horribly conscious of his microscopic member. He kept trying to get little glimpses of her body, but whenever she met his eyes he looked away in embarrassment.

'It's all right, you can look,' she told him, but all he wanted to do was hide his face in his hands.

At last they gave up. Deborah went downstairs and came up in her gown, with tea and toast, which felt like cardboard in his mouth. Afterwards he made an excuse and left, even though they had planned on spending the night together.

'It's all right, it's not the end of the world, it happens to loads of boys, it'll come back,' she told him. Jonathon smiled a tight little smile. She showed him out, sympathetic but disappointed, and very hurt that he wasn't staying; and he couldn't even tell her what was wrong.

31
thaw

Dino had spent the weeks following the disaster in a fog of misery and incomprehension. He was the golden boy, things like this didn't happen to him in the first place, and if they did, it didn't matter. Somehow he always came up smelling of roses. He'd lost his girlfriend, his parents and his self respect all in one day. He was heartbroken about Jackie – he truly loved her in his own way – felt helpless and confused with what was happening at home, and just plain used by Siobhan. If he forgot one misery, another came flying up to sting him. One of the most unbearable things was the way it had made him feel like a nerd – one of those insecure, uncertain speccy kids who wander round on the edges of things never fitting in. It was just awful.

It took a while for it to sink in that it really was over between him and Jackie. She'd come back to him, she always did. He sulked for a couple of days – it was a bit much just chucking him after what he'd been through, after all. When she showed no signs of contrition, he tried to speak to her and was rebuffed like a pair of dirty underpants.

Ben and Jon were both being fantastic – that was the only good thing that came out of the whole episode; he hadn't realised what good friends they were. He asked their advice about what to do about it, and was pissed off that they both thought he should leave it. After further pressing, they suggested begging forgiveness and declarations of love, so he tried bombarding her with emails, but after the first one, when she replied she was going to delete any others, he got no replies. He tried ringing her. She never answered her mobile and after a couple of poisonously hissing replies from her outraged mother, he gave that up too. He had no stomach for further humiliation.

It began to sink in. She didn't want him any more. And it wasn't just her. The whole school had turned against him. Suddenly the magic was gone. It was like going blind. Even complete strangers seemed to know that he'd become a tosser. Girls in shops showed no interest in him whatsoever. He'd become so used to them smiling and laughing and fluttering and chatting up to him, he'd just accepted it as something that happened. Now, they served him without a smile and moved on to the next customer as if, he, Dino, was just anyone.

It was shit; but there's more than one sort of heartache, and out of all his troubles the thing that was causing him the most pain wasn't Jackie. It was what was happening with his parents. Their relationship was like some vast giant asleep under the land. What he had thought of as hills and valleys, slopes and plains turned out to be the muscle and bones of the sleeping giant. Now it was stirring and all the little buildings and roads he'd built over the years were crumbling like ash. He'd had no idea how much he relied on them. Like his skeleton, he'd taken them for granted.

Despite what his mum had said about trust, it was obvious that neither of them believed his story about being set up. He gave it up after a few days and started to pretend that he had done it. It was so much easier. Anyway, if it was a choice between being a shoplifter or a mug, he'd rather be a shoplifter. He had hoped that after his arrest, his parents would postpone or even call off his dad moving out, but he came home from school just a few days later to find his mum poring over the local paper for flats. She even had the gall to ask Dino to help her. He stormed out of the room in a rage. After that, he was barely able to even stay in the same room as either of them. He was enraged with his mum for pulling his world to pieces, with his dad for letting her and with himself for being affected by it.

Things couldn't go on as they were. Dino was going out of the room almost as soon as they came into it. His mum tried to have a word with him, but he just sat there in stony silence. Eventually she lost her temper with him spectacularly, screaming and throwing mugs at the wall and pounding the table with her fists. Dino was amazed – he'd had virtually no insights into his mother's state of mind apart from that sordid glimpse through the window all those weeks ago. Afterwards, she was desperate with apologies – she had no idea she had that in her herself, let alone that she could show it to Dino. He coolly listened to her apology and left her to it. The incident convinced him that she was rotten to the core.

The following Wednesday afternoon, when Dino had a

couple of free periods at the end of the day, he came back to find his dad had come home early. He made his son a cup of tea and a sandwich, put them on the table in front of him and said, 'Let's talk.'

His dad used to make him sandwiches quite often a few years before, when his mum was re-training. He loaded the ham in and covered it with mustard, mayo and lettuce – Dino had forgotten how much he liked them.

'Yum,' he said.

'If I'd made more sandwiches and done less work, maybe it wouldn't be me who's moving out,' said his dad. He smiled wryly and folded his arms on the table.

'So what are we talking about?' asked Dino through a full mouth.

'Things. Me and you. Me and your mum. You and your mum. All that.'

'She's put you up to this,' accused Dino.

'We still decide things together. I took the afternoon off.'

Even though this was exactly what he wanted, Dino was embarrassed. 'Is it going to take long, I've got homework?' he asked.

'I don't know.'

'Go on then.' Dino busied himself with his sandwich.

'OK. Well, for starts, I don't want us to split up, as you know . . .'

'Then why are you going along with it?' demanded Dino, quick as a spike.

'Listen . . .'

'You don't have to.'

'Listen! She's stopped loving me . . .'

'Do you love her?'

'You're not listening.'

'But do you love her?'

'Yes.'

'Well, that's not fair, is it?'

'Dino, will you listen?'

Dino took a breath and picked up his sandwich. 'All right, then.'

'Right. Where was I? The marriage is over, it's as simple as that. She doesn't love me, I can't make her love me. She has the right to put an end to it. But I do think, I do think . . .' He raised his voice over Dino who was about to interrupt. '. . . I do think it's the wrong time – wrong for all of us . . .'

'But me in particular.'

'You included,' said Mike carefully. 'I think she should wait, give it another chance. But, she . . .' He was about to say, won't wait, but that was too easy. '. . . she, she feels she can't do it. The thing is, Dino, when I said that stuff about making sandwiches, it was a sort of joke, but not entirely. Your mum has done most of the childcare, the mothering. I did my bit, loads of it, actually. But she's been Mum, and she still is Mum and if things fall to bits, Mum stays and Dad goes. If I'd done the childcare it would be the other way round, but I didn't . . .'

'I'll bet,' sneered Dino.

'It's the kids come first. She's been the main carer.' He shrugged.

'So you get the shitty end of the stick.'

'I get the shitty end of the stick,' agreed his dad. 'She gets the house and kids and a great lump of my income, and I move away into some little flat, yes.'

'It's not fair. It's . . . pathetic. It's weak, isn't it?'

'Maybe. Or maybe it's being strong. It's certainly unfair, but I do know that kids come first.' His dad shrugged and smiled sourly. 'I don't say I like it. I don't say I agree with the way your mum's doing it. But since she is, this is what I'm stuck with.'

Dino couldn't believe it. 'But that's just crap! She has no right.'

Mike shrugged. 'You'll have to ask her about that.'

Dino waited. His dad sighed.

'She thinks it'll be better all round to get it out of the way and sorted, since this is what's going to happen anyway,' he said.

'So you're just going along with it.'

'There's not much choice.'

'You could refuse to go.'

'Dino, this has been going on a long time now. Years.' Mike paused again, not sure what to say. Secretly, he didn't just think his wife was wrong; he thought she was being a cow. She could have waited one more year. Mat was only nine, he had years to go at home, but he was a robust kid and Mike thought he'd be OK. But he knew his oldest boy; Dino was a lot more vulnerable than he realised. Kath said she'd been dying for years in this marriage, but another one wouldn't do that much damage.

'Men!' she'd exclaimed. 'You always want more!'

'We'll have to see what happens,' he told Dino. 'Maybe when she's on her own in here with you guys she'll realise it's not what she wants, I don't know. But the way things are at the moment, someone has to go and it ain't going to be her.' Mike glanced at his son. 'You can come with me if you like.'

'Can I?'

'You're seventeen. You can make up your own mind. I'd love to have you. I don't know if it's the best thing for you, though.'

'Why not?'

'Staying here would mean the least change. It's your choice. I'd like you to come – I'd feel better. But for your own sake I'd stay here if I were you.'

Dino swore he'd think about it, but he knew the answer already. This was a nice big house, it was comfy. He wasn't going anywhere.

At the end of it, Dino still wasn't sure whether his dad was being strong, weak or merely simple, but at least he seemed to know what he was doing. Like his dad, he'd have to put up with it, but he didn't have to like it. He was going to stay, but he'd do his best to make his mum's life a misery for forcing this on him in the meantime. He felt clearer about things, anyway.

About a week later, something else happened that cheered him up. There she was smiling her head off at the bottom of the stairs as he came down in the morning. She waved a letter at him.

'Come in and read this,' she said excitedly.

It seemed they'd been on to Miss Selfridge. His mum had

gone down there armed with school reports and an account of what had happened at home in the months leading up to his arrest. The manager had been sympathetic, but cool. It was out of his hands, he'd said – leniency was up to the police. Kath ploughed on. What was the point of prosecuting her son for a stupid prank, which he maybe didn't even commit, when there were so many other people who almost made a living shoplifting? Didn't the circumstances seem rather odd to him – just walking out like that? She could promise him it would never happen again, Dino had had the scare of his life, he was a changed boy.

The manager had listened politely and distantly, and said he'd think about it. She'd held out no hope – but here it was. He was prepared to drop charges, so long as Dino would do some charity work. It was a deal.

Dino leaped out of his chair and threw his arms around his mother. Sorted! It was going to be all right. No court, no prosecution, no having to watch those awful knickers brought out in public and waved before the courthouse. Bliss!

'I thought they had a policy of prosecution,' he said breathlessly when he'd calmed down.

'They do. But you see, you're a good boy, it does pay off. One slip like that – he must have seen the sense in what I said.'

That was one ordeal less, at least. On his way to school, Dino felt good for the first time in weeks. Life was picking up. No court case, the talk with his dad that night. He was feeling a bit more like himself.

32
beauty and the beast

The place to tell her was definitely at school. It was cowardly, but common sense. Ben was confident that she could eat him for breakfast any time, any place, but the opportunity to cram him down her gullet surrounded by one and a half thousand kids would be severely curtailed.

It wasn't going to be easy. Goodbyes hurt, and Ben was a soft heart. All he needed was ten minutes on his own with her – surely that would be long enough to get the word 'no' out of his mouth? For months now they had managed – *she* had managed – to get them on their own for at least that most days in the week, but Ali had such an instinct for getting things on her own terms, it was like a form of telepathy. Somehow, on this particular Monday morning, she was permanently busy.

'Sorry, Ben. I have a crisis in Year Eight.'

'When, then?'

'Don't be greedy. I don't know. Not now.'

Monday swept by. Next day, Tuesday, he had a date at her place in the evening. Ben quailed: it'd be like asking a hyena for a bone in its own den. He had to get her in school.

Tuesday morning he never saw her. Tuesday afternoon came and went. It was getting scarier and scarier. Words like hyena, dragon, hydra, beast, monster kept coming up into his mind as the evening drew near. It was unfair, he knew that. She had loads of nice qualities. There'd been months of loveliness, but now it was over. He made one last-ditch attempt to see her – a suggested meeting in a deserted classroom after school, something she always jumped at. It would be dangerous – after school, no one about; and, of course, her plans would be different from his. But it was better than doing it in her flat.

He collared her in between maths and a free lesson. Somehow he wasn't surprised when, with an unfailing instinct she managed to be busy then too.

'Crisis in Year Nine.'

'You're working up, it was Year Eight yesterday.'

'I have a parent to see. See you at my place. Here's the key, I may be a bit late.'

She thrust a key into his hand and rushed off. Ben stared at the little piece of metal in his palm.

'No,' he said. 'No.' The word seemed to have emptied itself of all meaning.

After school, he went for a walk in the pastures near her place to try and clear his head. Was it better to be there before her, or after her? Should he cut and run and tell her later by telephone? Leave a letter? Tempting! But impossible. It was just too cowardly. So what was wrong with cowardice? He who fights and runs away . . .

'No,' said Ben, and tried to imagine the word conjuring elementals, demons and dragons out of the fields, from behind the houses, like the hero in a computer game. The no-dragon against the yes-beast. Maybe it would even work.

'Give me strength,' muttered Ben to himself as a tessellated, green and red-winged serpent loosened its coils over the housing. The dragon benevolently spread its great wings. Ben set off for the flat.

She was already in.

'Where have you been?' she demanded as she opened the door to the sound of his key rattling in the lock.

'. . . went for a walk . . .'

'Christ. What a day! I thought you might have had the kettle on or something. Kids with their teeth falling out. Kids suddenly going to see their families in Pakistan for three months halfway through rehearsals. Great! Kids torturing one another with sparklers. I hate kids!'

Ben stared at her sadly.

'Go on then, put the kettle on, I need a cup of tea. Do you want a drink? There's beer in the fridge. Christ! What an awful day. I hope you're all right, the last thing I need is more bloody trouble.' She eyed him sideways and went to fling herself on the sofa like a huge, carnivorous beetle. Ben staggered into the kitchen to make tea.

'Placatory offerings,' he muttered to himself. Tea seemed hardly enough. Fresh meat would be better. Or a virgin. Give her something to gnaw on while he ran for it.

'What about you, how are you, you seem a bit off colour this week?' she taunted him from her lair on the sofa.

'OK,' lied Ben, and winced at how quickly he was being carried away from his purpose.

The kettle boiled. He dropped tea bags into mugs.

'No,' he whimpered. 'I have a choice. No.'

From next door came a terrible strangulated, groaning roar. It seemed to express agony, rage and lust all at the same time. He'd never heard anything like it. There was something chitinous about it, as if a giant insect had suddenly discovered its mouth had air, and was giving voice to the accumulated desires and appetites of its kind for the past three hundred million years. With a cry he dropped the tea bags and ran next door. Alison was stretching out her legs.

'What?' she said, looking surprised at his terror-struck face peering out at her.

'That noise . . .'

'What noise?'

'That . . . noise. Didn't you hear it?'

'It was just me stretching.' She leered at him. 'You're jumpy today.'

Ben stared in amazement at her and went back into the kitchen. What was going on? Jumpy? What had jumpy to do with such terrifying, primal agony? As he picked up the mugs, he noticed how the tea was shaking in the cups as if a dinosaur was approaching. The dinosaur was his own heart. He put the mugs down and walked three times round the room. Then he picked them up again and walked into the den. He put the mugs down. Put his hands in his pockets and said,

'Listen . . .'

'Go and get me a piece of cake, will you?'

'A piece of cake?'

'Yes, there's some almond slices in the tin. God! I feel like I've spent the day in hell. The day in hell. The day in hell,' she repeated, watching dispassionately as he struggled to speak over her and failed. Ben went back to the kitchen. He was feeling weaker by the second. He took out two almond slices, one for her and one for him, and took them back to the prostrate monster next door.

'Mmm. Hungry. God. Sit down, you're making me nervous.'

Ben was standing above her looking down at her, munching on his almond slice. With his mouth full he couldn't speak, what choice did he have? Eating: another mistake. He sat down and waited while he finished his piece of cake.

'Don't gobble your food.' She burst out laughing – it was a permanent joke to her to treat him like a little kid. Ben swallowed and stood up.

'Listen. I've been thinking about, you know, you and me, and . . .'

She began speaking a second after he did and just carried on. 'Christ, what a day, those kids need a tamer, not a teacher, what am I doing here, I should have gone professional, a dog deserves better than this, I feel AWFUL!'

She had to almost bellow the last word because Ben was not giving up this time, he just carried on speaking, his voice rising to compete with hers.

'I want to stop. This. Us. I don't think we should see each other ANY MORE.'

She carried on as if she hadn't heard, made no reference to the fact that he had spoken at all. 'Nice cake, I like almond slices. Boy, what I'm going to do to you when I've fed, this is just for starters, the main course is gonna come all over . . .'

He waited until she stopped. Had her eyes twisted like little stones in her head as he spoke? Had she gone deaf? Was she ignoring him? She drew a breath, and in the uninterrupted silence, Ben spoke again.

'I said, I don't want to see you any more.'

There was a terrible pause. No mistake this time. She sat there and stared at him, looking shocked and scared. Ben took a step back.

'You what?' she asked.

'I said . . .'

'I heard you!' she breathed. She took a long breath and began, fairly quietly at first. 'You choose now to tell me, now, now to tell me, now, after the day I've had? You fucking want to tell me about it now? Is that it?' Suddenly, she flung the remaining piece of cake on her plate at his head. It was soft, but Ben headed for the door anyway. There was no doubt; he'd done it at last.

'Don't run out on me, don't run out on me, Ben!' she begged, but he was off. She rose to her feet, scattering the plate and its crumbs around her feet, and ran after him. She grabbed his clothes as he fumbled with the door and he slapped her hand away with all his strength.

'Ow! Don't hit me . . .'

He was scared she was going to hurt him. He wrenched himself away and burst out of the flat and onto the landing.

He just had time to see the shocked face of an old woman struggling outside her door with four bulging plastic bags full of shopping. The bags fell over. Leeks and a carton of milk spilled out onto the floor. Ben leaped into space over the stairs and bounded down them three at a time. On the landing above him, Alison screamed.

'We have to talk!' she commanded, but Ben was gone, down three flights and out of the door like a rat down a hole.

'You could at least have helped this lady with her bags. Aaaahggh!' he heard her scream as he opened the front door and exited the building. Ben ran on. The houses and people and cars flashed by. It had been the hardest thing he had ever done.

Afterwards at home, he was sorry about how he'd done it. He'd only been thinking about how to make it easy on himself, when it was her he should have worried about. She'd been upset. Now he thought about it, hadn't there been tears on her face as she ran after him? He'd thought at the time she was after his blood, but maybe she just wanted to talk it through. Just blurting it out and running – it wasn't very clever.

He felt too jangled to give her a ring that day. He'd get her at school the next day, and say he was sorry he'd handled it so badly.

But he didn't see her the next day, which was odd; he nearly always managed to bump into her in the corridor. Thursday lunch time there was a rehearsal for the school play, in which he was as usual helping with the lighting. He was feeling awful for still not ringing her, and dreaded having to see her, but she wasn't in that day. It was announced at break that she was ill.

Ben knew at once; it was him. He'd done her in. But how? Headache, heartache or death, he had no way of knowing. Fantasies spiralled in his mind; the beast slaughtered in her lair. But she wasn't a beast. She was a person, someone who loved him and whom he had once adored; and he had hurt her.

He was still too scared to ring her that evening and she wasn't at school again the next day. By then he felt utterly craven, weak with failure to do the right thing. He swore he'd do it the next night, but when he got home that Friday there was a call for him.

She wasn't angry any more, he could hear that. Her voice was flat, wounded. She was sorry. She'd had a bad day, it came at the wrong time. Of course if that's the way he felt then he was doing the right thing. Could she just see him one more time? She didn't want to end like that, in a fight on the landing. Just this one thing for me. Don't let it end like this for me.

There were no signs of tears or bullying but his heart was going like a dinosaur again. He stared at the phone in his hand suspiciously, but he couldn't say no. It wasn't too much to ask, not much at all, but he couldn't get the thought out of his head that it was some sort of trap.

33
ben

The door was ajar. I knocked and she said, 'Come in,' in a little voice. I went in and she was sitting on an armchair with her hands resting on the arms looking very pale.

'Hi,' I said, and she said, 'Hi,' back and looked at me with a funny crooked smile. She seemed embarrassed. Something was wrong with her but I couldn't work it out just yet. She looked down very briefly as if she couldn't help herself and then looked away to one side. My eyes went down. The armchair had a brown cover on. I took a few steps towards her but she jerked her head back as if I was going to hurt her even if I tried to be gentle. Then I noticed that the chair arms were all red.

'Are you all right?' I asked, and she pulled a funny face as if she wasn't bothered. I walked over and poked the material. It was damp. It took another moment to sink in. Where was the colour coming from? Then I saw. It was coming from her wrists.

She'd slit her wrists.

I think I said, 'Jesus!' and I ran for the phone to dial 999.

She called after me but all I was bothered about was getting some help before she bled to death, just bled to death sitting there waiting for me. There were splashes of blood on the floor next to me and the phone was smeared with it. I got up to nine nine when she came up behind and pressed the button down to cut me off.

'What are you doing?' I begged.

'I don't need an ambulance. You can drive me.'

'Drive you?'

'It'll be quicker.'

'Will it?'

'Yes.' She shook her head and almost laughed. 'Don't worry, Ben. I'm not going to die.'

'How do you know?' I asked but even as the words came out of my mouth, I realised why. 'You've done it before,' I accused her. She'd never told me, but I'd seen the thin white scars on her wrists. I stood there with the phone in my hand wondering what to do, because I'd've very much preferred to call an ambulance and let them take her away from me.

'I can't drive,' I reminded her.

'You've got your provisional, I'll be sitting next to you.' She walked to the door. 'Come on. It won't take long.' She waved her hand at me and winced, and I could see the blood trickling out.

I was so scared I hardly knew what I was doing. I was scared of her, scared of the hospital, scared of the police, because . . . because you know why this had happened, don't you? I'd done it to her.

We got down to the car and set off. I was trembling, I

could see my hands shaking on the wheel. 'Why did you do that?' I asked her.

'Because I'm stupid.' She sat very still, holding her wrists on her lap, looking demurely down at them. She'd wrapped them in some blue-checked tea towels and the blood was slowly seeping through. After a little while she turned her head away from me and stared out of the side window. I kept having to brake hard and I was stalling and accelerating too quickly, and every time I did it, she stiffened up and pulled a face. She never said another word all the way there.

They made us wait for ages. A nurse came to have a quick look but there didn't seem to be any rush. I tried to speak to Ali but she just shook her head and said, 'No.' They left us waiting there for ages before they took her in and left me sitting there on my own.

'I'm not going to die,' she'd said. So what's the point of cutting your wrists if you're not going to die? I thought, I hope someone knows what's going on because I haven't got a fucking clue.

I sat there watching people come and go. There was this whole series of weird accidents coming in and out and I kept getting fits of the giggles. At one point the door burst open and this fat old Sikh man came in, clutching his bollocks and yelling, 'Nurse! Nurse! Oh, my God, oh, my God!' and these three younger blokes, his sons maybe, came banging in behind him and started prowling about. Poor bloke must have been in terrible pain, but I couldn't help it, I just started laughing.

I had to run outside to hide it. It took me ages to calm down. Then this kid came in with his mum, and he had both hands bandaged. She was tiny, he was about eight and he was only a little smaller than she was, and they both had this funny waddling walk and they looked just like a pair of penguins coming into the waiting room. I felt like I was on some sort of drug. But then things got boring and I just sat there, waiting for ages until they asked me in to see her.

She was lying on a bed with her wrists bandaged up, smiling weakly at me.

'Hi,' she said.

'Are you going to be all right?'

She nodded. 'Stupid thing to do.' She shrugged.

'I didn't mean to hurt you . . .'

'It's not your fault. You weren't to know what a stupid cow I am, were you?'

'What did the doctors say?' I asked her.

She laughed. 'They said, next time I should use sleeping pills if I want to kill myself. They said I'd stand a better chance of being successful.'

'They said that? They said that to you?'

'It's too hard to kill yourself by slitting your wrists, the arteries are too deep.'

I was outraged. How could they say things like that? They were supposed to be sympathetic. 'We should complain,' I began, but she shook her head.

'They were just angry because they had some real accidents to deal with.' She smiled weakly. 'Not a little pretend case like mine.'

They brought us both a cup of tea and then I drove her home.

Back at the flat she asked him to stay with her. He rang his parents and told them he was staying over with a friend. They were surprised but didn't try to stop him. He opened tins of spaghetti and heated it up for supper and they went to bed early. She lay next to him, neither of them sleeping for a long time, then she wanted him to make love to her . . . one last time, gently.

He lay on top of her and moved slowly and softly. She buried her face in his neck and made soft little noises. He was distracted by the sight of her bandaged wrists. After a bit he grew desperate and started banging at her hard while she spread her knees and gasped.

'Is that too hard?' he asked her.

'No, it's all right, don't stop.'

He banged away until the bed rumbled under them and he silently came. He got off and she rolled over to hold him so gently he felt awful after his roughness. She began to weep silently.

'I'm back, aren't I?' whispered Ben. He stroked her head and let her cry.

34
boy siren

Jackie didn't notice it at first. Support for her in the school had been rock solid for weeks. Dino was a two-timing piece of toad shit; she was a used innocent. It was obvious. But behind her back the wind had already begun to change.

Of course Dino had behaved badly – but Jackie really had led him right up the garden path, hadn't she? All those promises. Dumping him on the night of his own party because someone had been sick in the bed! What was that about? He should have chucked her for that! You had to feel sorry for him. And the shoplifting. And his parents splitting up. Now Jackie dumping him on top of everything. It was a bit hard. Look at him! He was so *upset*.

No one said anything about this to Jackie but she began to notice that her exclamations of his guilt and general nastiness weren't getting quite the applause she expected.

'Stay angry,' Sue hissed in her ear, when she caught sight of Dino smiling hopefully across at Jackie one morning about a month after she'd chucked him. Jackie flashed him a glare that would have withered brickwork and promptly turned her back. Thus it was Sue who saw Dino's reaction. What she saw in his face wasn't the usual anger, or contempt, or arrogance, or confusion. Something had happened. He wasn't disgusting any more. His eyes turned red, his lips pursed. She saw a sore heart. Dino was in pain. Sue felt a pang.

Pity? she thought, amazed at herself. Instinctively she threw herself in between Dino's face and her friend, as if to protect Jackie from the siren song, the broadcast beams of Dino's pain.

She hadn't realised. He was so *vulnerable*.

So's Jackie, and I *like* her, thought Sue to herself as she followed her friend away from the disgraced boy. Dino had been in pain for weeks and he'd just looked pathetic. What was so different? She couldn't help glancing over her shoulder to where he stood with his face an open door to his distress. It was so touching – he couldn't hide it! His eyes were wet, he was wiping them with the back of his hand. It was all so unconscious. Staring over her shoulder to check how fast his tears were flowing, Sue collided with Jackie who had stopped to watch her.

'What are you doing?' hissed Jackie.

'Making sure the bastard doesn't follow us,' said Sue quickly. Jackie stared suspiciously over her shoulder. Sue ushered her away, but it was already too late.

'What was that about?' demanded Jackie when they were clear.

'Nothing!'

'He was crying, wasn't he?'

'Did you see?'

'I thought so. Really crying?'

'Meaningless tears,' insisted Sue.

'They made you stop.'

'I was just surprised, that's all.'

'He was crying. For me,' said Jackie, casting a longing glance away in Dino's direction.

'Stop it. Remember! He isn't worth it.'

But Jackie was immediately and suddenly certain that those tears were wept for her. Every instinct in her body longed to take him in her arms and comfort him and tell him she understood and would make it all better. He was stricken; she had struck him.

The annoying thing about it was, for the past few weeks she'd been enjoying her life for the first time in months. All the things that couples tend to let go of – going out with her friends, dances, just hanging about gassing. She'd taken up fencing again. She'd hardly missed him at all, but now somehow his pain was back in her heart, the siren song was in her ears: I need you, I need you, only you will do. It was irresistible.

She didn't immediately start wanting him; he just began to populate her brain. During the day she found herself endlessly explaining to him in her mind why they had to split up. At night she dreamed about him talking to her, making love to her, walking or dancing or just being there for her. In one dream she was sitting having tea and cake with friends in one room, while Dino was being dismembered with a razor-sharp kitchen knife in another just down the hall. No one said anything, but they all knew it was going on. She could see people exchanging glances. Dino was in silent agony, dying. Only she could save him. All she had to do was put down her cup and walk through, but she was unable to get up out of her chair.

Sue was exasperated but unsurprised. It all seemed so pointless. It wasn't even as though Jackie had a broken heart. Sue herself was in more pain several times a year when she dumped one of her string of blokes for no apparent reason, unless it was boredom. It pulled her to pieces every time – it was even worse when one of them dumped her, as they occasionally did. But this obsessive interest in someone who was no good for you – for someone who, as far as she could work out, Jackie didn't even like, was beyond her. The point was to have fun, wasn't it? And one day maybe to fall in love. This was neither.

For a few more days she did her best for her friend, but she was rapidly losing interest. Dino had already moved from pariah to someone to be pitied, to someone really rather fanciable in just a few days. OK, maybe he was a tosser but – no one said it yet – so was Jackie.

'She's changed,' pointed out Deborah.

In other words, they deserved one another.

Sue was never very good with boredom. Enough was enough. Dino was obviously something Jackie had to go through. She was clearly beyond the help of medical science, and the kindest thing to do was put her out of her misery. If she had to obsess about Dino, she could do it with him, not her. Sue had had enough.

'I think you should talk to him,' she told her one day, suddenly no longer able to bear another word on the subject.

'Talk to him? Really? Do you really think that?'

'Definitely.'

'That's new. What's made you change your mind?'

'Boredom!' screamed Sue silently. But what she said was, 'I just think you have unfinished business with him.'

'Unfinished business?' Jackie's face flushed excitedly. She even let out a soft gasp of pleasure. 'Do you think so?'

'I really do. You need to talk to him, he needs to talk to you.' Sue nodded her head firmly. 'You need to talk to each other.'

'Really? You know, I think you might be right,' said Jackie. Her eyes sparkled excitedly. Sue was amazed that she didn't see any irony in this advice. It was like pressing the on button on a piece of kitchen equipment; off it went.

'Absolutely,' she said.

'Will you have a word with him for me?'

'Oh no, not me! Get someone else in on it.'

'OK.' Jackie nodded; she didn't seem to mind. 'Deborah will do it, I expect.' She smiled. 'He'll think I want to go back out with him. He's in for a surprise if he thinks that, isn't he?'

'Isn't he,' said Sue.

35
two's company

Every evening, Ben went to visit. Ali sat in her chair with her head up staring at the wall as if she'd lost her sight. He felt so stitched up. He kept thinking, She's done this on purpose, but it made no difference. On purpose, by accident, under your heels, over your head, because God wanted it or for no reason at all, whatever. She had him just where she wanted him. There was no way out. Just thinking about leaving her made him break out in prickles of guilt.

She'd cast a spell and frozen him solid. He wasn't going anywhere.

About halfway through the week, rumours began to spread through the school. Miss Young was depressed, she'd had an unhappy love affair, she'd tried to kill herself, an overdose, slit wrists. Gossip gossip gossip. Ben tried to see if anyone was watching him. Surely it was only a matter of time before he got caught.

'I didn't know,' he'd say to the head. 'I didn't realise, how could I?'

'It's a very serious matter. You took advantage of her. You more or less assaulted her, you couldn't have been closer to Attempted Murder if you wielded the knife yourself. This was a vulnerable young woman, deeply in love with you. You have trifled with her feelings, sir!'

At the flat, Ali clutched his arm and made him sit next to her and kiss her still face. He made her cups of tea, cooked her snacks, read to her, fed her tissues. Every time she wanted him to make love to her. When he left she clung to him and buried her face in his collar bone. There was no more talk of splitting up.

She'd told the school that she was depressed and her friends that it was the break up of a love affair that had sent her over the edge. She had in fact spun a long tale about her boyfriend over the past few months to them, painting a complicated affair with a man from out of town who travelled great distances to see her, a married man who she could never visit but only visited her. It gave her an air of sorry glamour, but everyone was surprised at how badly it affected her; she'd never mentioned love. They all trooped round to visit the heartbroken woman. Ben lived in fear that sooner or later someone was going to catch him.

People would often phone up while he was there, and sometimes there would be a ring at the door. Ali had an intercom to the door of the block; she always answered it but so far she hadn't let anyone in while he was with her. Who knows how long that would last? She was mad, wasn't she? Ben begged her not to answer at all, but it caused more problems than it was worth. Was he ashamed of her, she wanted to know? (Yes.) Had he got something to hide? (Yes.) Was he so selfish as to be more worried about himself than her, even though she was in such a mess? (Yes.) And anyway, what harm would it do if someone did find him round there? She seemed to rather like the idea. So he kept his mouth shut and suffered terrors every time the phone or doorbell rang.

During the second half of the week, she began to pick up. She started talking and laughing, cracking little jokes, cooking bits and pieces for him, little treats. By the end of the second week she wanted to take him out somewhere at the weekend, to the pub or for a meal or something. Have a date.

'We've never had a proper date, not a proper going-out date,' she said. Ben smiled and quailed inside. Terror! They'd be seen! He was fairly sure now she was more or less angling for that. What did it mean? Boyfriend and girlfriend, that's what. She wanted to go public.

They went out on Friday night to an out of town pub, had a meal, a few drinks, then back to hers. He felt like her pet. It was an ordeal, but at least they didn't get spotted. He mentioned his relief later in the evening and she got irritated about it.

'What's your problem, Ben?'

'Well, if we got found out, you'd lose your job, wouldn't you?' he asked disingenuously.

Ali shrugged. 'I'm fed up with that job. Teaching isn't for me. I've been thinking of packing it in anyway. I might go down and get some careers advice when I'm feeling up to it.'

'When?'

'No hurry. I'm on the sick, aren't I? Next week, maybe.'

Careers advice? *Next week?* Ben said nothing but his brain went into overdrive. What possible reason would he have not to see her then – apart from his murderous dislike of her which he could never admit? She was clearing the way for them, a couple in love; except that he wasn't. Did it matter that he no longer liked her? It certainly made no difference to her. He wasn't sure she knew what being in love was in the first place.

Ben knew when he was beaten. He was out of his depth. He hadn't a clue what to do or who to turn to. All he knew was, he was in hell and no way out. It was one of the situations you just have to make the best of, like nursing a child sick with leprosy, or your partner of twenty years who's broken their neck and can't move.

No. The magic word. What an ineffectual little spell it was against this witch. The word had gone from his mind as anything of significance, but over the weekend it began to be slowly replaced by another idea – not something necessarily useful, perhaps, but something that might lead towards something useful.

A problem shared.

Dino had impressed him no end, suddenly laying out his whole life to him and Jon that day. Ben didn't know if it had made any real difference to Dino's life, telling them everything so shamelessly. After all, they had no power over the shoplifting or his parents or Jackie or Siobhan/Zoë . . . but even so, Ben felt that just by listening carefully, he and Jon had helped. One or other or both of them were round there at least three nights a week. They went out together at weekends. As usual, even in the midst of great shite, it was lucky old Dino. He had friends, he had sympathy, he had people with an eye out for him. So why shouldn't it be lucky old Ben? He was so completely alone here – no help, no advice, no sympathy, no nothing. His being true to her was encouraged by her in the first place and now she'd buried him with it. Maybe it was time to be true to himself.

But who to talk to? Mum, Dad? No way! School? *No* way. Some official thing – the doctor? The Citizens Advice Bureau? It wasn't that sort of talk he wanted, not yet, anyway. It was a friendly ear he wanted, and that meant Jonathon and Dino. What a pair! Dino was in a mess at the moment: Jon was in a mess more or less all the time, but he did have his good sides. He had some useful insights into things, even though he didn't always seem to know the difference between an insight and a one-liner. He was a known loudmouth – but he could keep secrets when he really had to, and he *really* had to this time. He often got hopelessly carried away, especially when he was teasing, which he did far too much. He could be amazingly insensitive, but he could also be more sensitive than almost anyone else Ben knew.

As for Dino, he seemed to be improving, but he had enough on his plate without having to deal with this. After a little thought, Ben decided to leave Dino out. He was off his head just now. One at a time – he could always tell him afterwards if he wanted to. He felt bad about it; not so long ago he had been closer to Dino than he had to Jon, but things had changed lately. He told Jon after school that same day that he wanted to have a word with him. Jon looked horrified.

'What have I done?'

'Nothing.'

'Oh. Right. I thought I must have said something stupid to Dino.'

'No.'

'What is it then?'

'I just want to have a word.'

'Why?'

'Never mind why!'

'How can you have a word with me if you won't tell me what it's about?'

'Jonathon, this is serious.'

'Is it? Oh – I see. Sorry. What is it – *advice*?'

'No! Well, I don't know. I just . . . oh, fuck.'

'No, sorry. I'll be OK. I just don't know why you picked me, I'm not very good at this. Right, right now?'

'No, never mind.'

'No, really, I'll be OK. Come on, really, don't sulk, I wouldn't miss it for the world.'

Not a good start. But they went back to Ben's place and there he spilled the beans. He went through the whole thing – well, quite a lot of it anyway – from beginning to end. Halfway through Jonathon leaped to his feet.

'So – that night at the disco, it was all true? You really did lie down and get a blow job while you looked up her minge?'

Ben blushed. 'Never mind that.'

'But you did, didn't you? You lucky, lucky bastard! God!'

Despite himself, Ben smiled. 'Well, I'm paying for it now.'

'I should think anything would be worth it for that. Christ!'

For a moment it seemed to Ben that this might even be so. Jon was pacing excitedly around the room. 'Bloody hell,' he kept saying. 'Wow! I mean, what was it like? Miss Young! Christ! You jammy bastard. Is that really true?'

'It's true,' said Ben. And despite himself, he savoured his moment of glory.

Jonathon stopped and looked suspiciously at him. 'Why are you telling me this?' he wanted to know.

Ben rolled his eyes. 'Listen – you haven't heard half of it yet.'

By the time he got up to date, Jon was horrified.

'How awful! What an old bitch! What a cow!'

'Well, not a cow, not that bad, not really . . .'

'No, no, she really is!' Jon was pacing about again, this time in outrage. 'Christ. I mean, listen, Ben – she didn't do that to herself. She did it to *you*.'

'What?'

'Cutting her wrists, man!'

'She was trying to kill herself . . .' began Ben, but Jonathon shook his head.

'Bollocks, that's outrageous. That's just . . . abuse. She didn't try to kill herself. No, that's a cry for help. Or something. A cry for attention, in her case.'

Ben leaned forward. He knew this. As soon as Jon said it he knew he'd known it all along. He'd even said it to himself a hundred times, but then it had sounded like a shallow excuse. When Jon said it, it was real. In fact, it was obvious.

'Something like that. Fuck!' Jon was trying to calm himself, he was so excited. 'I mean, damaging herself isn't what she's after, is it? That's just a means to an end. She did that to *you*. Wow, who'd have thought it? She always looked so cool.' Jon shook his head. 'Christ. I can't believe this. It makes me feel dizzy just thinking it. Jesus! Mind you, I'd have thought it's worth any amount of shit to do the things you did with her – but that's big shit. That's the biggest shit I ever heard of. She's mad! Slicing her wrists just to put a lock on the door. She wants you. At any cost. No, scrub that – she wants *anyone* at any cost. Wow! Man! Incredible!'

Jonathon babbled away, trapped between amazement, envy and outrage. Ben tried to tease out some sort of advice about it.

'She's got you good and proper.'

'Yep.'

'She's had you good and proper the whole time,' realised Jonathon.

'The whole time,' remembered Ben; and through the mists of confusion he recalled his previous thoughts, which had been almost wiped out by the trauma. He'd never even once been able to say no when she wanted sex. He'd never once been asked about anything they did.

'I managed to avoid going on Thursdays for extra maths,' said Ben.

'Christ. She looks so normal. She must be stark raving bonkers. She's like some sort of carnivore. She really goes for it, doesn't she? That's awful. You poor bastard. How are you going to get out of that?'

Poor Ben shook his head and tried not to cry. Jonathon

didn't know whether to put his arms around him or what. He sat next to him and put his hand on his back.

'She's a monster,' he said.

'I can't do anything, can I?' said Ben.

'Well, it's not as bad as all that. She wasn't really trying to kill herself, it's just a trick. A pretty severe trick, though. That's the thing; how far will she go to stop you chucking her? Cutting her wrists, it's pretty dramatic, isn't it? But you have to leave her. Tell her she's better now, you haven't changed your mind, that's it.'

'But what'll she do next? That's the thing,' Ben muttered, his eyes filling up.

'That's her problem, not yours,' said Jon. 'It could be anything, but I bet it wouldn't be so bad – maybe she's done her worst. You've got to try. You can do it, can't you?'

Ben thought about it. It was unimaginable. 'No,' he said at last.

'Then tell someone, one of the authorities. You'd be doing her a favour, actually – she needs help. So do you.'

'Who do I tell?'

'The school?'

Ben shook his head. 'I can't do that.'

'Your parents.'

'Do me a favour.'

'Christ. Well, all I can say is, you need help. This is out of your depth. There must be *someone* who can do something. Unless you just want to stick it out until she gets fed up with you.'

'Thanks.'

'She will in the end, I bet you. The trouble is, I should think anything real that's horrible enough to see her off has been extinct for at least eighty million years,' said Jon, trying to jolly him along. 'Perhaps a geological event of some sort would help. A volcano. An earthquake. Ball lightning.'

'A pile up on the M1,' suggested Ben, wiping his eyes. 'Nuclear fission.'

'Something out of mythology. The gorgon Medusa. Something even more terrifying than she is. The Incredible Hulk. Superman. A giant anaconda. Another dragon even bigger and more terrible than she is. But where does such a creature exist?'

It was a good move, talking to Jon. It really helped. At first I didn't actually think he'd said anything I didn't already know, but at least he reminded me of what was real and what was me being paranoid. There were a lot of things that I'd forgotten about, I was so mixed up. Just having someone else say it for me made it real.

But I was still stuck. What he'd said about sticking it out until she got fed up with me sounded like the most likely scenario, but I didn't like it. It could go on for years. That's shit, isn't it? I mean, you've got to *do* something, don't you? You don't just sit there and let it happen. But maybe that's just wishful thinking. Maybe that's life – just letting stuff happen, and keeping your eye out for a chance to dodge the next batch of shit coming your way.

She'd really done me in. I hadn't realised how much until

I started crying that day, talking with Jonathon. I just sat there leaking tears while he cracked jokes to try and cheer me up. Everyone else had noticed already. My mum and dad kept asking me if I was ill, the teachers were the same – one of them even asked me if I wanted to see the school nurse the other day, I was so white. Even Dino noticed, which shows you just how bad it was.

'You are a bit pale, now I come to think about it,' he said. Which was quite perceptive for him – my skin looked like a pissy sheet, as Jonathon kindly pointed out.

So I'm buggered and she's loving it. She's being really nice – all tender and gentle, now she's got what she wants. It scares the hell out of me. She's all sorry for the way she was, sorry about cutting her wrists, sorry about being a bully. She's started using this little girlie voice, it drives me mad.

'Would oo like Ali to make oo a cuppa tea, nice Bennie?' she goes. I mean – she's in her twenties! It gives me the creeps.

Then, just when I'd more or less made up my mind that I'd just have to stick it out till she'd finished with me, I got an idea. It came from something Jon said, actually, a joke. You never know how what people say will come in handy. It was a really crazy idea. It was playing with fire – but that was the point, you see. What Jonathon said about a dragon even bigger than she was. I found one.

Poor old Ali! You've got to feel sorry for her. Jonathon went on about her being a monster, which she was, but she was the victim too. Somewhere down the line she was *really* done in – worse than me – and I had a good idea who had done it too. But I was out of my depth. I had to get out of there and

I was willing to do it any way I could. Maybe it was too late for her – maybe not. But it sure wasn't too late for me and I wasn't going to wait until it was.

It was a great idea. And it was cruel and it was selfish and it was cowardly, and completely terrifying, but I was going to do it anyway. I was round at her place when I thought of it. Mid-week. She'd popped out to get something, left me alone in the flat with orders not to let anyone in. The phone rang. Of course I didn't answer it, so then the answerphone comes on.

'Ali? Are you there, pick up the phone if you're there? Ali? I'm coming to visit you. It's been too long, you never ring, you could be dead as far as I'm concerned. My train gets in at five tomorrow afternoon. If you're not there to pick me up I'll catch a taxi. I know it's very short notice. You must ring me up more often if you want to avoid this sort of thing.'

The phone went down.

Her mother. I thought at once – monster. Not extinct, not mythological. She exists. And she was the only thing I ever saw that Ali was scared of.

I erased the message.

36
jonathon

Someone was telling me this stuff the other day. It's a secret, I can't tell you. I guess I've got a reputation as a big mouth – in fact I know I have because this person was reluctant to tell me this stuff for that very reason. So I promised, and I won't even write it down, but it was just about the biggest secret you can imagine. And it was from someone who I'd never have guessed was under such a strain. Just like me, except that for this guy, there's no way out. We sat down and tried to sort it out for ages, but there's just no way. The – this woman – she's got him right by the knackers and you just know she'll never let go until she finds another pair to hold onto. God! Poor, lucky bastard.

It makes you realise. Everyone's got their troubles. This secret – I mean! That's real trouble. And Dino too. I've been so crushed by this thing, I'd really started to believe I was going to have to die or spend the rest of my life in a state of misery, but it's not really true. I mean, Jackie's definitely not ever going to go out with him again. His parents really are going to separate. He can't change any of that. And this friend of mine is totally stuffed too, but I can do something for myself, however embarrassing it is. I can go to the doctor. The doctor will say, Fine, nope, nothing wrong – and I'll be OK. I have to do it. I just have to be prepared to get embarrassed.

This friend of mine. This problem he's got! Wow! You should hear about that. I could not believe my ears. I thought I had problems. I tell you, compared to what he has going on, imaginary cancer of the knob is nothing. I mean *nothing*. And it proves one thing. Sex is trouble. My mum always says, Sex rears its ugly head. Which I always supposed meant that she thought knobs are ugly, but perhaps she just means trouble.

I can't tell you. Really, it's impossible. It's not just being discreet, it's really serious stuff. Honestly, I can't say a word. It was so awful I got over-excited and started jumping around the place and Ben had to make me sit down and think about it. All I wanted to ask him was about what she – this woman he's got himself around with – how it started and what they did, you know? And how on earth he can do anything about that, I do not know. All he can do is ride it out. But I was really flattered, you know – that he'd spoken to me. He must have thought I was worth telling. He could have told any number of people. He's a popular guy with the girls and the boys. I'm just a gob, really, but he chose to tell me. It made me think, maybe I'm not so useless after all. Maybe I even helped.

The funny thing about it was, all the stuff I was saying to him, all the advice, could have been applied to me. Like, 'You need help.' I said that to him. 'You have to tell someone who can do something about it.' See? If I'd had the courage to tell him what I was suffering from, he'd have said just the same back.

But I didn't. He can, I can't. Apart from anything else, I suppose, he's got a real problem while mine's just a joke.

I dunno. Maybe I shouldn't go to the doctor. Maybe I should tell this friend. But – it really is too embarrassing. I mean, his problem, it's awful but it's cool. Mine's just crap.

Who else could I tell? My mother?

'I'm worried about my penis, Mother. It's all lumpy.'

'Ah, poor dear. Let Mummy have a look at it. There, we'll just put a plaster on that. There! Good as new. Now, go out and stick it in a nice girl like a good boy.'

No way! My dad? We'd both sit there in a silent rictus of embarrassment until I got up and left and the matter would never be referred to again as long as we both shall live.

Maybe I should tell Debs . . . but I know what she'd tell me to do, so I might as well do it anyway.

Doctor.

Fuck it. I just wish so much I didn't have to do this. It's so horrible – but the alternatives are so much worse. It'll be utterly unbearable, utterly horrible, utterly unpleasant but – but at the end when it's all over, I'll still be here, won't I? Oh, OK, the doctor might say it is knob cancer – only he won't, will he? I know he won't. This is juju to make the fear go away. But it's going to work, because – well. Because I believe in doctors, I suppose.

What's actually going to happen is this. I'm going to get a new knob and be very, very, very happy.

* * *

I'm going to tell you this as quickly as possible because it was the most painful experience of my life. I can't bear to think about it, hardly. The suffering was so intense, I'm not sure that I survived intact psychologically. I may be scarred for life.

I didn't get an appointment for starters. The earliest proper appointment was the next week – too late. So I went down for the emergency appointments at five o'clock. I got there early to get it over with and sat there for hours and hours and hours waiting for my name to come up, scared silly that the doctor would throw me out for wasting emergency time with a neurotic knob. Well, listen – it was an emergency for me, OK? For all I knew, in the next hour or so I might be facing life with no knob, or certain death or years of chemo and surgery and radio and . . .

Or a new knob. If it was just a vein and I was – please God – just mad and not cancerous. But that was the last thing on my mind at the time. I just kept praying that the doctor would be the kind of person who'd not mind you showing them your knob, without actually *liking* it.

They called my name. I walked in and there was the worst of all possible worlds. A young female doctor. Very attractive. Short skirt. Legs. It was so awful. As soon as I went in I froze. I couldn't say a word. I could see it all. She'd think I was a pervert. Even if she did agree to look at it, it'd probably get stiff while she was examining it. They'd be ringing around to see how many other surgeries I'd gone into to have my knob checked out. Prison, untreated cancer, amputation, death. Or possibly even just death there and then, because I was gasping for breath, my heart was cramping. I was going to choke to death on my own embarrassment.

'Hello, Jonathon. Sit down. What seems to be the problem?'

I stood there shivering. 'I have a problem,' I gurgled.

'That's why most people come to see us,' she smiled. 'What's yours?'

I stared at her in terror. Was she taking the piss? Did she know? What the fuck did she mean by that 'What's yours?' It was so . . . so informal. What's your poison? What do you fancy? How would you like me – over the desk, on the carpet? Please, please, don't let her try to seduce me!

'I . . . I have this lump. Well, this bump.'

'Whereabouts?'

'On. On. In,' I said. I just couldn't utter a word. I half stood up and looked at the door.

'Jonathon?' I made a little movement to go, but I'd frozen to the spot. She cocked her head sympathetically to one side. 'People come in here with all sorts of problems. I bet I've come across yours before. You'd be surprised.' She smiled at me and opened her palm towards the chair. 'Sit down. I'd tell you some of them, but what's said in this room is completely confidential. You should remember that. Nothing that gets said in here goes outside these four walls.'

I made a noise like a rat being grated alive.

'Please,' she said.

I followed her hand and sat down. She smiled.

'Something embarrassing?'

'Ah,' I croaked. I was trying to think of some other ailment

I could lay claim to. The pox? Testicular gangrene? Anything but this!

'It's very brave of you to come to talk to me about it. Some people go through years of agony just because of embarrassment. But embarrassment can't hurt you: untreated problems can.'

'Ah,' I gasped. So! I did have cancer!

'Is it in a private place?'

'Um,' I agreed.

'Testicles?'

'Nun.'

'Good.' She waited a bit but I couldn't speak. 'Well,' she went on. 'That leaves only two other areas, doesn't it? But down below?'

I nodded but my mind was going bonkers. *Two* other places? I couldn't work it out for a minute, but then it occurred to me; she thought I might have cancer of the arse as well! Did that mean she'd want to get up there too? My God! That would be even more embarrassing! Just seconds before I'd been unable to imagine anything more embarrassing than showing her my willy and now she'd found one within minutes of my coming in to see her. What next?

'At your age I'd say it's most likely to be your penis. Correct?'

'Ah. Ahes,' I said.

She nodded. 'Where is this lump, on the shaft of your penis, or the head?'

'Jjj. Shi.'

'The shaft. OK, if you'd just go to the couch over there and take your pants down, I'll have a look for you.'

This was it. Pants down! Mortified! I went to the couch. She was over by the work surface putting on the plastic gloves. Plastic gloves? I'd washed it. My knob is spotless. Or was this for the arse examination?

I got my jeans down but I couldn't do the final thing. She came and stood by me. 'Come on then, I don't want to take them down myself.'

Like a little boy I jerked to attention and pulled them down. Out came the meat and two veg. Poor Mr Knobby!

'Right,' I said. 'Here's the lump just on this side I know it isn't very big now but it gets a lot bigger and and and and and harder when I've got annnnurrrection.'

'Yes, I see.' She prodded it with a finger and stood up. 'That's a vein,' she said. 'Perfectly normal. Penises are very veiny things. This particular vein happens to be close to the surface, that's all. It means you've got a good blood supply.'

'So it's all right then?' I said.

'Perfectly normal.' She'd pulled the gloves off and went to the sink to wash her hands. What did she think she was handling? She needed to wash after the plastic gloves? Were knob germs that deadly?

'So it's all right then?' I asked again. I wanted to make absolutely sure, no mistake. I didn't want to have to go through this again.

'Perfectly fine. The thing about these sorts of things,' she said, washing her hands and looking over to me, 'is not to worry about them.'

'Yes. Yes. Right. I see, exactly, sometimes they just get a bit on top of you, I just wanted to get it cleared up. Exactly,' I said. 'Thank you very much. Goodbye.'

I ran out of the door. Just before I closed it behind me she said, 'Enjoy,' in a soft voice. As if she'd just given me something to eat.

On the way home I was dying, just dying. How had I ever managed to do that? It was awful, awful, awful. The hardest thing I'd ever done in my whole life. It wasn't until I was about halfway back, that I started thinking, Yes, that was very hard, very very very hard. And stupid and horrible. But now, my boy, you have a brand new knob. Thing is, to go and try it out.

37
deborah

Scared? I was terrified. No, really, it was dreadful. I mean, boys and their willies. And girls are supposed to be the delicate ones. Talk about a prima donna – just because he couldn't get it up. He hardly said a word to me for a week. I mean – I try to be sympathetic but the least he could do was talk about it. You know, I like sex too. I didn't like to say, look you're my boyfriend, I expect to have sex with you, what's going on? It was making *me* neurotic. I was thinking it must be because I'm overweight. Really, he was being a real idiot about it. Not a word, hardly.

Then, finally, out it came. He was scared he was impotent, he said. Well, I mean, how stupid. The first time he's ever done it he can't get it up and he's impotent! Loads of people can't get it up the first time. I didn't say of course, but actually I was really cross. I'm his girlfriend, he can talk to me, can't he? If he can't tell me then who can he tell? His mates – do me a favour. That lot. So I had to pretend to be all sympathetic about the ridiculous little thing, even though he'd kept me hanging around for so long I thought I disgusted him.

Boys.

I must admit, I don't really understand it, why they get so worked up about it. He tried to explain to me. He said it was because willies are such temperamental things. What, more temperamental than girls? I asked him.

'Look,' he said. 'If I was with you, and you didn't get turned on, I'd hardly know, would I?'

Well, yes you would, I told him, because I'd be dry.

'Yes, but, it wouldn't be so obvious. And if I tried to stick it in anyway, I probably could, couldn't I?'

'I hope you wouldn't!'

'No! But all you have to do is lie there – you don't have to make something all stiff, do you? If it doesn't work for you it just means you're not in the mood.'

So maybe you weren't in the mood, I said, and he said, 'I would be if I could, though.'

What am I supposed to make of that?

That's boys for you. You know, I do really wonder if it's maybe something to do with me – no, don't laugh – because this isn't the first time this has happened to me. Yes, really. This other one wasn't as bad as Jonathon though. At least he told me what was going on, how he felt. You'd have thought he was being sentenced to death. He was so depressed, I felt so sorry for him, but there was nothing I could do. We tried everything – no, you mind your own business what. Well, use your imagination. But nothing worked. It would be sticking up straight as a poker and then as soon as he got anywhere near you-know-where, down it would go. He got so desperate. You know, he wanted to look at some porn pictures while he was putting it in! Yes! No way, I told him. Imagine it – him turning the pages over my shoulder. I said, If I'm not good enough for you in the flesh, what do you think them paper girls are going to do for you? Well, I tell you how he justified it. Oh God, this is so embarrassing. He said, he said that if he could be looking at someone's fanny at the same time he reckoned it would stay up, and since it couldn't be my fanny, it had to be a paper one.

Oh God! Imagine! No, of course I wasn't angry. He was desperate, poor boy. He was dying. He did it from behind in the end, that seemed to work. Once he got back into his stride it was all right. It was all in the mind, you see. So when it happened to Jonathon, I thought, Oh no, not again! Jon was only my second, you see – that's a 100% per cent can't get it up rate! It doesn't exactly do a lot for your confidence. I have a problem too. Well, I'm not exactly six foot two and size 6, am I? I don't care enough to actually do anything about it, but I do like my food too much. Whenever I have problems with my boyfriends, I start to think straight away it's because of that. I do! I know it's stupid. Lots of boys like a bit extra, you know? 'I like to see a bit of movement,' my old boyfriend said! A bit of movement, oh dear, what am I saying? So I do worry about it, but it's just the same for everyone else, we all worry about our bodies. It's true. Even the thin gorgeous ones, they all think they're overweight. That's girls for you. With boys, it's their willies – with us it's our whole bodies. As soon as anything goes a bit wonky, I think it must be because I'm disgusting. It's a wonder people ever get to have babies at all!

So by the time we had another chance I was as scared as he was. I mean, if it went wrong again, what then? Maybe he'd never speak to me again! Maybe he'd have a nervous breakdown. He can talk the hind leg off a donkey, that boy, but hardly a word out of him for weeks. Oh, I love that boy. He makes me laugh, I'll go anywhere for a laugh. I'll do anything – within reason. No, don't look at me like that, I'm only joking.

There was another chance – my parents going out again – but I didn't dare say anything because he was so worried. I was just thinking, O-oh. I mean, it took him long enough to make up his mind if he wanted to go out with me in the first place. What if he didn't really want to? Maybe I was moving too quick for him. Because he comes on all talk and he's very clever and funny and all that, but deep down, I don't think he's got much confidence. And he thinks too much of himself. Does that sound strange? Maybe it is strange, but it's what I think. He's got a big ego and no confidence, exactly.

And then – it all changed overnight. Yes – just like that. Bang! One minute he could hardly move he was so worried, the next he was trying to push me out of my seat with his stiffie. He wanted to do it right there and then. I said, No way! Here on the floor with my mum in the kitchen? He just grinned, he was absolutely ready for anything. Something must have happened, but I don't know what. He never said. Never said a word. When I asked him, he just said he woke up one day and everything was all right. I said, Just like that? Well, I don't believe it. I wonder if there wasn't maybe some-thing medical, but what? Maybe he thought he had a dose of something – no really, well, there has to be something behind it, doesn't there? But he wouldn't say.

So, the big day came. My parents were out. Oh, they do car boot sales. Yes! *Very* handy! I told Jon to come round at eleven. No need to hurry, is there – it wasn't a job – not like being a postman or something! I wanted to make myself ready. I had a shower. I made my room up. Changed the sheets. That made me smile, because of what my mum always says.

'I'm a woman and when I change the sheets on the bed, it means something.' That's what she says, so if I ever see her changing the sheets in her room, I just give her a wink and she gets all flustered.

I put a little vase with some plastic flowers on the bedside table and tidied up. Actually, I think Jon'd have felt more at home if I'd heaped smelly socks under the bed and spilt tea and milk on the sheets – or worse – and kept the windows closed for a week. That's boys – the ones I get to go out with anyway. And I got some little bits in from the supermarket, some hummus and stuff and some rice and a bit of curry I'd made for the family at the end of the week. I always cook once a week, sometimes twice, when my mum's at work. And I made the room a bit dim – but not too much. I was worried that once I took my clothes off, he'd see all my lumps and bumps and that'd put him off, even though he says he likes my lumps and bumps. He says they're womanly. But I didn't want to make it too dim, you know why, because a lot of people, a lot of boys, they like to see what they're getting. It was a bit of a dilemma. Oh, God; this is embarrassing. Jon always likes to a have good old look, you know?

What am I like? Why am I telling you this?

So of course, I thought he'd be scared stiff again – I mean, scared not-stiff! But when he turned up, he was just great. He was in such a good mood. I was so surprised. He was jumping about and laughing and joking and teasing me. It was him who put me at ease! Normally he's so insecure. Sometimes you can see it in his face, he says the wrong thing or someone snaps at him and he looks confused and upset as if he doesn't know what's going on. He gets like that a lot. But this time, he'd been so weird for days and now suddenly everything was all right. I took him through to the kitchen and asked him if he wanted a drink, tea or coffee, and he said, No, why didn't we go straight through to the main course.

'I want to prod you with me stiffie,' he said, which made me laugh. He grabbed hold of me and kissed me and cuddled me and nuzzled my neck and tickled me. Such a good mood! So we went straight upstairs . . . and it was great. No problems. He made me feel good about how I looked, and how nice the room was. Well, he came almost at once, which was OK. He was a bit worried about that, so I told him I was flattered! That's how much I turned him on! And then we did it again almost at once and it was really lovely. Really lovely. He was so happy. I don't think I've ever seen him so happy with me before. Usually he's a bit cagey, you know? A bit anxious or withdrawn, ever since we've been going out together, but that day he was Mr Happy. Why? I just wish I knew. If he had some problem he got it sorted out, I can tell you! There was no stopping him after that! Every chance we got, he was all over me. It just goes to tell. Boys! What's going on in there? I think they're all mad. I know Jonathon is – oh well, so am I. You know what? I just fancy that boy so much, I think maybe I'm in love with him.

38
ben

I wasn't sure if I'd recognise her. The station wasn't exactly heaving but there were still a fair few people about and a lot of them were getting on a bit. I'd found photos of her – I'd stolen one, actually. Ali's flat was full of them, she'd never miss one.

'Still keeping her beady little eyes on me, even in the bedroom. Even in the bloody toilet,' she used to say. It was true – I never thought about it until she pointed it out, but there was a picture of her mum in every room of the flat. Sometimes two. Her mum had given her them and hung them up or put them out. Once you looked there were thousands of them, it was scary. They all seemed to stand out and stare at you and follow you round the room. I asked her why she didn't take them down, but she said her mum knew them all by heart and kicked up such a stink if they were moved, it wasn't worth it.

I pinched a piccie from a drawer, but I didn't know how recent it was. She might have changed her hair or her make-up or her whole face for all I knew, but I spotted her all right.

She was smaller than I expected, in a purple tweed coat and her hair up. She had one of those suitcases on wheels which was half as big as she was, but she was rattling along like some sort of rodent. I was a head higher than her but I had to hurry to catch up with her.

'Mrs Young?'

She looked over her shoulder at me.

'I'm a friend of your daughter. Alison. Can I have a word?'

She'd not stopped when I first spoke, but now she turned to look at me.

'You're very young for a friend,' she said. 'Do you go to her school?'

She had me sorted, first glance.

'Can I have a word?' I said again.

She looked up at the station clock hanging over the platform. 'I came to see my daughter.' She raised her eyebrows slightly, as if she was daring me to produce a reason worth her time.

'It's Ali I wanted to speak to you about.' She looked back up at the clock. You'd have thought just me turning up unexpectedly and asking would make her curious enough, but she really looked on the verge of walking off and leaving me. 'You really ought to know,' I said.

'Know what?' she asked at once.

'I can't tell you here,' I said. She pulled a face, but I had her now. 'There's a Costa Coffee over there,' I said. She pursed her lips and led the way there.

*   *   *

So where do you start? 'Well, I've been sleeping with your daughter but I want to chuck her now and I can't, so will you do it for me?'

I began with all the stuff about her being depressed and doing her wrists. That was the angle, you see. She was in trouble, I was worried about her, didn't know what to do. All that. Which was the truth – just not the whole truth. I mean, she was in a mess, and I was worried about her, but I was more worried about me. I wasn't the knight on a white charger. I was there for me. What a bastard. Well, OK. Being a bastard was all I had left.

Then she started asking questions and out it all came – Ali and me, teacher and pupil, having an affair. I wasn't happy about it, I said, but I couldn't see how to stop it since she was so . . . Well, what word do you use to someone about their daughter? Unstable, I said, and she almost hissed at me. I felt like a bigger and bigger shit every word I said. Because I was.

At last I ran out of things to say. She had pretty well the whole picture, or enough for her to fill in the gaps anyway. She sat there with her coffee cup in front of her – she'd bought for us both – and looked at me. I was waiting to see which way it was going to go. I was still hoping she'd understand me, I suppose.

'Young man,' she said, 'you have a lot to answer for.'

And I was surprised. I really was. I should have known, but I just wasn't expecting it.

'Me? What have I done?' I said, and I sounded like a whiny little schoolboy even to my own ears.

'Alison is a very vulnerable young woman and you've taken advantage of her.'

'Me?' I said again. I couldn't believe it. 'But I'm her pupil. She's my teacher.'

'Yes, every schoolboy's dream, I expect. Having an affair with an attractive young teacher. I suppose you had a great time boasting to all your mates about it.' She said 'mates' as if it was in inverted commas.

She began to get up. I was steaming. It was so unfair!

'But she was *in charge*,' I told her.

'Alison was never in charge of anything in her life,' she scoffed. And you know what – that pissed me off. All right, I know I was being dishonest in a lot of ways, and I know I should have just chucked her on my own, and I know . . . I know there's loads of things I should have done that I didn't do. And I know I was there for myself and not her, even though she was the one in trouble. But still. This was her bloody mother, and to her, Ali was just as big a piece of shit as I was. I was shit for taking advantage of her precious daughter, and Ali was shit for not being able to look after herself. I began to get a glimpse of why Ali hated her so much. I really wanted to tell her what I thought of her, but I couldn't get the words out so I just grinned.

'I'm glad you find it funny,' she sniffed.

'Mrs Young,' I said. 'Your daughter . . .' Suddenly I was so furious I just wanted to, you know, really hurt her. Or force her to understand. I wanted to say, Well, if she's fucked up, who fucked her up in the first place? But – what was the point? I just shut my mouth. Anything I had to say was just going to make it worse. The old bitch was going to go round and turn Ali into a lobotomy case all over again. I'd already given her the ammunition to do it, I wasn't going to make it worse than I had to.

I got up to leave. 'I didn't have to tell you,' I told her. 'I could have told the school.'

Mrs Young looked at me like I was an earthworm. 'Yes, and ruined her career for her. Well, you needn't worry about that. She won't be going back there.' And she said it with such confidence, I was sure she was right. She turned to go, and then glanced back.

'You are going to make some young woman very, very unhappy one day. I'm just glad I came to get my daughter in time.' And then she left, leaving me standing there with my mouth open, feeling like I'd just been discovered eating shit in public.

So – how big a bastard am I? Not in the way her mum was making out, though. I don't give a toss what she thinks of me. I suppose Ali is her little girl and I'm just another bloke who came along, shagged her and then dumped her when she was in trouble. What I did was about the worst thing I could have done to Ali. Her lobotomy-mother. There she is feeling hurt and vulnerable and suicidal, and I set the beast loose. Her worst nightmare. I suppose, really, the right thing to do was what Jonathon said – just wait and sit it out. Maybe I'd have been a better person if I'd done that. But – you've got to look after yourself, haven't you? Jon would have sat and waited, but not because he's a better person – because he'd be too scared to do anything else. Ali would have come out of it better, but he'd have suffered more. I suppose I could say, Well, maybe this'll teach her a lesson, maybe she won't do the same thing next time and all that. But I don't believe all that. It was her or me, and no way was it going to be me, that's all. I don't mind taking my share, but no way was I going to just sit there and wait until she was ready to throw me away, thanks a lot.

So I don't feel proud about what I did, but you know what? I'd do it again. If that means I'm a bastard, then that's what I am. You can't always be Mr Nice. She had it her way the whole time – but not then. Not at the end. I had it my way. Maybe I'm even a little proud of it, because if it's a choice between being shat on and pissed on and used and being a bastard, I'll choose being a bastard any time.

And guess what – it worked. It worked like rocket fuel. That was it. She didn't come back to work, she was out of her flat by the end of the weekend and gone. Totalled. She didn't stand a chance. A couple of days later there was a supply teacher at school, the play was cancelled and then next half term there was a new drama teacher. Bang. Amazing!

So that was it. I was free. For ages I kept expecting her to pop up and murder me, but she never did. At long last I started to think maybe things were picking up. Summer was coming. Dino had started going on about this uncle of his who worked on a pleasure cruiser up in the Lakes, on Windermere, and that maybe he could get us jobs up there over the summer. You know? That sounded cool. Booze, girls.

People on holiday having fun. A bit of money in your pocket. Even the hard work sounded OK.

I started chatting to Marianne again the other day and I got the feeling that she was still interested. But it's too soon. Out of the frying pan – not that she's a fire in any way, but I just don't need another girl to go out with. Maybe after the holidays. I expect she'll be with someone else by then, girls like that just get snapped up. Well, that's the way it goes. I just want to get away for a while. Somewhere. 'Cause, you know what? I'm free, that's what. Free as a bird.

39
dino

I was standing by the lockers with Jon and Ben watching Deborah go back to report to Jackie.

'She wants to go back out with me,' I said. Jonathon laughed. 'Do you know something I don't know?' I asked.

'Apparently.'

'What's so funny, then?'

'She's going to go out with you again, is she? After all that?'

'She's been telling everyone what a complete shit you were. And she was right, wasn't she?' said Ben.

'Bet you, that's what it is.'

They looked at each other, it made me giggle. They thought I was just being smug, but it was true. Because, you know what? I don't know what it was I lost for a while there, but I've got it back now. I could feel it. I could see it in the way people looked at me.

'Why else does she want to talk to me? Check up on my homework, I don't think so.'

Pause.

'He has a point,' said Ben.

'Well, if it is true then that's all my faith in girls gone for ever. That would be pathetic.'

I shook my head. 'It's nothing to do with that,' I told him. 'She just fancies me something chronic, that's that.'

Ben laughed. 'And if she does, will you?' he asked.

I pulled a face. 'Dunno.'

'Another chance to enter her golden doors,' pointed out Jon.

'Another chance to get mucked around,' I said. 'She's not very reliable, is she? She wasn't exactly there for me, was she?'

'Not reliable?' said Jon, and they both fell around laughing, which pissed me off. So what's so funny about that?

'Yes, not reliable, what do you think?' I told him. And I was certain I was back on form then, because I had poor old Jon blushing away like he'd forgotten to zip up.

'I was just saying, you know.'

'Dino,' said Ben in his patient voice. 'You two-timed her. She was upset.'

Ben and Jon, they can go on a bit sometimes, but they're good mates. One thing I've learned from all this shit, all that stuff about who's It and who's not and all that, that's for kids. Look at Jonathon – he's got about as much cred as a pair of Y-fronts but he's been a much better mate than Stu and Snoops and the rest of them. And Ben – he still hasn't got a girlfriend, he hardly seems to be interested any more. I wonder if maybe he's even gay. See? None of that stuff matters when it comes down to who your friends are. They're my mates – they showed that. And the rest of 'em are just so much crud.

But I was right about Jackie. I knew from the way she was

looking at me. You don't smile at someone like that if you think they're a shit. She must have realised the sort of pressure I was under.

And I do know what I'm going to say to her, despite what I was saying to Ben and Jon. She's still the best-looking girl in the school, and I still fancy her something rotten. And we never – you know. It'd be a shame not to, wouldn't it?

We met outside the school gates and walked down the lane. She was all happy and smiley. It was great. It was, How are you, how you doing, how's your mum and dad, good news about the shoplifting, all that sort of thing. I didn't say anything much, just answered her questions. We were both smiling away at each other. After we were about halfway down she linked arms with me.

'Don't think this means anything, because it doesn't,' she said. 'We're just being friendly, OK?' But she said it in this little-girl sort of voice, kind of teasing, you know, so you couldn't really take what she said seriously. 'You made me very cross,' she scolded.

'Sorry about that,' I said, and she slapped at my arm lightly.

'You're not sorry at all, I can tell. Don't you ever dare do that again,' she said. There was a pause. 'I was really hurt,' she added.

'I really am sorry,' I said, smiling away, and she smiled back, kind of rueful this time, and then she held tighter onto my arm and sort of wriggled into me.

We got to the end of Crab Lane without anything

happening. Jackie was sighing and standing there like she was waiting for something, so I carefully put my arms round her and she smiled up at me. She looked so happy, her eyes were all bright and shiny, it made me feel really horny. I kissed her. We had a good long snog, it was great. Then she sighed and leaned her head against my chest.

'Does this mean we're going out again?' she asked.

'I suppose so,' I said.

'You're a bad boy, Dino, I ought to . . . never mind. Kiss me again.'

So I kissed her again and . . . that was that.

'We better make a date,' she said. So we made a date for the next night. Sue was standing over by the bus stop; she looked really pissed off, she actually rolled her eyes at us. Jackie was still doing this little-girlie thing, all wriggly and silly and making a bit of a fool of herself, really. But it was a lovely horny snog, and what do I care about Sue, anyway?

So, that could have been that but . . . you know what? I went home, and I thought, Do I really want this all over again? It was just going to be the same kind of thing, really. Her all over me one moment and then all cold the next. And . . . well. There were other girls. Actually, to tell you the truth, I had already asked this other girl out at the weekend. Everyone fancies her, she's really nice. Now I was going to have to tell her it was off. I was thinking, maybe I preferred this other girl to Jackie. I used to think Jackie was all steady and straight, but she isn't really, she's all over the place. This other girl, she's pretty straightforward, which is probably more like what I need right now.

I didn't do anything just then. Next day it was all over the school about me and Jackie getting together again. No one could believe it, which was cool. I managed to avoid her most of the time, but by the end of the day I was pretty sure it was a mistake. So that night I gave her a ring and I told her it was off. I did it as nicely as possible. I still fancied her, but I didn't think it was going to work. She took it quite well. She was all pleased to hear from me and then all quiet and shocked when I told her. I felt bad about it, but it was better to do it that way than let it drag on. I guess we'd just mucked one another around for too long.

40

sue

Rage. Tears. Hacking of air with the hands. Make-up all over her face. Ashes. Despair.

'How could he? After I *humiliated* myself for him!' she wailed.

It lasted about a week and then she was over it.

41
finale

The idea was for them all to go to the cinema, or bowling or swimming or something – Jon and Deborah, Ben, Dino and Jackie. Except that Dino had given Jackie the push and was being very secretive about maybe someone else coming along.

'So I'll be the gooseberry again,' said Ben. But he came along anyway. He was thinking, if they went bowling he'd go too, if they went to the cinema he'd leave them to it. He did think about asking Marianne to go along with him – but it was too soon. Relationships. All that closeness. It was too much.

They met in a café by the leisure complex and sat at a table drinking soft drinks and eating crisps. About ten minutes later, Dino turned up with the new girl on his elbow.

'Hi,' he said self-consciously.

'Hello,' said Jonathon.

'Um,' said Ben.

'Hi, Marianne,' said Deborah.

Dino smiled happily. Marianne said hello and gave Ben a cool smile and a tilt of the head.

'So what are you two up to, then?' asked Jonathon, to try and break the silence.

'We're going to walk about a bit, don't know really, see what happens,' said Dino. He was just so pleased with himself. Isn't she lovely? Isn't she gorgeous? Aren't you all pleased for me? Don't you all wish you were me?

Deborah started a brief conversation with Marianne about what there was to do in town. Dino stood and smiled anxiously at his two friends, who seemed to be a bit put out, he couldn't think why. After that, he and his new girl said goodbye and headed off for the door.

'See you later,' he called.

'Later,' said Jon. He waited until they were out of the door.

'The fucker,' he said.

Ben smiled and bobbed his head, blushing pinkly.

'What's up, you two were really off with him?' said Deborah.

'That's the one Ben fancies,' said Jonathon.

Ben shook his head. 'That was ages ago,' he said, but his blush turned from pink to bright red.

'Oh, really, but, oh, that's so mean,' said Deborah. She pulled a face. 'Isn't that just so typical Dino?'

'He didn't know I still fancied her, did he?' insisted Ben.

'He knew,' said Jonathon, outraged on Ben's behalf. After all that running around looking after him! And after all that Ben had been through – he'd only just shaken free and now Dino had waltzed off with the one girl he really fancied!

'But he didn't *know*, did he?' said Ben. 'I mean, he was telling me I should ask her out only a couple of weeks ago and I wouldn't. Remember? I told him I didn't want to.'

'But . . .' began Jonathon. But it was true. Dino knew nothing about Alison Young. He had no idea why Ben hadn't asked Marianne out.

Neither did Deborah. 'But why didn't you ask her, I bet she'd have said yes,' said Deborah. 'You've got to ask, Ben, what's she supposed to do, wait for you or something?'

'No, no, it's right.'

'I don't care if he knew or not, he's still a shit. It can't be an accident,' insisted Jonathon. 'How can he be so accurate except on purpose?'

Ben grimaced.

'It's typical Dino,' said Deborah.

'It's just amazing. Bang on the nose. How does he do it?'

'It doesn't matter,' said Ben. He really didn't want to talk any more about it.

He stayed and chatted a little longer. Jon and Debs tried to convince him to stay, but that was it, his heart was jolted out of place, the last thing he wanted was to hang around with a couple. He finished his drink and went off, leaving Jon and Debs to do their stuff on their own. He turned back to look at them through the window and saw that they'd leaned close together already, noses almost touching across the little wooden table. Sweet. He'd never seen Jon look so happy. He wandered off into HMV and looked at a few CDs he wanted but couldn't afford to buy, then caught the bus home. His parents were out shopping, his brother was at a friend's, he had the place to himself. Ben walked into the front room and stood there, gazing at the wall.

'Fuck,' he said. 'Fuck fuck fuck. Shit wank bollocks!

ARRRRGGGHHH!' He ran over to the door and kicked it as hard as he could. It split. He was going to have to answer for that but he didn't care. He ran around the house yelling and throwing cushions and kicking walls and trying not to break anything valuable. Finally he flung himself down on the sofa. He felt like weeping or screaming or laughing or all three. He put his teeth into a hideous grimace and grinned like the devil at the ceiling.

In a minute he put his hands behind his head, sighed, and closed his eyes. Not that he'd had any intention of asking Marianne out, and it was totally unreasonable to expect her to wait around for him; but it just had to be Dino who got her, didn't it, and it had to be then, just days after he'd broken free. Like Jon said, it was too accurate to be an accident, but he was willing to bet Dino had no idea what he was doing.

Ben got up and looked at himself in the mirror. He had a good face, small even features, tight curly black hair. His eyes were bright and red with anger – he'd been close to tears – but he looked OK. The world was full of good-looking girls. Someone else would be there. Dino and Marianne wouldn't last for ever and he'd still be there. What was the hurry? He could wait if he wanted to, or not.